The
Royals
Upstairs

OTHER TITLES BY KARINA HALLE

CONTEMPORARY ROMANCES

The Swedish Prince (Nordic Royals #1)

The Wild Heir (Nordic Royals #2)

A Nordic King (Nordic Royals #3)

The Royal Rogue (Nordic Royals #4)

Love, in English (Love in Other Languages #1)

Love, in Spanish (Love in Other Languages #2)

The Forbidden Man (Love in Other Languages #3)

The One That Got Away (Love in Other Languages #4)

Where Sea Meets Sky

Racing the Sun

Bright Midnight

The Pact (McGregors #1)

The Offer (McGregors #2)

The Play (McGregors #3)

Winter Wishes (McGregors #3.5)

The Lie (McGregors #4)

The Debt (McGregors #5)

Smut

Heat Wave (Hawaii Love #1)

Nothing Personal (Hawaii Love #2)

Before I Ever Met You

The Royals Upstairs

KARINA HALLE

BERKLEY ROMANCE
NEW YORK

BERKLEY ROMANCE
Published by Berkley
An imprint of Penguin Random House LLC
penguinrandomhouse.com

Copyright © 2024 by Karina Halle
Excerpt from *The Royals Next Door* copyright © 2021 by Karina Halle
Penguin Random House supports copyright. Copyright fuels creativity,
encourages diverse voices, promotes free speech, and creates a vibrant culture.
Thank you for buying an authorized edition of this book and for complying
with copyright laws by not reproducing, scanning, or distributing any part
of it in any form without permission. You are supporting writers and allowing
Penguin Random House to continue to publish books for every reader.

BERKLEY and the BERKLEY & B colophon are registered trademarks of
Penguin Random House LLC.

Library of Congress Cataloging-in-Publication Data

Names: Halle, Karina, author.
Title: The royals upstairs / Karina Halle.
Description: First edition. | New York : Berkley Romance, 2024.
Identifiers: LCCN 2023052841 (print) | LCCN 2023052842 (ebook) |
ISBN 9780593334218 (trade paperback) | ISBN 9780593334225 (e-book)
Subjects: LCSH: Royal nannies—Fiction. | Guards troops—Fiction. |
Bodyguards—Fiction. | LCGFT: Romance fiction. | Novels.
Classification: LCC PR9199.4.H356239 R697 2024 (print) | LCC PR9199.4.H356239
(ebook) | DDC 813/.6—dc23/eng/20231120
LC record available at https://lccn.loc.gov/2023052841
LC ebook record available at https://lccn.loc.gov/2023052842

First Edition: September 2024

Printed in the United States of America
1st Printing

Book design by Ashley Tucker

To my father, Sven Halle—I miss you every day.

To my brother Kris Halle—I hope you have found peace.

And to all the Halles who make Todalen, Norway,
such a special place—tusen takk!

The
Royals
Upstairs

One

. . . . . .

JAMES

IT'S BLOODY COLD, I'LL TELL YOU THAT MUCH.

I'm standing on the side of a runway in what feels like the middle of Norway, and I've been freezing my bollocks off for a good twenty minutes at least. It's early December but there's already a fresh layer of snow on the ground, and though it's nearly three in the afternoon, the sun is already setting, suspending the air in this murky kind of twilight. My new employer, Magnus, the Crown Prince of Norway, arranged for a private jet to take me from London to this tiny airstrip, and I'm supposed to meet one of his advisors who will take me to the nearby Skaugum Estate, where the prince and princess live, my future home for the foreseeable future.

I gather my coat collar tighter around me, snowflakes sticking in my hair, wishing I had brought a scarf. When I did my research about Norway, everyone always said that it wasn't as cold as the stereotype and that it rarely snowed in December, but boy were they fucking wrong.

Finally a black SUV screeches to a stop outside the chain-link fence, and a man practically falls out of the vehicle, his shoes slipping on the ice. He holds on to the hood, arms splayed, legs slowly sliding apart before he manages to take another step. He straightens up unsteadily, then looks at the ground between us, seeming to have second thoughts.

"Mr. Hunter?" he yells over in a light Norwegian accent.

"That's me," I tell him. "Are you Ottar?"

"Ja," he says. "Would you mind if I stayed here? I don't think my shoes can handle the ice."

I stare at him for a moment. He's on the portly side, though he has a boyish face and black glasses. But the more I stare at him, the more I realize that half his face is banged up. Maybe it's best that he stays where he is.

"Not a problem," I tell him, picking up my suitcase handle and carefully walking over to the fence and going through the gate. At least my black boots have an ample amount of tread, which is more than he has. I don't know why someone here wouldn't know how to dress for the elements, but I guess I'm about to find out.

"Mr. Hunter," Ottar says, smiling hastily as I approach, sticking out his hand. "It's a pleasure to welcome you to Norway."

I stop and shake his hand. "Please, call me James," I tell him. Now that I'm up close, I can finally get a good look at him. He's got a black eye and a bunch of scratches along his cheeks. "I don't mean to pry, but are you okay? You look bloody mangled."

He laughs and then points at his face. "Oh right, my face. Long story. But I'm fine. Here, let me get your bag."

Ottar takes my suitcase from me and then starts the very long, laborious process of walking alongside the SUV, his hand propped against the car for support as he tries to balance on the ice.

"I can just put it in the back seat," I tell him.

He attempts a dismissive wave, but that movement alone sends one leg flying forward and the other leg flying backward, and it's only by the grace of a Norse god that he doesn't end up doing splits.

"Hellvete," he swears.

"Are you sure I can't help?" I ask, biting back a smile.

"I'm fine, I'm fine," he says quickly, letting out an awkward laugh. "Just hurt myself the other day, so I'm a bit, uh, overly cautious, as one might say."

One might say that he has a reason to be overly cautious and that the best course of action is to just abandon the suitcase and make it back to the safety of the driver's seat.

But I'm a man with my own pride, and I'm not about to interfere with the pride of someone else. So I wait, leaning against the SUV, watching as Ottar very carefully makes it to the back of the car and then opens the trunk, throwing my bag in. There are a few more twists and turns and near splits, and then he manages to pull himself back to me.

"Shall we?" he asks, opening my door with a triumphant smile.

And that's when he totally loses ground, holding on to the handle for dear life while the rest of him slides under the door, heels first.

Bloody hell.

I reach over and grab him by the elbows, hauling him up. He's not light as a feather, I'll say that much.

"Tussen takk," he says sheepishly, his cheeks going pink. "That's Norwegian for *thank you*. You know any Norwegian?"

I step inside the car. "Not a word." I'd had a brief affair with a wild Norwegian woman but only got away with knowing swear words.

"Ah," he says. He shuts the door, almost falling again, then finally pulls himself into the driver's seat, letting out a massive exhale of relief. "I'm sure you'll learn fast. At any rate, everyone speaks English fluently, so it won't be a problem if you don't. Except for Einar, Magnus's bodyguard. But you probably wouldn't get more than a few words out of him anyway."

He starts the car and thankfully the tires have more tread than Ottar's shoes.

"Sorry I was late," he says to me, eyeing me in the rearview mirror. "I run on Magnus's schedule, and that can be off at times. You'll find out soon enough." He pauses. "I really didn't expect them to hire someone this fast."

I give a light shrug, looking out the window at the passing scenery. Farm fields covered in white and orderly forests of pine fly past in the dying light. It's pretty here, I'll give it that much, even if I feel a bit discombobulated about the whole thing.

See, Ottar's not alone in thinking everything had gone so fast. It's literally been a couple of weeks since my former employer, Prince Eddie of England, told me that he and his wife, Duchess Monica, were taking their daughter, Madeline, back to Canada.

Now, I'd gone with them before. Four years ago they'd moved to a tiny island off the very wet west coast of British Columbia to prepare for Duchess Monica's pregnancy and escape the rubbish media of the UK, and I went along with them as one of their personal protection officers. We did our time there on the island, enjoying the much-needed peace and quiet, then came back to London for baby Madeline's birth.

Then Eddie and Monica decided that they didn't want to raise Madeline in the same environment that Eddie was brought up in, so they decided to move back to that tiny island and asked if I would go with them.

I ended up saying no. As much as I loved working for them, the island felt like early retirement. Suffice to say, I opted to stay behind, which then meant I was out of a job. And being a PPO or bodyguard, it's not like you can start perusing the job listings on Craigslist and hand out applications.

Thankfully Eddie helped out. He nosed around and found out that Prince Magnus and Princess Ella of Norway were looking for a bodyguard, specifically for Ella and their children. Supposedly, one of the kids, despite having his mother and a nanny, is quite the troublemaker and is hard to keep an eye on. One thing led to another, and Eddie arranged for Prince Magnus to hire me without even meeting me. I guess Eddie's word goes a long way in the royal world—enough so that I only found out I had the job just the other day.

"I'm grateful that Prince Eddie was able to put in such a good word with Prince Magnus, especially on such short notice," I tell Ottar. "But from speaking to Prince Magnus on the phone, I got the impression that the role won't be too dissimilar from what I was doing before."

"Yes," Ottar says, rather uneasily. He gives me a crooked smile. "I can see how you would think that."

I frown. "What do you mean?"

"Oh, nothing," he says, adjusting his grip on the steering

wheel. "Let's just say that I'm sure when you worked for the duke and duchess that they ran a pretty tight ship."

"I suppose," I say. "Not as uptight as the rest of his family, though."

"Right. Well, Magnus . . . does not run a tight ship. Ella tries to, but it's hard when she's trying to balance her children and running her environmental group . . . the palace can be chaos on even the calmest days."

"I see," I tell him. This doesn't really surprise me. Prince Magnus is famous for being the wild prince, especially before he settled down and married Ella. Some media outlets even report that their marriage was an arranged one to try to counteract a slew of bad publicity the prince had gotten. Extreme sports, sex tapes, being a drunken idiot—it was hard to go a week without reading something about Magnus in the papers.

Now, since he got married and had children, he seems to have calmed down. He's become a public spokesperson for ADHD, which he has, and runs an organization devoted to eradicating the stigma attached to being neurodiverse. He's actually one of the most-liked royals there are because of how open he is with the public.

"Don't get me wrong," Ottar quickly says, "I think you'll enjoy working here. Everyone is super friendly. Just . . . be prepared for the unexpected."

"Is the unexpected what happened to your face?" I ask.

He nods, looking chagrined. "The other day Magnus wanted to go cross-country skiing. I'm an awful Norwegian because I'm not the best on skis."

"You don't say," I comment wryly.

"It's true. It's like I have two left feet. Anyway, Magnus then decided to turn it into a downhill skiing expedition, and wherever he goes, I follow." He gestures to his face. "I had a run-in with a tree. Or two."

"You're not his personal protection officer, though," I point out.

"No, but it's my job to try to keep him in line. When I can. I'd never let him go off and do something like that on his own, even when Einar is with us. I've even been BASE jumping, if you can believe it."

I'm not sure that I can believe it. "Sounds like you have your hands full."

He smirks at me. "I do. But so will you."

"Princess Ella? Every footage I've seen of her, she seems as calm and collected as they come," I tell him.

"She is, thank god. But you're not just protecting her. You're protecting her and her children, Bjorn and Tor, and they are a handful. Bjorn especially. Takes after his father in every single way. Then there's Ella's lady-in-waiting, and the nanny, and they both take the term *headstrong* to the next level. Now you see? You're not just protecting Ella but the rest of them too. In some ways, at least there is only one Magnus."

I mull that over. Suddenly everything seems a lot less simple than it did a few days ago. But I'm nothing if not adaptable. I'm sure everything will be just fine, and it's not like I don't know how to handle a few headstrong ladies.

Ottar takes the car off the road and down a long driveway covered by trees.

"Where are we going?" I ask, staring at the frozen fields beyond the trees.

"To Skaugum," Ottar says.

"I thought we were going to the palace?"

"This is the Skaugum Estate," he says. "But you can call it a palace if you'd like. Traditionally it was the summer palace."

I twist in my seat, looking around me at the bucolic scenery, feeling a bit panicked. "But I thought the palace, the estate, was on the outskirts of Oslo."

"We are on the outskirts of Oslo," he says.

"But there's nothing here!" I exclaim.

"Yes. That's why it's the outskirts. Don't worry, it's only forty-five minutes to the city." His forehead creases as he turns to glance at me over his shoulder. "Did you think you would be living in Oslo? The king and queen live there at the palace, but Magnus and Ella wanted a more private place to raise their kids."

Bloody hell, did I ever get this wrong. The reason I didn't want to go with Eddie and Monica to that tiny island is because I didn't want to work in the middle of nowhere again. The isolation was fine the first time, but it wouldn't be good for my mentality the next time, especially in the winter. I wanted to stay around city lights, and people, and women, and traffic.

And yet as the SUV pulls up to a grand white palace, in the middle of nowhere, I realize that I'm about to live in isolation all over again. No more city lights, no more people, no more traffic, or stores, or civilization.

No more women.

Just me and the apparently wacky arm of the Norwegian royal family.

This is not getting off to a great start.

"Well, here we are," Ottar says, parking the car. "Oh, and look, there are the kids. You can meet them already."

I give my head a shake, trying to snap out of it and put my misgivings aside, and slowly get out of the car. Lucky for Ottar we're on packed snow and there's no way for him to fall.

"Hei, Bjorn, Tor," Ottar yells over at two kids in snowsuits on the front lawn. "Come say hi to our new friend. He's going to be living with us."

I close the car door and look over at the kids. They're staying put, both of them immersed in building a snowman. Okay, so a woman is building a snowman for them, but her back is to me so I can't tell who it is, whether it's the princess, the lady-in-waiting, or the nanny.

One of the kids is pretty young, a toddler, and is sitting in the snow, shoving the white stuff into his mouth; the other is standing by the snowman, staring at me with demon eyes.

Oh. This must be Bjorn.

Ottar hauls the bag out of the back and pauses beside me. "Sometimes they can be shy," he says. Then he winks. "Appreciate it while it lasts."

Bjorn rolls up a snowball, while keeping his eyes locked on me, and I'm certain he's about to throw it in my face.

Then at the last minute he turns and whips it at the woman's head, bouncing off her down hood, snow flying everywhere.

"*Bjorn,*" the woman says to him, exasperated, and a string of sternly worded Norwegian follows.

Suddenly my whole body feels like it's been jerked back into the past. The woman's voice is so acutely familiar that I have to blink a few times to try to ground myself to the present.

This *can't* be.

"Who is that?" I find myself whispering.

"Oh, that's their nanny," Ottar says.

And it's then that she turns around so that I can see her face. I know her name before Ottar can even give it to me.

"Laila," he says.

Laila stares at me, eyes going wide as the moon, her face paling to match the snow.

I feel like I'm in a tractor beam, stuck here in this staring contest that I know at any minute is about to get ugly. I'm glued in place, locked in her gaze, my body swimming in feelings— lust, desire, even a bit of fear.

Holy shit.

It's her.

And she's just as shocked as I am, her unblinking gaze sinking into mine, memories passing through me, making my blood run hot.

"Wait," Ottar says slowly, pointing between us. "Do you two know each other?"

Laila lets out a derisive snort, the first of us to snap out of it.

"I can't believe it," she says, her round eyes going narrow, and that familiar burning sensation of her glare comes back to me. "It's *you.*"

"In all the royal palaces, in all the world," I tell her, my voice shaking just a little, "I walk into yours."

"So, how do you know each other?" Ottar asks carefully, probably just realizing that we don't know each other in the best way.

I give Laila a look, raising my brow to say, *Well do you want to tell him?*

But she learned her lesson from the last time. We both did.

"We used to work together," she says crisply, her posture stiffening, a coldness coming into her eyes, the kind that burns. Then she turns her attention back to the snowman, like I never existed. I guess she's had a lot of practice.

The two of us had what Lady Gaga would refer to as a *bad romance.*

And that's putting it mildly.

The last person I ever expected to see again was Laila Bruset, my wild Norwegian woman.

"James?" Ottar says to me.

I blink, staring at Laila's back, wondering what the hell I did to deserve this.

Actually, scratch that. I know what I did to deserve this.

My stomach sinks. I look at Ottar, and he gives me a forced smile.

"Shall we go inside and meet the rest of the family? I'm sure you'll have plenty of opportunities to connect with Laila."

Out of the corner of my eye I can see her practically bristle.

"Of course," I tell him, raising my chin. I'm going to have to pretend that everything's fine going forward if I want to keep my job. I'm going to have to pretend that the woman I had a very passionate and tumultuous affair with isn't the royal nanny and my future coworker. Thankfully, I've made pretending into an art.

Ottar takes my suitcase and heads down the driveway to the palace, stomping confidently through the snow. The estate is big, though it reminds me more of a rich person's country mansion than a royal palace. It's white and sprawling, with pillars, but there's a bit of a rustic quality to it, like it needs a fresh coat of paint. That puts me at ease, just to know that the royal couple isn't as hoity-toity as they could be.

But that ease is short-lived, because I look over my shoulder at the snowman on the lawn and see Laila's cold eyes following my every move as I go up the front steps, so much so that I nearly trip and fall.

"Easy there," Ottar says to me good-naturedly. "It can be slippery. Wouldn't want you to fall."

I give him a tepid look in response, just as the front doors swing open.

"Ahh, you found the new recruit," Prince Magnus says with a flourish as he steps out, arms held as wide as the smile on his face. "James Hunter."

I'm about to bow, as is the courtesy when meeting a royal, but before I can even do that, Prince Magnus throws his arms around me and gives me a rib-cracking embrace. While I'm in top shape, the man is built like an ox on steroids. Must be a Viking thing.

"So nice to finally meet you," he says, slapping me hard on the back.

"Likewise, Your Majesty," I tell him, trying not to wince.

He rolls his eyes. "Please. Call me Magnus. Not Prince Magnus, not Your Royal Highness, and definitely not Your Majesty. You're part of the family now."

"Right," I tell him, feeling a wee bit unsteady, like I'm still standing on ice. His energy is pretty intense.

"It's nice to have a Scotsman joining us," he says with a wink. "You know we're probably related, going way back, since Scotland was the first step for us Vikings."

"Back then with all the plundering?"

"Yes, the plundering and the ravaging of the local ladies and all that unsavory stuff." He grins at me. Not only is he built like a Viking, he looks like one too. Though he's wearing a long gray cable-knit sweater and jeans, I know he's famous for his tattoos. Then he's got the scruffy beard and the longish wavy dark hair. "Like I said, you're family now."

"Speaking of family," Ottar says to Magnus as he walks into the house, "it turns out that Laila and James know each other. Gave him quite the surprise."

Magnus stops in the front hall and gives me a curious look. "You didn't know she was working for us?" He then glances at Ottar. "Laila was the nanny for the duke and duchess, just as James was their PPO. I believe they worked together for about two years?"

I nod, clearing my throat. I hate that this whole thing has caught me completely off guard. "That sounds about right."

The thing is, if I had given all of this a little more thought, if I'd had a little more time, I'm sure I might have come to this conclusion. When Eddie first told me I had a chance to move to Norway, memories of Laila drifted through my head. She'd left her position as nanny to the Fairfaxes because her beloved grandmother, who lived in a tiny village in Northern Norway, had gotten sick and she wanted to be with her. I know it was a tough decision for Laila to make, but since her grandmother raised her and they were especially close, she didn't have much choice.

At that point, Laila thought I was an outright wanker, so we weren't really on speaking terms anyway. The most I would get out of her was a stiff nod of recognition as we passed each other in the halls. One day I found out that she was gone and that was that. Never heard from her, or about her, again. Until now.

"Must be a relief to see a familiar face," Magnus says to me. "That's why I put your room right next to hers."

Bloody hell.

Two

......

JAMES

"COME, I'LL SHOW YOU TO YOUR QUARTERS," MAGNUS says, motioning for me to follow. We turn down a long hall, the walls dark wood and adorned with paintings of forests and pastoral scenes, interspersed with the occasional vintage photograph in a gold frame and wooden heirlooms.

"We have a house for the rest of the servants and help," Magnus says as we walk, our boots echoing down the dark hall. "But we like to keep our closest members close to us. Downstairs you'll find your bedroom, Laila's, Ottar's, and Ella's lady-in-waiting, Jane. Jane has been Ella's closest friend and advisor for a long time, though she's a handful, I'm warning you," he adds with a conspiratorial grin.

At this point I'm wondering who *isn't* a handful in this house.

"Upstairs has the guest bedrooms, plus mine and Ella's, the kids' rooms, and a nursery . . . not that we're planning on any more, but you never know. Perhaps one day we'll add to the chaos."

"And your personal bodyguard?" I ask.

Magnus laughs. "Einar. He's around. He has his own little cabin out in the trees. He prefers to be alone when he can, lord knows why since he's locked in his brain most of the time."

We stop outside a door, and Magnus opens it, striding on in.

It's a nice room, on the large side. A king-size four-poster bed in teak, dark blue walls with gold designs along the top. A window that looks out onto the white fields and the rows of frosted pine trees beyond. The isolation already feels suffocating, and there's a bit of a draft, ice on the edges of the windowpane.

Ottar takes my suitcase and places it on the suitcase holder, struggling with the weight.

"That's all you brought?" Magnus asks incredulously, pointing at the suitcase.

I shrug. "You get used to living out of a suitcase."

"I bet, but you worked for Eddie for how many years?"

"Four." What I'm not about to get into is how I've basically lived out of a suitcase my whole life. Growing up in various foster homes will teach you to never put your roots down for long. I'm actually surprised I lasted as long with the duke and duchess as I did.

"Besides, I pretty much wear the same suit every day," I add.

"Suits?" Magnus says, brows raised. "No, no. You don't wear suits when you're here. When we're out and about, yes. I don't know why every member of the protection force has to cosplay as James Bond, but fine, I get it. But here? In this house? In your home? No. No suits. You wear what you like."

"I *only* have suits," I tell him. And I like suits, *especially* for the James Bond aspect of them. When I was young and living in threadbare hand-me-down clothes salvaged from a donation bin, I'd always admired the businessmen on the tube going to their jobs, dressed in their suits, looking so distinguished, like they had a real place in the world, something I had always lacked. Besides, they hide my gun.

He gives me another hearty slap on the back. "Not a problem. Tomorrow, we'll go into the city and get you something nice to wear. Now come on, the tour continues."

A shopping expedition for myself on my first full day on the job? I don't think so.

"I'm really okay with my suits," I tell Magnus, following him out of the room. I look at Ottar for support, but he just smiles and nods, as if this is a normal thing.

"Nonsense," Magnus says, then raps his knuckles along the wall and points to the room next to mine. "This is your lady friend's room," he says, then glances at me over his shoulder. "I don't have to tell you to keep it in your pants, do I?" Before I can even respond to that, he continues. "Good. Just wanted to make sure."

Oh fuck. Why would he even bring that up? Maybe he thinks that sleeping together is a predetermined thing just because she happens to be stunningly attractive. Or he thinks we've already slept together and he wants to warn me that we're not allowed to do it again. Or he knows the truth. We slept together, things blew up in our faces, and now we're mortal enemies.

"Don't worry," Ottar says to me with a wag of his brows. "He's warning Lady Jane to stay away from me all the time. She finds me irresistible."

"Speaking of Lady Jane," Magnus says as we step inside a large country-style kitchen, "here she is. She's been part of

Ella's life as her personal assistant for such a long time, she's one of the family."

A woman I assume is Lady Jane is sitting at a table in the corner, the biggest mug of tea I've ever seen in her hands.

She looks up at me in surprise and smiles, lowering the bowl of tea. "The fresh blood is here!"

Lady Jane is a robust woman with a round face, big smile, and bright eyes, her dark blunt bangs above them acting like a frame. I already like her, even though she's only said a few words.

She gets out of her seat, the chair moving back noisily on the tile floor, then comes over to me, both hands out to shake mine. "I'm Jane, Ella's lady-in-waiting. You can call me Lady Jane, or Jane, makes no difference to me since I'm not an actual lady," she says in a Liverpool accent as she looks me over with a wry twinkle in her eyes. "My, aren't you a handsome one? And Scottish too. Oh, Ella and I had a ball when she was studying at St. Andrews. I have to say, it's a relief to have someone from the UK here among all these Europeans. Even if it is Scotland."

"Nice to meet you," I tell her, but she's shaking my hand more than I'm shaking hers. "The name is James."

"James Hunter," Magnus supplies. "So now we have to figure out whether you want to be called by your first name or your last name."

"I'm fine with either one." When I worked for Eddie and Monica, they called me James. When I worked for the Belgian royal family, back in the day, they addressed me as Hunter.

"Aren't you agreeable," Magnus says, then looks over his shoulder. "Ella! There you are. Where have you been hiding?"

I turn to see Princess Ella standing in the doorway to the kitchen. She's wearing skinny jeans, a Fair Isle sweater—the super-itchy-looking kind—and big fluffy socks, her blond hair braided to the side. She's very delicate-looking, like a fairy princess instead of an ordinary one, but I can tell from the lift of her jaw that she's a force to be reckoned with.

"I was working," she tells Magnus as she walks toward us, fixing her blue eyes on me.

"So you're James," she says, her voice soft, a mixture of a British and German accent. "It's nice to meet you."

I already know she has a different approach than Magnus does. I bow. "It's an honor to be serving you, Your Majesty."

"Well, thank you," Ella says.

"I told him to knock it off with the formalities," Magnus tells her.

"And I'm glad he didn't listen to you," she says. Then she smiles at me. "But Magnus is right. We're pretty relaxed around here, and we like it that way. Please call me Ella."

"Very well, Ella," I tell her.

"Where are the boys?" she asks Magnus.

"Out front with Laila," he says.

She gives me a wary smile. "Have you been properly introduced?"

"To the boys? I'm afraid not."

Her eyes go to Magnus for a moment, then come back to me. "That's right. You already know Laila, don't you?"

I'm starting to think that Laila has said some not-so-positive things about me.

"I do," I tell her. "We lost touch after she left the Fairfax household. It's nice to be working with her again." I say that all so smoothly, finishing it with a charming smile, that I have even nearly fooled myself.

"Great," Ella says, and then beckons for me to follow her. She glances at me over her shoulder and frowns. "Are you going to be warm in that? You should at least get some gloves in case the boys cajole you into a snowball fight."

I pull my leather gloves out of my coat pocket to show her.

"I suppose that will do," she says as we head to the doors, grabbing a puffy coat from the rack. "You'll get used to the winters here. I grew up in Liechtenstein, and I thought our Alps were cold. Here it can go to a whole other level of—what is Magnus fond of saying again?"

"Colder than a witch's tit," Magnus pipes up from behind us, striding quickly to catch up, pulling on his own coat.

"We have that saying in Scotland," I tell them.

"See, I knew we were related in some way," he says, laughing.

"But it's the darkness here that gets you," she says with a sigh as we carefully walk back down the steps, eyeing the sky. "In another twenty minutes it will be pitch black outside."

We stop at the base of the stairs, and Ella puts her hands on her hips. "Hey, boys, maybe it's time to come inside before you can't see anything. We have a friend here we'd like you to officially meet."

I swear I hear Laila's sigh as she bends down to scoop up the youngest boy, holding him in her arms.

"Come on, Bjorn," Laila says, reaching for the other boy's hand.

But Bjorn is not having it. He's rolling up a snowball again, his tongue sticking out of his mouth in a devious manner.

"Hey, Bjornsy!" Magnus booms. "Do what Laila says."

Bjorn then giggles and yells, "No!" He throws a snowball at Laila's head before turning and running off across the lawn toward the woods.

Magnus mutters something in Norwegian and starts running across the snow, chasing down his son.

"I don't know what gets into him," Ella says, coming over to Laila and taking her other son, Tor, from her arms. "Here, I've got him. Why don't you and James get reacquainted?"

Laila opens her mouth in protest as Ella walks back up the steps with her son, then closes it on second thought.

"So, *Laila*," I say to her, having to be the bigger person here and hating it. "I honestly had no idea that you'd be working here."

She pastes a stiff smile on her face, her hood moving back just enough for me to make out more of her features in the dim light. Bloody hell, she's still ridiculously beautiful. She's got these huge dark hazel eyes that tell you everything she's thinking (and right now she's thinking how much she'd like to dunk my head in a snowbank, that's for sure), and the kind of lips that know how to make a man feel pretty damn good. She reminds me of a young Julia Roberts, only with honey-highlighted hair and more attitude. If you can get her to laugh, though, it's a momentous occasion.

"I didn't know you'd be here either," she says sharply. "When they said they got a new protection officer from England, I never thought it would be *you*."

"I got him!" Magnus yells at us, trudging through the snow with Bjorn on his shoulder, literally kicking and screaming. "Laila, take the rest of the night off. We'll take care of the demon spawn. You guys just relax."

He gives me a wink and then carries the shrieking demon spawn up the stairs and into the house.

Laila gives me a veiled glance. "I guess I should be thanking you for getting me a night off," she says. "Then again, you're about to ruin every one of my days for the foreseeable future, aren't you?"

Laila starts off for the house, but I instinctively reach out and grab her arm. "I really don't want us to get off on the wrong foot," I tell her. "Can we start over again?"

She pulls out of my grip and folds her arms across her chest. "How so?"

"Like we're meeting for the first time." I stick out my hand. "Good evening, I'm James Hunter. I'll be working as the protection officer for the Norwegian royal family. And you are?"

She stares down at my hand.

Then back up at me.

This isn't going to be easy.

Three

. . . .

LAILA

I LEARNED AT A VERY EARLY AGE THAT LIFE WILL UTTERLY
rip the rug out from under you when you least expect it, and
hell if it wasn't raising its ugly head again because *holy shit.*

How is this happening?

How the hell am I staring right into the face of the last person on earth I wanted to see?

James Hunter. A person whose name I have trained myself
to never repeat inside my head is standing right in front of me,
a face I thought I'd erased from my imagination. Somehow he's
walked right back into my life, like he's been teleported here.

My mind and my body are functioning on two vastly different levels. My brain and my heart are racing, while my body is
as frozen as the ice on the ground.

I stare down at James's hand, wondering what my next move
should be. Every instinct inside me is telling me not to shake it,
to kick him in the shin and then storm off toward the house.

But my instincts often get me in trouble. It's logic that I

need to start listening to more, not what my gut tells me, because I swear my gut just wants a little excitement from time to time.

I have to do what my brain says. And it says that the only way I'm going to get through this is to make nice with him. Or at least pretend to make nice.

I hold out my hand and quickly shake his. His grip is strong, and far too familiar for my liking, and I try to take it back right away. But his hold is as persistent as he is.

"I mean it," he says to me, and I hate how rich his Scottish accent is.

"I know we both have a lot of baggage behind us, but I'd like to keep it behind us for the sake of our jobs. I can't imagine being here," he continues, looking at the house, the fields, the woods, "and having an enemy."

I snatch my hand back, burying it in my jacket pocket. "I'm not your enemy," I tell him.

But he's giving me a look that says, *Oh yeah, then what am I, love?*

Okay, he has a point. You'd think I would have had enough time to figure it out, but after I left the Fairfaxes, I put him out of my head. It was next to impossible when I was seeing him every day, but the moment I was gone, I did my best to put everything behind me. His transition from lover to enemy was pretty natural.

Besides, I had my grandmother to look after. She very quickly taught me the significance of life being too short and not letting the bad things take up too much space in your head.

And James Hunter was a very bad thing.

"So now what?" he says to me, shoving his hands into his

pockets. "If it's your night off, and I don't officially start until tomorrow, do you want to get a drink somewhere?"

I stare at him. "Are you kidding me?"

He frowns, puzzled. "What?"

"What?" I repeat. "I'm not going to get a drink with you."

"Why not?"

"Why not?" I have to think about that for a moment. There are a million reasons why—so many that it's hard to pin it down to one. "Because I don't want to," I eventually say.

He lets out a dry laugh. "Fair enough. So much for trying to start things off on the right foot."

Ugh. I guess he is trying. I should too. Even though he's the one who broke it off with me and turned into a complete douchebag right after, so really, it's about balance.

"Just because I can suck things up and tolerate you being here doesn't mean I want to get intimate."

His brows go up. "Who said anything about intimate?" He grins at me, and damn it, I hate that his smile still has the power to knock the air from my lungs. In fact, nothing has changed about him at all. I had foolishly hoped that if I ever saw him again, perhaps a wart would have popped up on the end of his perfect nose, or that he'd lose all the tight, lean muscle I know he has under his clothes, or maybe he'd lose a couple of his perfect white teeth, forever screwing up his smile. Maybe he'd lose some hair while he was at it. But no. His hair is still thick, shiny, and dark. The smile is still gorgeous, his face is smooth and blemish free, maybe a bit more of a beard than the last time I saw him, but it suits him well, and his body seems as in shape as ever.

"There's nowhere to get a drink around here anyway," I tell

him, averting my eyes before his ego gets a boost. "I'm guessing you didn't know that part of the job description. Total isolation."

"You're right, I didn't," he says, and I can't help but feel a little smug about that.

James is a city guy through and through. He likes going out to bars, to restaurants; he likes to date as many women as he can on his days off. I'm not sure how much of that is his actual personality or if it's a method of distraction (you'd think I would know James on a more personal level, considering, but when you're in it for the sex, you tend to skip over that stuff). Either way, we're in the middle of nowhere and I know it will drive him crazy.

"And so now you're stuck here, with me," I tell him, trying not to smile.

His dark brows knit together. "In case it isn't clear, Laila, I don't have a problem with you. You're the one with the problem."

That was the wrong thing to say.

I make sure he knows that.

I give him the death glare. I swear I see him shrink back, just a little.

"If I have a problem, it's because you . . ." I stop myself abruptly, closing my eyes, trying to remember the Zen yoga training that Ella makes me and Lady Jane do every Saturday morning with her, as if that's enough to get me through the week without losing my damn mind.

"I what?"

I exhale slowly through my mouth before opening my eyes again, fixing my gaze on him. "Nothing."

I watch him closely for a moment, trying to see if he's squirming. He knows what he did. He knows how he broke things off between us. He can't possibly think any of that was okay, that he's not at fault.

To his credit now, he does seem a little squirmy. He worries his perfect lips between his teeth, lips that I've had all over my body.

"Look," he says, tilting his head as he stares down at me. He's always been a giant next to me, even though I'm tall. "I'm serious about wanting to start over. I know I messed up in the past. I know things ended between us badly, and I know that I'm mostly at fault for it."

"Mostly?" I question, folding my arms across my chest.

His eyes go sharp for a moment. "Aye. Mostly. But I'm here now, and you're here, and either we bury the bloody hatchet and start again, or we make ourselves miserable for the next while. And I need this job, Laila, just as much as I assume you need yours. Who knows how long that will be, but we have to accept that we're working together."

I sigh, tilting my head back to the sky for a moment. The first stars are starting to appear. "Okay."

"We already shook on it, but do you want to hug it out?" he asks, holding out his arms.

I balk, giving him an incredulous look. The nerve of this guy. "You have got to be kidding me."

"What? Prince Magnus already gave me a hug. You can't tell me that this is inappropriate." He flashes me a grin.

Before I even have a chance to say anything or try to move away, James comes in and envelops me in a big bear hug.

I freeze in response, shocked and not wanting to give in either. But still, just for a moment, my eyes flutter closed and I find myself resting my head on his chest, breathing in his familiar scent of cedar and salt. My god, I can't remember the last time a man hugged me, let alone touched me.

And it's with that worrying thought that I abruptly rip myself out of his grasp. I didn't want to—I would rather have stayed there for a while, just letting the comfort overtake me and smother all my problems—but it had to be done. Of course, now I feel colder without it.

"Okay, so you had your hug," I tell him, staring at the snow between our feet. "You had your handshake. And we've agreed to bury the hatchet. Sounds like you've gotten everything you wanted."

"Not quite," he says, eyeing the house. "To be honest, I'm not sure I would have taken this job had I known how isolated we would be. Please tell me that you get to the city at least a few times a week."

My left brow goes up. He hasn't changed at all.

"What?" he asks.

"Nothing. You just have the wrong impression of my job. Again. If you were Magnus's bodyguard, Einar, then yes, you'd go at least once a week into Oslo, and not just to see the king and queen but probably to go out and do fun things. But Ella . . . she's more of a homebody. She goes out only for business and royal duties. And the kids, well, we try to keep them here as much as possible."

"But if my duty is to protect Ella and the children . . ."

I bite back a smile. "Then my job is pretty much your job now." I let that smile loose once I see how crestfallen he looks. "Going from protecting the regal Prince Eddie of Fairfax in the throes of London, jet-setting around the world, to being stuck in an isolated manor watching over two zany children, their no-nonsense homebody mother, and their irritable nanny."

"Does she have to be irritable?"

I laugh, which I immediately regret. All my life I've been known for having the loudest laugh. I'm surprised herds of reindeer aren't suddenly flushed out of the forest from the noise.

He's smiling at me now. Not so much that shit-eating smirk he wears so well, but something gentler, something that softens his eyes.

It makes me want to be . . . *nice* to him.

What a ridiculous idea.

"Look," I tell him. "I don't have the energy to go into the city tonight, and even if I did, I don't think it's a good idea. If I were you, I'd just get myself acquainted with the estate and the rest of the staff and try to settle in." I head off toward the house and pause, looking at him over my shoulder. "There's a bar in the library where most of us spend our evenings. Feel free to help yourself."

I go up the steps, and even though I'm bundled up like Stay Puft, I can feel his eyes on my ass. That part of him definitely hasn't changed either.

I decide to be smart and spend the rest of my night off in my room, skipping dinner because listening to everyone ask James questions and hearing him talk with that damn sexy brogue of his is bound to piss me off further. Then again, the longer I stay in my room, attempting to read a psychological thriller from the growing collection on my bookshelf, the more my brain wants to stew on what's happening out there. And the more I start thinking about James, the more I start realizing that everything about my job has now changed, possibly forever, or at least until one of us quits. And quitting is not an option.

Though, to be honest, my role as nanny has not been the

easy job I thought it would be. Ella and Magnus are lovely, very down-to-earth people, and I do appreciate the zany family atmosphere here. Everyone is easy to get along with and friendly (if a little up in your business), and I crave that sense of stability, especially when it feels like things with my grandmother are so precarious.

But the boys . . . *whew.* I want to love them, and I hang on to the belief that in time I will grow closer to them. But Bjorn is an absolute terror who doesn't listen to me no matter what I do, and while Tor is young, he's impossible to keep happy. He cries at the drop of a hat. As a result, we don't go into public that often. When we do, the Norwegian tabloids always either comment on me, being the poor forsaken nanny who is in over her head (case in point, when Bjorn smashed a chocolate ice cream cone in my face, creating a wonderful photo op), or they make fun of the kids. I know it hurts Magnus and Ella to read it, and in time, the boys will realize how unfairly they've been treated.

Anyway, I can see why a protection officer is needed, because the older the boys get, the more they'll be out and about, and the more that we'll need protection. I just never thought it would be James taking on the role, swooping back into my life like a disgraced knight in tarnished armor, about to upturn everything for good.

I WAKE UP with the lights on in my room and the paperback on my face.

Crap. I fell asleep.

And from the way my stomach is growling, perhaps skipping dinner wasn't such a good idea.

Then I remember the reason why I skipped dinner.

James Hunter.

Why, oh why, is he here? I know he already used the whole "of all the gin joints" *Casablanca* line, but seriously, why did he have to walk into mine?

I groan and roll over, glancing at my phone. It's almost midnight. At least everyone should be asleep. I'll just go into the kitchen and see if there are any leftovers. The cook, Sigrid, probably made extra food, not knowing how much James would eat.

I get up, put on my slippers, and head out into the hall. It's dark down this wing, save for a few sconce lights, and I'm extra careful not to alert James in case he still sleeps lightly.

Shit. How annoying is it that I know how he sleeps? (Naked, actually, and on his stomach, facing away from you, arm tucked under the pillow.)

I make my way to the kitchen, not at all surprised to see Lady Jane sitting at the table in her fluffy leopard-print robe, drinking a giant cup of some lavender Valium concoction. She often battles her insomnia at this time of night.

"There you are," she says to me, and pats the seat beside her. "Here. Come sit down. Let me make you a tea. Or food. You hungry? Oh, you must be hungry. You didn't have any dinner. Are you feeling all right? Feverish?"

I can't even get a word in before she's coming toward me and pressing the back of her hand on my forehead. "You do feel a little warm," she says.

"I'm fine," I tell her. "Just came to get a snack before I go back to sleep."

One of the benefits of living in the same house as the royals, and having them treat you as family, is having unfettered access to the kitchen and bar. Anything you want, any time of day, you just go right on ahead and get it. When I worked for the Fairfaxes, we (the help) were sectioned off in our own house and quarters, so we didn't have quite the same "family" atmosphere as we do here. It's one of the reasons why, even when the going gets tough, I like working here.

"But you weren't at dinner," Jane says, sitting back down. "Magnus said he gave you the night off. I thought maybe you'd gone out."

I laugh, opening up the fridge. "That would be a first."

"That's what I said, though I also thought you would deserve it." She pauses. "You know I worry about you, Laila."

"Why?" I ask, pulling out a dish of cold roasted lemon potatoes. That's good enough for me. I close the fridge door and give her an expectant look. Lady Jane has looked after Ella for a long time, and now that she has Magnus and her children, I feel Jane's overbearing tendencies being directed toward me.

"Well, because you're so young and single."

My eyes roll to the ceiling. Good lord. "Twenty-eight isn't so young."

"I'm thirty years older than you," she points out.

"Well, you don't act like it," I tell her, grabbing a fork and taking the potatoes over to the table. "If anything, I should be worried about *you*. Why are you still single? Huh?"

Her eyes narrow wickedly. "You know why. No one is good enough for me."

"Maybe it's the same for me," I tell her, spearing a potato with a fork.

"You're not going to warm that up?" she asks, looking horrified.

I shrug. "Too lazy."

She doesn't look impressed. "So you think no one is good enough for you? No, I don't think that's it."

I point my potato at her. "Hey, I have standards."

"I'm sure you do. But in the four months that you've been working here, living in this house, I haven't seen you go on a single date, haven't even heard you talk about a single boy."

"Boy," I snort. "I date men, Lady Jane. Just not at the moment. I'm busy, if you can't tell."

"You have your days off."

"And you really expect me to date a guy on Sundays only? Never mind the fact that I'm seeing my grandmother on those days?"

"It just doesn't seem right," she says after a moment. "You know, Ella was single for so long before she and Magnus became involved. I know she wasn't quite sold on him in the beginning, but I was just so happy for her to be with someone."

"But I'm sure Ella would have been fine if she stayed single too."

She sighs and has a loud sip of her tea. "I suppose. But you know, she was never as happy as she was when she fell in love with Magnus. Even if she would have been fine, I would have hated for her to miss out on all the good stuff."

"Well, *I'm* doing just fine," I tell her, feeling defensive. "There's absolutely nothing wrong with being single. Besides, I'm focused on this job right now, this career. The rest, the falling in love and getting a boyfriend, that can come later." Or, like, never. The less hassle in my life, the better, in my opinion. The more detached from people you are, the safer you'll be. I learned that the hard way.

"Hmmph," she says, leaning back in her chair and fixing me with her gaze. "You know what I think it is? Someone broke your heart."

Oh boy. Here we go. Even though Lady Jane is Ella's lady-in-waiting, she's become this meddling mother figure for everyone in the house. I'm not saying it's all bad, but if you have a problem, she will definitely try to solve it for you—regardless of whether you want her to or not.

"No one broke my heart," I tell her, and I'm not really lying either. I don't think I'd fallen in love with James; I'd just fallen in very strong lust with him, and he took that lust and twisted it around until it snapped in two. I had all the rejection of a broken heart but with twice the bitterness.

"Uh-huh," she says, taking another sip of her tea.

I finish my potatoes quicker now, afraid of where this conversation might go.

"So James is a nice man," she says in a cheery voice. A little too cheery.

"He is," I say, smashing the last potato in my mouth so I don't have to talk.

"I have to admit, I found it kind of strange that you worked together for so long in London, hadn't seen each other for at least a year, and then his first day here, you don't even show up for dinner."

I attempt to swallow. Was I that obvious?

I shrug, getting to my feet and taking the dish to the sink to wash it since the dishwasher is already running. "I was tired. How often do I get a night off to just be alone in my room?"

She thinks that over. "Maybe. Or maybe you don't like James."

I give her a very fake incredulous look as I rinse the dish, squirting out the soap. "What are you talking about?"

Her eyes dance beneath her blunt bangs. "That's it, isn't it? You don't like him. Something happened at the Fairfaxes', and now you hold a grudge."

How is she this astute? She must be reaching.

I need to keep my cool.

As much as Lady Jane is a servant, part of the staff, like the rest of us nonroyals, I know I can't confide in her. If I ever told her the truth of what happened between James and me, not only would she watch our every move like a hawk, but I have no doubt she would tell Ella. The lady can't keep any secrets. And then Ella would go about finding another nanny. One who can control her beloved children better and hasn't slept with the new bodyguard.

I dry off the dish with a towel and shake my head. "You're the one who needs to get out of the house," I tell her. "You're making up fantasies."

"I'm not. I'm just observant."

I put away the dish and walk over to the table, resting my palms on top and leaning toward her. "Lady Jane," I say. "I don't have a problem with James. There is no grudge. I honestly didn't know him very well. We weren't together much. I was always with baby Madeline; he was always protecting Eddie. He was outside of their lives; I was in the middle of it. We'd be friendly when we saw each other, but that was usually in passing. Honestly. I don't know James well, but I like him just fine, and I'm glad that he's working for the prince and princess."

I hold her eyes until it feels uncomfortable, and then she deflates, shoulders sinking. See, she wanted us to have a problem. What a drama queen.

"Oh, all right," she says. "I guess I'm just imagining what's not there."

"That's right. And I'm sure the two of us will be having many dinners together in the future."

And with that I leave Lady Jane with her tea and head back down the hall to my room. I quickly use my en suite bathroom, then get into my pajamas and crawl into bed.

As I do so, the headboard of the bed jostles against the wall.

And then I hear a knock back.

Oh my god. James. His bed must be right up against mine. I'd gotten so used to having no one in that room.

"You up?" I hear very faintly through the wall.

Shit. How is it that I can hear him? How thin are the walls in this place?

I raise my fist, about to bang on the wall, but then stop myself. I don't want him to think I can hear him, and I don't want to start playing some silly game with him.

I turn around, more carefully this time, and switch off the light. I pull the covers up to my chin, totally conscious of even breathing now, hoping that I don't snore.

"Good night, Laila." His voice comes through the wall.

I put my pillow over my face.

Four

. . . .

LAILA

Two years ago

"GOOD NIGHT, LITTLE PRINCESS," I WHISPER TO BABY Madeline as she stretches her arms above her head, yawning deeply as her eyes flutter closed. A sense of relief pours through me, knowing she's finally going to sleep. Duchess Monica is lucky that her daughter sleeps through the night, but I've never met an infant who rebels against her bedtime like Madeline does. Even though I've been putting her to bed at a reasonable hour every day this week, she'll literally just lie in her crib and stare at me, as if I'm her entertainment and she's waiting for me to do a dance, which of course I end up doing. I have to admit, it's flattering to have a royal baby think the world of you, but I think she's just working through the fact that her mother, who normally puts her to bed, has been gone every night this week. I know from experience that when the nanny first steps in, there are always a few growing pains, no matter the age of the child.

I give the plush rabbit I'm holding a squeeze, pressing it to my chest for a moment. I have no doubt there are a million nanny cams in Primrose Cottage, but all they would see is the new nanny holding on to the stuffed rabbit before giving it to the princess. They don't see that the rabbit gives me comfort too.

I reluctantly place the rabbit in the crib with Madeline, who is finally fast asleep, and smile, then take in a deep breath and steady my nerves. It's funny how free and real I always feel when I'm with the children in my care, but the moment I have to step away, the mask slides back on my face. I've only been working for the Duke and Duchess of Fairfax for a week, and while everything seems to have gone well, I'm eternally aware that with one slipup I could lose my job. Every time I start a new position I walk on eggshells for months, and with a high-profile role such as this one, the feeling is tenfold. Even though the Fairfaxes have been gone most of the week, traveling in the US for charity work, I know I have to uphold a good image in front of the rest of the staff. I guess I'm fortunate, in a way, that my bosses are gone my first week at work—I've always worked better without constant supervision or micromanaging—but to me that means I have to try even harder to act like I deserve this job, like this is a test of sorts.

You're doing good, I remind myself as I pick up the baby monitor and step into the hallway, closing the door until it's almost shut. Lately I've been trying to counter every negative thought that pops up with something encouraging, but in my brain it's always easier to believe the negative.

I turn around and run right into someone tall and solid. A scream dies in my throat as the person reaches out and grabs my shoulders.

"I'm so sorry," a man says in a Scottish accent, and in the dimly lit hallway, it takes me a moment to realize this is James, one of Duke Eddie's bodyguards. "I didn't mean to startle you."

He lets go of me, and I take a step back, pressing my hand against my chest.

"I didn't even hear you," I say, trying to calm my heart.

"Side effect of the job," he says in a light voice.

I've seen James before with the duke, but obviously when he's working there's no time for small talk. When he's on duty he's all brooding and stone-faced, but now that I see him close up, I realize he's not as serious as I first thought. There's a small scar running up the side of his face, drawing attention to his dark brown eyes, with a seductive slant. His full lips curl into a slow smile, and I notice how lush they are, his teeth perfectly straight and white.

"You always work so late?" he asks, his accent giving him a deep, raspy voice, the kind of voice that tickles some pleasure spot at the back of my brain.

"She doesn't know the meaning of bedtime," I tell him. "I think she misses her mother."

He nods and leans casually against the wall, the tie tucked under his tailored jacket and the top few buttons of his shirt undone. The jacket is unbuttoned, like he started undressing on the way to the servants' quarters, his shift over.

"But the later she goes to bed, the more she sleeps through the night," I admit, and he smiles, a bright smile that makes the dim hallway flicker a little.

"I'm James," he says, extending his hand. "I'm afraid we haven't had a chance to be properly introduced."

"Laila," I tell him, reaching out, and he grasps my hand in his. His hand is warm and his grip is strong, not enough to cause me any distress but enough to hint at what he's capable of. I catch a whiff of his cologne and it's earthy, woodsy, like the pine forests of my childhood.

Damn. I knew he was good-looking already; I mean, there's something about a bodyguard and the way they prowl and protect with utmost confidence that would make the most cynical person swoon, not to mention I'm a sucker for a guy with brooding dark looks, which I blame on an early obsession with Mr. Rochester from *Jane Eyre* (who, in hindsight, is a bit of a problematic hero, but hey, we like what we like).

He lets go of my hand and nods down the hall. "Walk you home?"

I find myself biting my lip in coy response and nod. "Sure."

My goodness, what the hell has come over me? I think back to my pep talk before I stepped into the hallway, the mantra I've been repeating to myself: *You're doing good, don't mess it up* (translation: the last thing I need to do is look all googly-eyed and hormonal the moment a handsome guy shows up in my life, especially if I'm working and living alongside said handsome guy).

I give my head an internal shake as we walk down the hall. I'm pretty tall, but walking beside him makes me feel like I'm in his shadow.

"So you've only been working here for about a week, right?" he asks, and I nod. "Where were you working before this?"

This should feel like small talk, but it genuinely sounds like he's interested.

"I was a nanny for a high-profile diplomat in Sweden," I tell him. "But they weren't a great fit for me, so when my recruitment agency told me about the Fairfaxes, obviously I was interested. I'm still in shock that they actually picked me. The competition for this job was fierce."

He holds open the French door at the end of the hall for me, and we step out into the night air. He wasn't wrong about me working late; it's dark outside save for a few fairy lights in the trees beside my quarters and the sconces lighting the path. The air smells like night-blooming jasmine and it's pleasantly warm. The heat waves this July have had England melting all over the place, but you don't really notice when you're inside all day with the baby. Besides, where Primrose Cottage is, just outside London, some topography with the Thames and the surrounding hills makes it feel cooler than the city.

"Are you Swedish?" he asks. "You sound Swedish."

"Norwegian, actually," I tell him, trying not to get annoyed at being mistaken for a Swede since I can't blame him for thinking so. "But my accent is a little morphed from working in so many different places over the years. I tend to mimic without realizing it."

"Aye," he says, his accent coming on thicker. "Wish I had that problem. When I worked in Belgium, I thought my brogue would lessen, but that isn't the case with us Scots. Certainly not me anyway."

I glance up at him, the lights casting shadows on his face, illuminating his features or casting them in dark relief. His jaw is angled, hard and sharp under a five-o'clock shadow, but his lips are soft and full. He is beautiful, and for a moment I feel like I'm a character in a movie and the director just told me to act smitten.

"I've always been a fan of the Scottish accent," I tell him before looking away so that the light doesn't show me being an utter simp for him. I clear my throat and focus on the stone path in front of us. "So how long have you been working for the Fairfaxes?"

"A few years," he says. "I was with them when they moved to the island in Canada."

"That must have been a trip," I say. I remember that before Madeline was born, when Monica was being lambasted by the press simply for her Hollywood background and the color of her skin (though of course no one in the media would admit to the blatant racism), she and Eddie went overseas to a small island in British Columbia to escape the scrutiny. It seemed to work because after that I heard very little about them, like they finally got the peace they needed.

"It wasn't London, that's for sure," James says. "I was more than happy to come back here. I need the city lights and the people to keep me going. Protection officers aren't meant to relax."

"That's kind of sad in a way," I tell him. "What do you end up doing for fun, then? I mean, you don't work all the time. I know you have shifts with the others."

When he doesn't say anything I glance at him. He appears deep in thought, the light from the fairy lights making his eyes seem to glow. "Well, usually I try to make sure that I'm out and about when I'm not on duty. There's a few pubs I like to visit, some friends I try to get a drink with when I'm off."

"Must be hard to make friends as a bodyguard?"

"Aye," he says, nodding. "It is. That's why I think it's important to try to get out and socialize when I can. I need the distraction. And you? Do you end up having much of a social life when you're a nanny? Seems you work as many hours as I do."

"I try not to," I tell him. "I mean, I don't know that many people here, and I don't want to make enemies on my first week."

He spits out a laugh that's more of a bark. "Enemies, huh?"

I shrug, giving him a quick smile. I said it as a joke, but it's kind of the truth. I imagine it would be hard to have a social life as a nanny, but I've always leaned into being a loner anyway. It's easier that way when I feel I can't let my guard down around people, and with my mask on, I still come across as odd sometimes, which makes making friends hard. Growing up in a tiny village where everyone not only knows your name but also what you eat for breakfast, I went from being Laila the Pitied ("Oh that poor girl, losing both her parents so young") to Laila the Strange ("Oh that weirdo with her dark music and empty stare"). I was always branded as "different." And if different stands out in a tiny village, you can imagine it stands out when you're a nanny for a prestigious or royal family.

Which is why you better not view James as a friend, I remind myself, even though the way my body is reacting to him is not very friendlike.

"I'm just boring as hell," I tell him. "When work is done, you'll find my nose in a book."

"Oh yeah?" he says, brows raised. "What kind of books do you like to read?"

Tell him the truth, a small voice says inside me, the voice I usually shut up.

"Psychological thrillers," I say. This isn't a lie, but my preferred reads are young adult and middle grade books, and at my age, if you tell most people that, they'll look at you like you have two heads.

"Ah," he says. "*Gone Girl* and the like. Stories of complicated women who doff their husbands."

"Something like that."

The servants' quarters is a modest building down a short path from the main one that looks like it used to be a barn before being converted. It's made of the same stone as the main house, though its arched windows have mullions instead of diamond panes. A single door is in the middle of the front of the building, an art deco–patterned bronze, and has the family crest above it. James holds the door open for me and we step into the hall.

"You met the rest of the workers yet?" he asks, lowering his voice now since it's late. The building is two levels, with four bedrooms down on the first floor and four more on the second, which is where my room is. As far as I know all the rooms have an en suite, so you never really run into people here.

"Just the cook and gardener," I tell him. "They seem nice." Well, the gardener is nice. The cook doesn't say much and gives me the stink eye, but James doesn't need to know how sensitive I am to things like that.

"Well, all us PPO live on the first floor," he says. "I'm sure you'll get used to us coming and going. For now, it seems like we're on the same shift."

"Wait," I say, stopping at the foot of the stairs, a red velvet carpet running up them. "Why aren't you with Eddie—I mean, the duke—right now if he's in America? All that distraction seems right up your alley."

He runs his hand over his jaw, his facial hair making a scratching sound in the quiet of the building. For a split second I wonder how that hair would feel on my soft skin, but I push that intrusive thought away. Totally not wanted.

"They gave me time off," he admits, looking sheepish. "Frankly I don't know what I did to piss him off, but . . ." He trails off and then straightens up, his face growing impassive, like he just caught himself telling me something he shouldn't have. "I appreciate it, though. I'm such a workaholic I probably wouldn't take any vacation if they didn't make me."

"I get it," I say with a nod, because I totally do.

He jerks his thumb over his shoulder toward a door that I assume is the one to his room. "I was going to change and then head out into the city since I don't have to be up at a certain time. Do you want to join me?"

My stomach does a strange flip, something I'm not used to feeling. I can't recall the last time a guy asked me out, even just as a friend or a coworker, which is what I assume James is doing here.

"Wish I could," I tell him, waving the baby monitor in front of his face. "But I'm on duty around the clock until they get back."

He frowns. "There's no backup nanny?"

I shake my head. "Technically nannies are the backup for the mothers."

"And you've only been working here a week or so, right?"

"Launched right into the deep end," I say, mimicking a flying motion with the baby monitor.

He gives the banister a quick tap with his long fingers. "Well, perhaps when Monica comes back and if we both happen to have a night off . . ."

I stare at him for a moment and his mouth quirks up sheepishly.

"You know, if you felt like making some enemies."

I laugh loudly, then clamp my hand over my mouth, hoping I don't wake anyone up. My laugh is very distinctive. "Okay," I tell him. "That sounds like fun."

I can feel my cheeks burning for no reason at all, so I shoot him a quick smile and head up the stairs before I laugh at something else he says. What is it about this guy that makes me feel like a schoolgirl?

"Good night," he calls after me.

"Good night," I say over my shoulder, trying to ignore the fluttering in my chest.

I quickly go to my room and shut the door, letting out a deep breath. Even though I haven't been here long, I've already started to associate my room with a sanctuary. I'm aware that my room could be searched at any time, that it's not really mine but comes as part of my employment, so I keep everything as organized as possible. Still, I go to the closet and bring out one of my stuffed animals—Knut, a fluffy polar bear that my grandmother bought me after she took a trip to Svalbard to visit a friend. It's managed to stay pristine white over the years, though the eyes are worn down and have lost their shine.

I put the baby monitor down and hold Knut to my chest as I sit on the corner of my bed, trying to gather my thoughts. James seems like a nice guy. I mean, he's definitely hot, and there's something about his energy—the way he seemed to observe me like he was trying to see past my mask made my stomach flutter. But I know the last thing I need is to start feeling anything for anyone I work with, no matter how mild. Hell, I don't let myself feel anything for anyone; the idea of having to keep my walls up seems exhausting at this point, and I've been burned too many times to let them down again.

"So that settles it," I say in a hush, as if he could hear me from downstairs. *When—if—he invites you into the city next time, say no. Easy as that. Better to stop this before it starts.*

I give Knut a little squeeze, as if the bear just gave me a pep talk, then I put him back in the closet and get ready for bed.

Five

· · · · · · ·

JAMES

I SET MY ALARM FOR SIX IN THE MORNING, EXPECTING TO have to jump into action by seven. But by the time I shower, trim my beard, get dressed in my suit, and step out into the hall, the house is dead quiet. Not a single sound except for a clock ticking from somewhere.

I make my way on the creaky hardwood floors of the hall down toward the kitchen, expecting at least the cook to be up and making food. But no. Nothing.

Am I in the bloody twilight zone? Did zombies attack in the night?

I leave the kitchen and then make my way to the front doors, opening them. More snow has fallen overnight, and everything is cold and pristine. I step out onto the grand porch and crane my neck to get a look at Einar's cabin. Smoke is rising from his chimney, so at least that means he's up.

The air certainly has a bite to it, so I step back inside and close the doors, just in time to see Laila walking down the hall toward the kitchen.

"Hey," I whisper to her, striding over.

She takes one look at me and keeps walking, like she's embarrassed to know me. I guess she figured out that I can hear her through the walls and she's a pretty loud snorer.

I round the corner into the kitchen, grabbing her elbow lightly.

"Where is everyone?" I ask.

Her brows rise. "Sleeping?" she says, as if it's normal for an entire royal palace to sleep in. She looks me up and down discerningly. "Are you on the way to a business meeting?"

She turns and goes to the kettle, flicking it on. She's wearing pink-and-white-striped pajamas, her hair in a messy pile on top of her head. With sleep still in her eyes and not a lick of makeup on her face, she's far more gorgeous than she should be.

"It's almost seven thirty," I tell her, glancing at my watch.

She leans back against the counter and folds her arms. "I don't know what to tell you, suit boy, but this isn't jolly ol' England. This is Norway. And for whatever reason, this house likes to get up late. Even the kids. Thank god, because I can use the beauty sleep."

"Well, it suits you well," I blurt out. I cover it up with a charming smile. "The beauty sleep."

She gives me a withering look, not amused. She never took my compliments well, rebounding like she's Teflon.

"Though I must say, I didn't get enough beauty sleep myself," I quickly add. "On account of the thin walls and someone's predisposition to snoring."

Her cheeks go pink. That was one thing I loved about her,

the fact that she blushed easily, especially with well-placed dirty talk.

Stay focused, James. You're going to run your new job into the ground if you're not careful.

"You're going to have to move your bed to the other side of the room," she tells me, raising her chin, refusing to be embarrassed even though her cheeks don't lie. "Or wear earplugs. Also, I don't snore."

She turns around and grabs a mug from the cupboard.

"Yes, you do," I tell her, stepping closer. "Especially after some wine or whisky. Then you're a bloody banshee, shaking the whole damn bed."

When Laila and I had our little trysts, I didn't often spend the night since my own room was downstairs. But when I did, I had to put the pillow over my head. I'm a light sleeper by nature, and her snoring would make the room rumble. Still, there was something about it that I found endearing—like how could such a beautiful woman produce such a horrendous noise?

"James," she hisses, whipping around, fire in her eyes. "It isn't starting over again if you keep bringing up how we knew each other before."

"Everyone knows we know each other."

"Not in *that* way, they don't," she says, her eyes darting out to the empty hall and back. "*Never* in that way, or I might lose my job. And you might too. And if you truly want me to bury the very big hatchet that I personally sharpened just for you, then you can't ever mention that we were . . . uh, together."

She has a point. "Aye." I raise my palms in surrender. "Fair enough. I'll try to erase you from my memory. Got to say, it won't be easy."

"Oh really? Is that so?" The bitterness in her voice makes me step back. "Because you were so fucking good at it before."

Ouch.

Out in the foyer, there's the sound of the front door opening.

She gives me one last nasty glare and then turns around, pulling instant coffee out of the cupboard.

"You're still drinking instant coffee?" I say. "What's wrong with you?"

"I'm used to it," she grumbles, spooning it into her cup.

"God morgen," Sigrid, the cook, says cheerfully as she comes bustling into the kitchen, all smiles. "Good morning to you, James."

"God morgen, Sigrid," I tell her. "Best that I learn Norwegian sooner or later."

The sooner the better, since I don't think Sigrid speaks a lot of English. She just nods at me and goes about in the kitchen, getting ready for breakfast.

Laila leaves the room with her mug of disgusting instant coffee (black! She even drinks it black!) and I make myself a quick cup from the Keurig, like a proper person does when the French press isn't available, dousing it with cream.

Then I set about trying to find where Laila went.

I look in all the rooms, then head to her bedroom, knocking on the door.

"*What?*" she asks through the door, her voice sharp.

"How did you know it was me?"

I hear her exhale and then she opens the door, staring at me with a pinched expression.

"What do you want?"

"I want to drink my coffee with you," I tell her. "You're the only one up *and* the only one I know. Can I come in?"

The struggle behind her eyes is real. I can tell she wants to shut the door on me, but luckily she relents.

"Fine," she says, opening it just wide enough for me to squeeze past.

I step inside the room, and she closes the door. Then thinks better of it, and opens it, leaving it that way.

I know what she's doing. She's being smart. If someone were to walk past her room and hear us talking with the door closed, perhaps they'd get the wrong idea. Also, this is her way of keeping me in line, reminding me that we're starting over again and nothing from the past is to be mentioned. I'm on the same page as her, but she wouldn't believe it.

I walk around the room, taking it in. It's the same size as mine, mint-green wallpaper with silver filigree accents. Her bed is small, piled with thick Nordic quilts, and pressed right up against the wall where mine is.

I stop by a framed photo of her and Helge, her grandmother. The photo is different from the one she used to have in her room in London. In this one, Laila has her arms around her, and though both are laughing, Helge looks much smaller and frailer. I feel a familiar pinch in my chest, that conflicting feeling of wishing I had someone like that in my life, who raised me and loved me, and then being relieved that I never have to deal with anything like the loss of someone I deeply love. I already went through that when my parents gave me up, and then when my wife left me, and I'm making it my life's mission not to go through anything like that again.

"How is your grandmother?" I ask, my voice automatically going soft, not sure if I'm being too personal.

"She's good," Laila says.

I look at her, and for the first time since I've been here, I notice the lines of grief around her eyes.

She takes a sip of her coffee, slender fingers wrapped around the mug, then gives me a quick smile. "I mean, she's as good as she can be," she says.

"I'm really sorry," I tell her, putting my hands in my pockets. "I know how much she means to you. When I'd heard from Eddie that you left . . ."

"You were probably glad I was out of your hair."

I shake my head. "Not even a little. I worried about you. I wanted to reach out to you to see how you were, but . . ." God, why does this feel so bloody awkward?

She gives me a dismissive wave. "It's fine."

"Magnus mentioned over dinner last night that she has dementia and she's in a care home. Does she still know who you are?"

I expect her to brush me off with that question, but instead her features soften, looking defeated.

"She does," she says quietly. "Sometimes. Other times no. But on her good days, it's like I have her back, if only for a short while." She looks away, having another sip of her coffee, silence humming in the room. "But those days are getting few and far between. I wish I could just pop by and see her every day, you know, especially when she's having a good day. But I can't. So I just have to hope that on Sundays she'll happen to remember."

Laila isn't the kind of girl you see vulnerable all that often. In fact, in our time working together she's always put up a tough front, like nothing bothers her. I feel like I'm seeing more of the real her now than I ever did then. We might have been sharing our bodies with each other, but neither of us ever opened up in a personal way, aside from the occasional comment here and there.

I should be honored that she's confiding in me now, considering how things ended between us, but I can tell she's realizing her mistake. That softness in her eyes disappears, her shoulders straightening.

"I better get ready for the day," she says stiffly, her eyes going to the door.

Just as Prince Magnus walks past.

"James!" he exclaims, as if we're long-lost friends and he hasn't seen me in years. "Good morning to you! How did you sleep?" He doesn't come in the room, I guess respecting Laila's privacy.

I give Laila a parting glance and then step out into the hall.

"Slept great, sir," I tell him. "I've been up for some time."

"Oh, stop with the *sir* business. It's Magnus," he says, whacking me on the back. He's in his pajama pants and sheepskin slippers, having thrown on a fleece sweater with a picture of a Christmas tree on it—a sweater that is only meant for ugly Christmas sweater parties and certainly not meant for an heir to the throne. "And we don't stick to a schedule around here in the mornings. Unless we have to. And then I have a million alarms and wake-up calls. Need a coffee refill?"

He takes my mug out of my hands and saunters down to the kitchen, just as Laila shuts the door on me. I hurry on after him.

"So, James," he says, sticking my mug under the Keurig. "How would you like to accompany me into the city today?"

I put my hands behind my back. "Of course, sir, anywhere you wish."

He gives his head a shake, his messy hair jostling, and I can tell he doesn't like the whole *sir* thing, but I can't help it. Especially if we're going out of the house and I need to be on patrol, I can't think of him as a friend or anything like that. I know I considered Eddie a friend, but it complicates things a bit when you're their employee, and this time around I want to keep things as uncomplicated as possible—especially with Laila back in the picture.

"Great. How about we leave in an hour or two? Gives us enough time to eat."

He hands me my mug, and I thank him.

"Will it just be you?"

He nods. "Yes, me, you, Ottar, and Einar. The boys will stay behind, and I'm sure Ella isn't interested."

On the one hand I'm excited to be on duty outside the house. On the other hand I wish Laila was coming with us. I'm not sure why. It's not like I can bug her or talk to her in a public setting when I'm on duty. I guess there's this sad little part of me that likes to remind her of what my role is and what I can do. What can I say? My job brings out the alpha male in me.

I don't dwell on it for long. Sigrid sets up a buffet, as apparently she does every morning, allowing everyone to get their food whenever they want. After a breakfast of cold cuts, smoked salmon, thin slices of dark brown bread, and tons of butter and cream cheese, we're heading out to the SUV.

I take the front seat beside the stoic Einar at the wheel, who is much older than I am and looks like the product of very angular people, with his sharp jaw and razor cheekbones. He's also wearing eighties-style ski-goggle sunglasses, despite the day being very dim and gray.

Ottar is in the back seat with Magnus, calling stores to see if they can close them so that the prince can do his clothes shopping in private. Naturally, the stores all comply, because they all want to be the place where the Prince of Norway shops.

Meanwhile, I'm just happy to be heading into the city.

"What kind of a drinker are you, James?" Magnus asks me.

I twist in my seat to look at him. "I beg your pardon?"

"What kind of drinker are you? You're Scottish, so that's a start. You know I have this bar I go to, total divey, hole-in-the-wall place. I should take you there after your shopping spree."

I frown at him. "*My* shopping spree?"

He laughs. "You thought we were going shopping for me? Look, I know you saw me in *that* sweater this morning, but I can assure you I have a lot of clothes. Proper clothes. Not to say I won't take a look if they have some new Tom Ford in, but no, James boy, this is about you."

Einar glances at me, and though I can't see his eyes underneath those ridiculous sunglasses, I know he's feeling sorry for me. Poor new bodyguard, has to have the prince buy him new clothes.

"Your Majesty, really, I'm fine." I throw the *Your Majesty* part in there to remind him that in the end, I'm here to protect him. Not to be a guinea pig in some makeover.

"James," he says, slapping his fingers along his knee. "We're going. Consider this your uniform."

Guess I can't argue with that. I look down at my gray suit and navy tie and wonder where I went wrong. It seems everything I learned being a PPO for Eddie and others has been thrown to the wind.

The drive to Oslo doesn't take as long as I thought it would, and when we start getting into the city proper, my spirits rise a bit. I haven't had any time to explore Oslo, and even though I am officially on duty, I can't help but take note of what look like cool restaurants, museums, or bars. We eventually stop at a store in what seems to be an upper-class, boutique area of the city and park the SUV at the back, and I slip into my security role. Whether you're protecting the Prince of Fairfax or the Prince of Norway, the job is always the same. My focus sharpens so much that it's almost an out-of-body experience. I float to the store, every sense heightened, my eyes seeing everything, my ears hearing everything. The sense of power I get from having the role of protector never fails to get my adrenaline and endorphins running.

The owner of the store opens the back door, and Einar takes the lead and strides in, casing the joint. I stay behind Magnus, between him and Ottar.

The store is empty aside from three employees dressed in black. Their faces are so impassive that I'm sure Magnus's shopping trips happen more often than I think.

"First off," he says to me, "we're going to get you a few new suits. Nice ones."

I look down at my suit again. "What's wrong with this one?"

"It's fine," he says. "If you're working for the British monarchy. We're in Norway now, James boy. Birthplace of death metal."

Oh my god, where is he going with this?

"We're a little darker," he says, quickly running his hands through a rack of suits. "A little crazier. Unpredictable. You need to dress for the culture."

If he pulls out a kinky leather suit, I'm going to be pissed.

"Here," he says, snatching a suit from the rack and holding it out to me.

To my relief, it's something Alice Cooper would never be caught dead in. Just a simple black suit, maybe a bit of a blue sheen to it, the lapels narrower than I'm used to. But harmless, really.

"What size are you?" he asks. "No, wait, you go by UK sizing. We'll get you measured."

And thus comes the slightly embarrassing scene where the tailor, who has ear hair growing out of his head like an overgrown field, measures me with Prince Magnus, Ottar, and Einar all watching. When he's done, he jots a bunch of numbers down, goes back to the rack, and pulls out the suit in another size.

"Denne," he says in Norwegian. Whatever he's saying, it's a command more than anything.

I thank him, "Tussen takk," happy to remember my Norwegian from the other day, and then get changed in the dressing room.

The suit is a lot tighter than I'm used to. Normally this would be a problem, since I have to have a lot of movement, but it moves beautifully. Maybe it's the material, but it almost feels athletic. Hides my gun well too, thanks to the drape of the suit jacket.

And, well, it shows off my junk just a little bit, for any discerning eyes out there. This certainly isn't a suit for a modest Brit. For a brash Scot, aye, it will do the job.

I step out into the room, feeling like a million bucks already.

"You see!" Magnus exclaims. "Now you're almost cool."

I snort. "Almost."

"You'll never be as cool as Einar, though," Ottar says, grinning.

"Not with those sunglasses," I tell him.

Einar just grunts in response.

After we decide on the new suit, we get into the sweaters, dress shirts, five-hundred-dollar T-shirts, and jeans. I have to say, even though I still find the whole shopping experience with my boss—a royal on top of that—to be a little weird, it's also kind of nice. I've never had anything like this done for me before. Growing up, I was lucky if the hand-me-downs and Salvation Army finds I was given didn't have holes or stains on them. Most of the time they never even fit me properly. So this is an entirely new experience.

And true to Magnus's word, we end up going to a bar in another part of town. Of course it's just after two in the afternoon, but that doesn't deter him.

Einar and I go in first and check the place out. He wasn't kidding when he called it a dive bar. The name is Harold's, and it's not dirty or anything, just extremely small and dark, without any flourishes except for some tiny gold-framed paintings of whales on the dark green walls. To be honest, it's my kind of place, except for the lack of suitable women in here. There are two men and an elderly lady sitting at the bar who exchange a nod with Einar, and from the way he nods back at them, and the bartender, I'm guessing they're considered safe.

Magnus walks in and gives a few high fives to the customers, greeting them like he knows them really well, and then we go and sit in a booth at the back. Einar locks the front door and remains stationed by it, hands clasped at his front.

"I take it you come here often," I tell Magnus.

He folds his hands across the table. "Before I met Ella, I lived in an apartment not too far from here. I would come here all the time." He gestures to the three over his shoulder. "That's Maud, Guillermo, and Slender Man. And the bartender is Harold. Also the owner, if you haven't gathered."

"I'm sorry—Slender Man?" I ask peering over his shoulder.

One of the men is extremely skinny and tall, with a long gray face and black suit, so I guess I can see where he got the name from.

"His real name is Erik," Magnus supplies. "I'd introduce you, but he's been going through a divorce for years now, and he'll take the wind out of your sails if you get him going."

He frowns at me for a moment, weighing something in his head, and I have a feeling I know what it is.

"Something to drink?" he then asks, derailing me.

"No thank you," I tell him.

"Are you sure? It's not a problem. We'll just count here on forward as an evening off."

I shake my head. "Thank you, but no thank you. With all due respect, sir, even if I was off duty right now, I am your protection officer, and I have sworn a duty to protect you no matter what. We're out here in public. I need to keep a clear head and do my job regardless."

A smile slowly spreads across his face. "Well done. That's what I was hoping you'd say."

"Wait, was this a test?" I ask as Ottar gets up and heads to the bar.

"Not really. I would have been fine if you had some aquavit with me, but the reason I hired you is to keep me, and my family, in line. Seems you're going to do just fine." He pauses. "But the bar at home is a different story."

"I'll take that as a warning."

Ottar comes back with water for me, and glasses of aquavit for him and Magnus. The stuff smells terrible, and this is coming from a man who will drink almost anything.

Magnus raises his glass to me. "Let's skål to James Hunter," he says. "To your bravery and selflessness in the line of duty. I still don't think I'm worth taking a bullet for, and I'm definitely not worth missing out on aquavit at Harold's, but I commend you for it."

I raise my glass of water and knock it against his and Ottar's. I have no doubt that my work going forward will never have a dull day.

Magnus slams back the glass of aquavit, making a face, and Ottar does the same, matching him. "You really ought to try this," Magnus says, though he's wincing and can barely speak. "Nectar of the gods." He coughs, face going red.

"I'm sure there'll be many an aquavit in my future." I'm more than grateful for my tap water.

"Speaking of Slender Man and divorce," Magnus suddenly says after he recovers, swinging the conversation back in time. "You were married once, weren't you?"

Talk about a non sequitur. I'm so taken aback by the question, I don't even have time to feel defensive.

Oh, wait. There it is.

"I was," I say carefully, feeling my hackles go up.

He studies me, giving me a sympathetic tilt of his head. God, I hate those head tilts. They always accompany the words *marriage* or *divorce*. "Is it hard to talk about?"

I clear my throat. Lift my chin to give the illusion that it isn't. "No, not at all. It's just in the past."

"She was a Belgian woman, correct? What was her name . . . Anne?"

"Anika," I say hesitantly. "You seem to know a lot."

He gives me a tight smile. "I had to do my due diligence when I hired you of course, to make sure there were no skeletons in your closet, or nothing that could impede your duty. May I ask what happened? You're my age, aren't you? Thirty-four? Pretty young to be divorced."

This is something I don't talk about, with anyone. So the fact that Prince Magnus is asking me so boldly says a lot about where I really stand in our power dynamic, because he knows I have to answer him. Of course I don't have to—I can tell him it's none of his business—but I also know that could make things worse. Despite all the pleasantries and his easygoing nature, we're in the "probation" period of the job.

"I'm going to say hi to Maud," Ottar says, clearing his throat before getting out of his chair and going over to the bar.

"Now Ottar is gone," Magnus says to me. "I don't blame you for being cagey. He has a big mouth. So tell me. What happened?"

I sigh, twisting the glass of water between my hands, averting my eyes from his intense stare. "Nothing too dramatic," I admit. "It was my first job for a royal family, and I was protecting Princess Adeline of Belgium. Before that I was in the army, worked as security after that, and then I lucked out and landed the gig with the Fairfaxes. It's a different game in Belgium. The monarchy isn't as worshipped, or hated, as it is in the UK, but even so, I took my job very seriously. Eventually I met Anika.

Fell in love." For the first time, but I don't add that. "We got married. And I guess I couldn't deal with having two lives. One committed to protecting the princess, the other committed to my wife."

"Ah."

"Don't get me wrong," I say quickly. "I was committed to my wife. Fully. It's just that my duty took me away from her more often than not. I barely saw her. I tried so hard to find the balance, but it was impossible. I was madly in love with her, make no mistake about that, but being in love . . . wasn't enough. Not for her anyway. So she left."

Actually, she left me for another man, one she'd been having an affair with for a very long time. That man was able to give her everything I couldn't. That man was enough for her. I wasn't.

"It can't be easy being a bodyguard," Magnus eventually says with a wince. "I know that being a royal is hard, and I was extremely lucky that my path crossed with Ella's. I have no idea where I'd be right now, or what kind of person I'd be, if I hadn't met her. She's changed me, helped me . . . saved me in more ways than one. But I often forget how hard it is to be involved with the monarchies. How little a life you get. I hope you know that I'll do whatever I can to make sure that you still get to have your own life when you're not protecting mine."

"My duty is around the clock," I remind him.

"It is. But even so. I'm trying. I look at Laila sometimes and wonder the same about her. She's so young that it feels like a waste that she's locked up in that house with us and the boys."

I swallow hard. "It's her job too. She knew what she was getting into. And from what I know, she wants to be here."

"You're right. And sometimes I think people like you, like Laila, purposely take these kinds of jobs to avoid forming any attachments." He drops that last bit of info like a bomb, a knowing glint in his eye as he studies me, as if searching for the truth.

I let out a sour laugh. "You're a philosopher all of a sudden." He taps his fingernail against his empty glass. "I blame the drink." He pauses, something weighty coming over his expression. "I didn't want to just talk about your divorce, James. I wanted to talk about the period after your divorce."

I press my lips together, hard. Talking about my divorce is one thing, but talking about the aftermath? That's a whole other ball game of *personal*.

"I took some time off, that's all."

"That's all? You traveled the world for two years."

"It's a big world."

He clears his throat and gives me a somewhat sympathetic look. "When I talked with Eddie about hiring you and asked him about your previous work experience in Belgium, he told me it was more than just a sabbatical. That it was for your mental health."

Damn that Eddie. That's what I get for confiding in him, and that's exactly why PPOs and the people they work for *shouldn't* become friends. Should have figured that it would travel along the royal grapevine.

I nod, taking in a sharp breath through my nose, steeling myself for what I'm about to say, though it won't be much. "I wasn't doing . . . great. The divorce caught me off guard. I quit my job and went traveling. To clear my head. It worked."

"You sure about that?" he asks after a moment, studying me.

I meet his gaze dead-on. "Absolutely sure."

I don't know how long our staring contest goes on for, though in the back of my mind I know it's not normal for a bodyguard to be staring down the prince he's supposed to protect, but then Magnus raises a brow and gives me a wry smile.

"Good. Then it's all settled."

He turns in his seat and waves at Harold. "Harold, another please!"

Whew.

Six

. . . . . .

LAILA

Two years ago

"HAVE YOU HAD DINNER YET?" DUCHESS MONICA ASKS
me as she takes baby Madeline from my arms.

I shake my head and give her a wan smile. "Haven't had a
chance," I admit. Food is the last thing on my mind when I'm
busy like this, and even though all staff have access to the
kitchen, it always feels a little wrong to go and get food for myself outside of mealtimes, like I'm scavenging a rich person's
house or something.

She tilts her head and gives me a dry look as she eyes me.
She's not much older than me yet acts like my mother sometimes, not that I don't appreciate it every now and then. It's nice
to feel looked after, especially since I only ever get that from my
grandmother, and she's back at home in her village in Norway.
Which reminds me, first vacation I get, I'll be flying there to
see her.

"Laila," she admonishes me. "You need dinner. If I'd known, you could have eaten with us."

I feel a little like a child who has gotten a scolding. "I'm fine." Besides, even though I've eaten dinner with Eddie and Monica a few times since I started a month ago, I always feel like a charity case. Don't get me wrong—the Fairfaxes are the most down-to-earth royals you could ever meet, and they always make me feel welcome. But I'm also very aware of my role in this house—that they are not only royals and I'm a commoner but that they are also my employers. Mistaking kindness for friendship is a mistake I've made before, and I know better than to get close to someone who can fire me.

"Is she off duty now?" James's deep voice says from behind me.

I turn around to see him in the doorway of the nursery, the sight of him in his suit making my heart flutter against my will.

Monica blinks at him, adjusting her grip on Madeline, who is playing with her mother's long dark hair. "Laila? Sure."

"Actually I've got another hour," I say, glancing at my watch, wondering what James is getting at.

"It's fine," Monica says to me. Then she narrows her dark eyes at James. "You're not corrupting her, are you?"

His mouth curls. "I wouldn't dream of it," James says solemnly, though his expression says otherwise.

I can't help but smile. I've worked for the Fairfaxes for long enough now to know that their interactions are always full of banter and humor.

"But I'm heading into the city to see Piper and Harrison before they leave tomorrow," he continues. He fixes his eyes on me. "And I was wondering if you wanted to come along."

Harrison was the Fairfaxes' PPO when they lived in Canada, and Piper was the neighbor of the house they were renting. Piper and Harrison got off on the wrong foot but eventually fell in love with each other. Enough that Harrison ended up quitting his job and opening a bakery on the island. I met the two of them when they came by the other day for tea, and they are absolutely adorable, although they seem to be polar opposites, with Harrison very stoic and Piper a bright ball of sunshine.

"Oh, right," Monica says with a wistful look in her eyes. "I can't believe they're leaving so soon. A week doesn't seem like enough time to have a proper visit."

"He has pies to bake, and she's got children to teach," he says. "I promise we won't stay out too late," he adds, knowing full well he'll do whatever he pleases.

That's one of the many differences between us that I've picked up on over the last month. While I haven't had much interaction with James, it's obvious that he likes to stay out late on his days off, and sometimes when I can't sleep I'll look out the window and see him coming home in the middle of the night, drunk and weaving down the path through the yard. I have to admit, I often feel a twinge of jealousy, wishing that I could just go out without having anxiety over it.

"All right, then," Monica says, giving James a suspicious look. "But if she's not in her room at ten, I'm coming to get her," she adds with a wink.

"I'll make sure she's in bed on time," James promises, making the sign of the cross over his chest.

"And make sure she eats something," Monica adds adamantly. She grins at me. "Try to have a little fun, Laila."

I shouldn't be so surprised that Monica is encouraging her

employees to fraternize, considering Monica wasn't born a royal and it goes with her easy personality. Still, it catches me off guard. After all, I hadn't even agreed to this yet. It's like she knows I'll say yes anyway.

"I should go change," I concede, looking down at my uniform of a navy A-line dress that's riddled with stains from Madeline. I look at James. "How much time do I have?"

"No rush. Take your time," he says. "I'll be in the study."

He turns and heads down the hall. Naturally he doesn't have to change. He's in a suit, as always. In fact, I don't think I've ever seen him in anything outside of a suit. Even when he goes to the bars, he's always impeccably dressed.

Definitely makes you wonder what's underneath the suit, I think, though I push that image out of my head. Yet another intrusive thought when it comes to him.

As if Monica can hear the chatter in my brain, she nods at the door. "Go, Laila," she says imploringly. "You deserve to have a night off. Have fun."

I decide to heed her advice. I thank her and head down the hall and across the yard to my quarters. August is coming to a close, and though there are a few hot days scattered here and there, the evenings are cool and the air smells like hay from the neighboring fields beyond the estate.

I take the world's quickest shower, not getting my hair wet, and change into jeans and a loose tank top. I wear a pair of sandals that I bought on Amazon, and I do my hair, rubbing in some anti-frizz stuff before pulling it back into a low ponytail. I don't want to go overboard, but I want to look nice for my first night off since I started working here.

When I get to the study, I find James sprawled out in one of the armchairs, reading a book. A piece of his dark hair flops against his forehead, and I have this sudden urge to push it back.

He looks up as I enter the room, setting his book down on the table beside the chair, and takes a moment to appraise me. The grandfather clock in the corner ticks away the seconds.

"You look lovely," he says.

"Thank you," I say bashfully, leaning against the wall beside the door. I can't remember the last time someone called me lovely. Monica often tells me if I'm looking pretty, but it's been a long time since a man has said it. I clear my throat, feeling a little awkward. "Sorry I took so long." I peer at the book, trying to recognize the title. "What are you reading?"

"Something you'd probably like," he says, getting to his feet. "Wife threw her husband off a moving train . . . or did she?" He adds with a mock suspicious squint.

I can't help but smile. "Got to love a damaged heroine."

"They are my favorite," he says affectionately. "Shall we?"

Primrose Cottage is located on the same sprawling estate as Berkstead Castle, where the king and queen spend their weekends and summers, but the land is so massive that even when they are on the property, you never see them. I get the feeling that even though the tabloids report that Eddie and Monica have patched things up with the king and queen, their relationship is still strained and has been ever since they ditched England for Canada. Even the arrival of Madeline hasn't done much to pull them back together, except in public. I wouldn't be surprised if one day they end up leaving England again.

Outside, the night air blows with a soft wind and there's a town car waiting for us. A perk of working for the Fairfaxes is that we don't have to deal with public transportation. Instead we have drivers that take us wherever we want to go, as if we are royalty ourselves.

The driver comes around and opens the car's back doors for us.

"I'd drive us into town myself," James says as he gestures for me to get in, "but then I can't properly imbibe."

I slide in. "You have a car?"

He nods and comes around the other side, buckling in as the driver closes the doors. "I do. It's a piece-of-shite old Peugeot, but it works. There's something about being on an estate like this, outside the city, that feels a little claustrophobic, even when you do have people like my good man Charles over here to drive you."

"Appreciated, sir," the driver, who I now know as Charles, says, winking at him in the rearview mirror.

He drives off, and I have to admit, I feel a bit of a thrill as Primrose Cottage and the towering Berkstead Castle behind it begin to fade into the background. The city! London! I had forgotten how exciting it is to be living near it, I've been so worked up with my job.

"Would you look at that," James says. "Your face is lighting up."

I glance at him, suddenly very aware of how close I am to him. Our eyes are inches apart, and I can see flecks of a lighter color in his dark eyes. The car is cast into a strange watery light as we pass under lampposts, and the scene feels dreamy. There's a thread of tension between us, and even though he probably doesn't notice it at all, I do. It makes the hair on my arms rise.

I swallow thickly. "My face?"

He reaches out and puts his fingers under my chin, tilting my face so it's facing him dead-on. He's so close my breath catches. I can smell him, the soap from his morning shower and the faint woodsy smell of his cologne. It makes me want to inhale deeply, but I can't do that when my eyes are locked with his.

"This very face," he says. "Makes your eyes dance." His hand drops away and I feel bereft.

Suddenly the car bumps over a pothole and I jolt, coming back to reality. James looks at me and grins, obviously enjoying the fact that he managed to startle me.

"Sorry," he says. "I didn't mean to put you on the spot. You're obviously excited about something."

I blush, the tension building. "It's just that I've been so busy with my job that I've forgotten how great it is to be living near London."

He nods, his grin turning softer. "I figured that. Which is why I thought it would be good for you to get out of your head for a while. Live a little."

So he's already picked up on how inward I get.

"Let me guess, you think the night will end with me dancing on top of bars."

He laughs. "I would pay to see that."

I give him a look. "Just so you know, I don't actually dance on bars."

"Just so you know, I don't pay either."

I giggle at that and lapse into a mix of small talk and silence, though both become more comfortable as the ride goes on. Eventually the city limits approach and the density thickens. The car comes to a stop. I glance out the window. We're in a very upscale part of London, down the road from Harrod's. The car pulls up to a red light. I watch a woman in a beautiful ball gown cross the street in front of us, followed by a man in a tux, and I can't help but marvel at them, wondering where they are going.

"This is amazing," I say quietly, eyeing the cabs jutting across traffic, the gleaming red double-decker buses that trundle below brick buildings, the flashing lights of the theater. "Why don't I come here more often? I feel like I'm in a movie."

James puts his hand on my shoulder, sending a warm thrill through me. I glance at him, and he gives me a smile. "Then let's make this the best movie we can."

Okay. That was cheesy. That was the line a guy would give you on a first date, and this definitely isn't that.

"What?" he says, his dark brows arching dramatically. "Too much?"

I make a gesture with my thumb and forefinger. "A little."

Charles parks the car and comes around, opening our doors like we're royalty. He tells James to text him when we're ready to come home, and I suddenly feel giddy, like I'm a teenager again, playing hooky from school or something, or heading to a party I've been forbidden to go to. Or at least, I figure that's what it feels like to be a normal teen. I never had much of a childhood, and my teenage years were a struggle.

"Where are we going?" I ask as James puts his hand at the small of my back, the warmth of his touch coming through my top, and guides me down the street to our left. The air smells like a mixture of car exhaust, cigarette smoke, and rain coming soon, and it's more humid than it is in the countryside. All around me are lights and people and the sounds of the city. I can feel their presence in the air, pulsing through me. My ears ring with the vibration of a thousand conversations. I can smell food frying, hear music playing. I can see the soft light pouring from the buildings, casting shadows from all around.

"Just a restaurant I'm a fan of," James says as his hand falls away. "Hope you like Italian."

"Who doesn't?"

"Well, you strike me as a woman of many surprises," he says. "Now if we could just get you to tell me what they are . . ."

I give him a coy glance. "Maybe you'll find out."

Laila, stop it, I tell myself. *Just stop.*

He gives me a sexy, crooked smile. "Maybe I will."

Ugh. What the hell is happening here? He's flirting with me, and I'm flirting with him, and that's just a horrible idea all around. I promise myself to have no more than one drink with dinner, because something tells me this man has the power to make me do very regrettable things.

We reach the restaurant, a tiny Italian place, and James holds the door open for me. I step inside and immediately feel transported to the streets of Rome, or so the décor implies. The walls are decorated with photos of the Italian countryside; there's a display of masks and an ornate vase with an olive tree in it. Along the left side of the restaurant are a few booths; at one of them I recognize Piper and Harrison. Her eyes go wide when she sees me, and she smiles, while Harrison twists in his seat to look as we come over.

"Laila," Piper says. "I didn't know you'd be coming."

She gets out of her seat and comes and gives me a hug. I go stiff and lightly pat her back, surprised at her sudden affection. I only talked with her and Harrison for a little bit when they were visiting Eddie and Monica, but I guess she's the hugger type. I'm definitely not.

"She's on her fourth glass of wine," Harrison says good-naturedly, getting to his feet.

Piper sighs and releases me before reaching over to smack him on the arm. "Hey, I'm not drunk, I'm friendly," she scolds him, exaggerating the last word.

Harrison gives her a wry smile and then nods at me. "Nice to see you again, Laila. Glad you could join us."

"Finally convinced her to leave the house," James says.

I give him a puzzled look. "Finally? This is the first time you've invited me."

"There were others. Perhaps I wasn't direct enough," he says.

"James? Not direct? That's a new one," Harrison says with a laugh.

James sits down beside him, and I slide into the booth beside Piper.

A waitress who has been hovering nearby pounces on us with the menus, rattling off the specials, but I'm not listening to her. I'm thinking of what James just said. When on earth had he invited me out to town with him? Sure, he did so the first day we really met, but after that . . .

And then I realize he's been doing it all this time, and no, he wasn't direct enough. There was one night when he asked me what I was doing and I said I was going to bed. Another morning I passed him in the halls and he said I ought to go out and enjoy the fresh air. Yet another time after dinner he announced he was heading into town and followed that with an awkwardly long pause, as if waiting for me to say something.

"Miss?" the waitress says to me.

I tear my eyes away from James and blink at her. "Sorry, what?"

"What will you have to drink? Wine with the table or . . . ?"

"We got another bottle of red," Piper says as she nudges me and nods at the empty bottle in the middle of the table that the waitress is removing. "It's delicious."

I give her a quick smile. "Red wine can give me a headache sometimes," I admit, then tell the waitress I'd like an Aperol Spritz. Trendy, yes, but a drink that's perfect for the last days of summer.

"Looking forward to going home?" James asks the couple.

Piper sighs. "Yes and no. It's been amazing here. It's the first time we've done anything like this since . . ."

"Since I moved to the island," Harrison finishes. "It's hard to find staff on the island, so I've been reluctant to leave the bakery. But now I've found a worker I can really trust. Hopefully she'll still be there when we return."

"And I'm looking forward to fall and being back in the classroom," Piper says. "New year, new students, the fall fair, pumpkin spice everything. But I have to say, it's been so nice to just be overseas, in a big city, seeing life through other people's eyes, you know? Sometimes I start to feel closed in if I stay on the island for too long. Like I can't think clearly, like I don't have a lot of freedom to be . . . me."

Even though I've never lived on an island, I know exactly what she's talking about. The feeling of being caged, of not being able to be your true self.

"What about you?" I ask Harrison. "Island life affecting you the same way?"

He manages a small smile, his gaze focused on Piper and soft with affection. "Not at all. It was good to come back to Mother England, but I don't feel closed in, not with her by my side."

"Aw, come on, mate," James says with a derisive laugh. "No one wants to hear how happy you are."

He's right about that. Don't get me wrong, Piper is adorable and Harrison is the strong, silent, sexy type, and I'm happy for them because they're very clearly in love. But sometimes when I'm around happy couples, it just reminds me of how I'll probably never have that in my life.

Harrison scoffs at James. "Right, as if you aren't breaking women's hearts left and right every time you come to the city."

James rolls his eyes at that, but Piper stiffens up beside me, and I can tell she's attempting to kick Harrison under the table, as if I shouldn't hear about this. I mean, I don't care what James does, though I never gave much thought to who he was seeing when he went into the city. I guess the guy does date, he just doesn't bring them home.

I shift in my seat and plaster on a smile to hide the strange prick of jealousy in my gut, just as the waitress returns with the much-needed drinks.

We all toast bon voyage to Piper and Harrison, and the rest of the dinner flows nicely. Between bites of cacio e pepe and the heavenly burrata salad, I feel my shoulders drop, a weight lifted. It feels like I actually have friends, and the more I dwell on that the more I grow warm inside. It makes me want to open up, to ask them silly questions, to relax and let my guard down a little.

But I manage to keep myself in check, and though I want to drink more than just the Aperol Spritz, I limit myself to one.

When the meal is done we walk Piper and Harrison to the tube (she was insistent on taking it one last time, who knows why) and say our goodbyes. They tell us they'll be back soon, which I doubt, and if either James or I want a real vacation, we should come visit them in Canada, but I doubt that too, unless Eddie and Monica decide to go.

Then they're gone and it's just James and me outside the Knightsbridge station. The rain I smelled earlier feels close, an electric charge to the breeze, signaling change.

"I think it's going to rain," I tell him.

"We better go inside a pub," he says with a grin.

I sigh. "I should really get back home. I promised Monica I'd be in bed early. Hell, *you* promised her that."

"Yes, early. Early in the morning," James corrects, his eyes glinting in the city lights.

I laugh. "I'm not dancing on any tables, remember?"

He takes a step closer to me just as a fat drop of rain bounces off my nose. "Ah, I knew you were a glutton for punishment, Laila."

"What do you mean?"

"Accompanying me out to drink, when you said you were going to bed early."

"I haven't agreed to anything," I tell him as the rain starts to come down steadily. I really need him to ring up Charles and get the car to come get us.

"Come on," he says, his voice lower and more seductive than it was a second ago. "Let's go have a pint."

I look at him, his eyes on me, his expression enticing. Damn, he is a persistent one. "I really should go back. And you should too."

"Why?" he asks, and as he does so, he takes his suit jacket off and holds it over me to shield me from the rain.

Okay. If that's not the most chivalrous gesture, then I don't know what is. Is he purposely trying to make me swoon, or is this really him?

"We," I begin, trying to find the right words, "shouldn't fraternize."

"Fraternize?" he repeats, taking another step closer until his energy engulfs me and I'm pretty much pressed up against him. "What century are you from?"

"You know what I mean," I say, staring up at him like I'm entranced, feeling my resolve start to weaken.

"Are you worried we'll start sleeping together?" he says, his eyes alight as he jumps right into the awkward.

I'm not sure what expression I have on my face—probably shock—but he laughs. "I'm joking, Laila. You don't have to look so serious. It's just a friendly drink, nothing more."

I'm relieved to hear that, but even so, I don't trust myself around him, and with the rain coming down harder, I need to make a choice or we'll get soaked.

"Come on," he says, gesturing with his head down the street. "I know a quiet and cozy pub right there. I'll call Charles now, and we can wait there until he comes. Deal?"

I take in a deep breath and nod. "Deal."

Seven

. . . .

LAILA

"COME ON, BOYS, LET'S GO INSIDE," I SAY TO TOR AND Bjorn, holding my hands out for them. Usually Tor would cry at the thought of leaving his snowman-in-progress, and Bjorn would probably kick me in the shin or something in protest, but I can tell they're getting cold and tired. The snow has been coming down steadily all day, and though it was a lot of fun playing in it at first, building igloos and snow castles and having a snowball fight, it hasn't let up at all. If anything, I think it's doubled down in the last hour, and my eyelashes have ice crystals on them.

The boys come over to me, Tor taking my hand while Bjorn burns past me through the snow like the Tasmanian Devil toward the front steps to the house, just as Ella is stepping out.

"I've made hot chocolate," she calls out to us, rubbing her hands over her arms for warmth. "My god, it won't stop," she says staring up at the white sky as the flakes fall down.

Bjorn tears up the steps in his snowsuit, running past his

mother and into the house. Tor lets go of my hand when he sees Ella and tries to make a run for her as well, a big smile on his chubby cheeks, but immediately face-plants. I scoop him up and bring him over to her, plunking him in her arms as her sweater gets covered in snow.

"Goodness, Tor, I can't tell if you built the snowman or if the snowman built you," she says, brushing the snow off his hat.

He giggles in response, and once inside, Ella puts him back down and closes the door. "You're going to need some help," she says, because I always appreciate a little help when it comes to taking off the kids' snowsuits.

She goes hastily down the hall to wrangle Bjorn and then brings him back over to me like a lost puppy dragged by his collar, and we quickly get the boys out of the suits, their clothes dry underneath, thankfully.

"Hot chocolate!" Bjorn yells, escaping his mother's grip and running down the hall to the kitchen, Tor toddling after him.

"Hmmm," she says, blowing a strand of hair off her forehead. "I should have left it a surprise. I thought I would need to bribe them to come in."

"Whatever works," I tell her, unwrapping my scarf and taking off my own coat.

"I hope Magnus doesn't run into any troubles," she says, a faint line between her brows.

"With what?" I ask, hanging up my stuff.

"Well, he went to Oslo with James, Ottar, and Einar. He had lunch with his father, but he should have been back by now."

"Have you tried texting him?"

"I texted, I called," she says, then gives me an apologetic

shrug. "Knowing him, though, his phone is probably dead because he forgot to charge it last night and he hasn't even noticed. Out of sight, out of mind. Anyway, what can I say, I'm a worrywart."

We walk off to the kitchen to make sure the boys aren't burning it down while I briefly wonder if I should text James. Then I remember I deleted his number in a fit of rage. He probably has a different number now anyway.

It's been a few days since he graced Skaugum Estate with his smarmy presence, and while I've gotten pretty good at avoiding him since he does spend a lot of time with Magnus (even though he's not technically his bodyguard, Magnus likes making friends), there are times when he's unavoidable. It's common for everyone to gather in the library after dinner to have a nightcap or two before bed, and while I got away with ducking out the first night, it's going to start looking really weird if I never show up, especially since I was there like clockwork before. A nice highball of Scotch has been a lifesaver at the end of the day. Besides, Lady Jane was already getting suspicious of me missing that first night.

So I've had to sit there by the roaring fire, sipping Scotch and pretending that I'm listening to the conversation, when really all I can think about is James sitting near me. I don't even have to look at him, I just feel him. That sexual energy he carried with him before is just as strong as ever, and it seriously messes up my train of thought. And by messes up, I mean totally derails it into a fiery explosion.

And besides the nights by the fire (thanking the lord that so far we haven't been left alone, because his energy plus cozy fireplace vibes definitely screams *sex*), I've had to see him at dinner twice, and I'm always bumping into him in the halls. Not to mention the fact that every single night I can hear him going to bed. I have my noise-canceling headphones on with a brown-noise app blasting out my eardrums, and I swear I still hear every little sigh. Honestly, I'm not sure how I'm supposed to just carry on and work, I'm really not.

I step into the kitchen to see Sigrid handing the boys hot chocolate. I'm not sure sugar is a good idea, especially when they're so hyped up (so much for the snow and cold tuckering them out), and when they're done, Ella knows she's made a mistake.

"Oh dear," she says, as Bjorn starts doing laps around the kitchen table. "Sorry about that," she adds to me, wincing.

"Would you believe me if I said I was used to it?" I tell her.

Ella laughs. "You're so good with them," she says warmly. She nods at the window, which is now covered in a layer of icy snow. "I was watching you earlier. You really play with them in a way that I can't seem to. Sometimes I think I'm just too boring and rigid to really access that part of my brain, but with you it seems to come so easily."

As I listen to her, it's hard to stop myself from getting defensive. Ella means this as a compliment, and I remind myself to take it that way. Everything she says is something I've heard before, though not from an employer. People I grew up with, friends in my early twenties, a handful of relationships where I let myself be the real me, and they all ended with people telling me I was strange or childish. They'd point out that I was silly for having plush toys, for talking to animals like they were human, for becoming obsessed about random things. They all ended with me feeling absolutely crushed, furthering this belief that deep down there is something fundamentally wrong with me and that there is no real safe place for me to exist.

"They bring out my inner child," I tell her.

"Well, they bring out my inner adult," she jokes as Bjorn starts hammering his fists against her jeans and making a yodeling sound.

Anyway, I know what to do with them now that Ella is here to help. The first step is to let Bjorn run wild through the house and do what he wants, while sequestering Tor in the playroom with a bunch of coloring books. After a while, when Bjorn gets tired, he'll feel left out and come and join Tor, and everyone can get peace and quiet for a little bit.

"I'm going to do some coloring with Tor," I tell Bjorn, taking Tor's hand. "Do you want to come?"

"No!" Bjorn scream-laughs like a banshee and runs off.

Ella rolls her eyes. "I've got him."

"Good luck," I call after her as she stalks off after him.

"Hey, Tor," I say, peering down at his white-blond head. "You want to color?"

"Yeah," Tor says, nodding profusely.

I take him across the way to the playroom, which is any kid's dream and honestly my favorite spot in the whole house. There're plenty of toys, a baby grand piano, stuffed animals galore, and a long bookshelf. There's a big purple plush chair and a large window looking out to the expansive front yard, now piled high with snow.

I had a small room to play in as a child, but the problem was that I was always left alone. My mother never, ever played with me, even when I begged, and my father pretty much pretended I didn't exist. I grew out of the dolls and such when they died, having to suddenly grow up and be thrust into adult mode, so to see the boys having room to play and people to play with . . . just makes me feel like I'm in alignment, something I need to remember on days when the job feels hard.

"Let's go into the castle," I tell Tor, grabbing the colored pencils and books off their mini desks and bringing them into a tall, round tent in the corner that resembles a turret. I crawl into the corner, then make room for Tor, spreading the pencils and books out in front of us.

Then, for the next thirty minutes, both of us color to our hearts' content. I've colored in an octopus in shades of green and purple, with magenta highlights, and Tor, well, he's made a mess, but it's an artistic mess that I tell him is worthy of being framed.

Ella comes by with Bjorn, dropping him off and saying she's going to get some work done, but now Bjorn doesn't want to color with pencils; he wants to make snowmen out of clay, so I go about getting the room set up for that. It makes a mess, but I truly believe children should be allowed to be as messy as they want. They won't get away with it when they're older.

Not long after we've settled down for some clay sculptures, I hear the front door open and the stomping of boots and Magnus's booming voice swearing away, calling the snowstorm a drittsekk or "shitbag."

"Uh-oh! Bad words," Bjorn says with a grin, then abandons his art and runs out of the room to see his father, with Tor following behind.

I go after them in time to see Ella coming downstairs and Magnus and James brushing mounds of snow off their jackets.

"What happened?" Ella asks. "I tried to reach you all day."

"Phone died and roads were total shit on the way over, and the car is stuck down at the bottom of the hill," Magnus says, shaking his shaggy hair so snow flies everywhere. "Ottar and Einar grabbed shovels to dig it out. I'm telling you, I've never seen it come down so hard."

"I better get a shovel too," James says, turning for the door, but Magnus reaches out and stops him.

"Relax," Magnus says. "Stay put. They've got this. I'm not going to have both PPOs breaking their back."

"I'd hardly call snow-shoveling backbreaking work," James says dryly. "We do have snow in Scotland, you know."

"In that suit?" Magnus says, looking him up and down. Then he looks at me and notices the sticky and dried clay all over my hands. "You stay. Help Laila entertain the boys."

Oh no. Please no.

"She doesn't look like she needs any help," James says.

"Because I'm fine," I tell him. Tor motions for Magnus to pick him up, so he does, giving him a hearty squeeze and tickle that makes Tor laugh, while Bjorn scoops up the melting snow from the coats and starts flinging it at James so it lands on his suit in splatters.

"Bjornsy!" Magnus booms, to which Bjorn giggles and runs away. "I swear to god, that child is someone I wronged in a past life."

"Anyway," I say, gesturing to James, who is brushing the snow off his tie, "I don't think his suit could handle my job either."

That brings out an annoyed frown from James, and I smirk back at him.

Ella lets out a laugh before she heads up the stairs. "Okay, well, Magnus, James"—she nods at the kitchen—"Sigrid just made some hot chocolate for the boys, so if you're nice to her, she may make you some more."

Magnus places Tor back on the floor. I take his son's hand and laugh quietly as Magnus and James beeline it toward the kitchen, not so different from when Bjorn and Tor went for hot chocolate earlier.

"Okay, Bjorn," I say to him. "Tor and I will be making a clay zoo if you want to join in. Competition for scariest animal."

"No scary!" Tor yells out, looking close to tears.

"Okay," I tell him. "Cutest animal."

"*I'm* the scariest animal," Bjorn yells, baring his teeth, and runs into the playroom. Well, at least he's game.

We settle down again and get lost in the world of creation. Bjorn has quite the aptitude for sculpting, getting hyperfocused when he's working on the details of the creatures (and yes, *creature*, because whatever godforsaken thing he's creating is not a zoo animal). It's nice to see him finally calm down and get lost in something. Makes me feel calmer too.

"Will this do?" a Scottish brogue says.

I look over my shoulder to see James at the door dressed in a white T-shirt and dark jeans, and I almost do a double take. I don't know if I've ever seen him out of a suit; it's either that or . . . naked. In fact, he might as well be naked, considering the way the jeans sit on his hips, how the thin fabric of the T-shirt clings to him, showing off his biceps and muscular forearms. God, I am such a sucker for those arms.

I hope I'm not drooling.

"You have other clothes?" I exclaim. "I had no idea."

He gives me a dry look. "Very funny. Turns out, yes. And

rumor has it you're having a scariest-slash-cutest animal competition and I would like to enter."

Hmmm. Why is he doing this?

"Yes, come play," Tor says, waving his clay blob around, speaking in Norwegian.

"What did he say?" James asks me.

"I should lie and say it's that you should turn around and leave, but alas, he wants you to come play." Meanwhile Bjorn is so wrapped up in his winged monster that he hasn't even looked up to acknowledge James.

James seems to hesitate in the doorway, as if he's debating whether he should turn and go. I swear I see a flash of fear or worry in his gaze, like he's actually concerned that he might piss me off.

Then that look twists into the grin I know all too well, like he's won something, and he saunters into the room.

I sigh and move over on the floor to make room. "Are you trying to prove a point? Like you can get down and dirty if you want to?"

I realize what I've said too late.

His grin widens and he winks at me. "Oh, you know I can, love."

My eyes narrow. "Don't call me that," I whisper harshly.

He raises a palm in surrender, then looks to the boys. "Aye, so what are we doing here? Bloody hell, Bjorn, that's one creepy-looking mogwai."

Bjorn finally looks up, his tongue out the side of his mouth in concentration, and nods, then goes back to sculpting what I can now see are the mogwai's ears, not wings.

"How were you able to tell that was a mogwai?" I say to James quietly.

"I stream shows, you know," he says wryly. "It's called having downtime. *Gremlins: Secrets of the Mogwai* is a lot of fun."

"Cartoons?"

He shrugs and dips his hand in a bowl of water, sprinkling it on a lump of clay. "Sure, why not?"

The funny thing is, I love cartoons too. Well, mostly anime, but there's something so soothing about watching something meant for kids. I'm just surprised that he does too, let alone admits to it.

"And what are your favorite cartoons?" I ask, watching as he begins to squeeze the clay. My god, it's reminding me of the way he used to squeeze my hips, almost to the point of bruising when he was really having at me.

Wow, inappropriate. Look away, girl.

I look back down at my own clay, only to find I've dug my nails into it. Thank god James doesn't seem to notice, though, as he says, "Really enjoying *Baymax!* at the moment. You know, the big puffy robot."

"Baymax!" Tor yells, raising his clay-covered fists in the air excitedly.

"We're aware of Baymax," I tell him.

"I bet you've seen a lot of kids' movies and the like, over and over again as a nanny, aye?" He glances at me, and I make the mistake of meeting his gaze. His gaze is striking, enough that it makes me dizzy for a moment. He really shouldn't be so close to me, with his eyes and his scruffy, manly jaw, and the scent of his woodsy cologne. The correct distance for him would be across the room. No, down at the other end of the house. At the end of the road. Buried in a snowbank.

"Perks of the job," I admit, my attention going back to my

clay. I originally had the intention of making a horse, but now it's starting to resemble a triceratops. That's fine, I can pivot.

"Do you think you'll have kids one day?" he asks, and it takes me by such surprise that I drop the clay, staining my jeans.

I stare at him wide-eyed, fumbling to pick it up. "Me?"

"Yeah," he says with a frown. "You're such a natural. Is that an inappropriate question?"

"Maybe . . ." I mean, it is when he's asking.

He lifts a shoulder in a shrug and goes back to working at his clay. "I get it. It's none of my business."

We fall silent for a few moments until Bjorn suddenly gets up and abandons his mogwai, heading over to the coloring books in the castle tent.

"Are you done?"

"Yeah!" he yells.

"Are you sure?" It only looks half-done, but it isn't new for Bjorn to abandon things when he finally gets bored of them. "Because I'll have to enter it in the competition as is."

He mumbles something and starts coloring erratically.

"Well, then, I give up," James says, putting down his mound of clay and gesturing to it. "I mean, this is supposed to be a bear and it's just a blob with eyes."

"Baymax!" Tor says cheerfully, pointing to the blob.

We work on our clay for a little while longer, Bjorn now in chatter mode as he colors from the castle, telling us a story about a dragon and Baymax and some kind of frog—I don't know, his story went off the rails for a bit.

"Sorry if I got intrusive," James says in a low voice, leaning in for a moment so I get another whiff of pine and amber.

I shake my head. "It's fine. It's not a heavy topic or anything.

I just . . ." I bite my lip for a moment in thought. "I actually don't want kids. Is that weird? I have a feeling it's weird considering I love being around kids and I love being a nanny, but . . . no. I don't want them for myself. I never have."

"That's not weird," he assures me. "It's honest. It means you know yourself."

I hope he's right about that. Sometimes it feels like I don't know myself at all.

I give him a quick smile. "And you? Do you want children?"

He ponders that for a moment, poking his finger into the clay. "You know what? I haven't thought about it much. Maybe it will change when I meet the right person one day. Maybe it won't. But I think deep down I know my answer is no." He gives me a smile that's borderline vulnerable, making him look boyish. "With the childhood I had, could you blame me?"

"Not at all," I say, resting my hand on his arm. His skin is so soft and warm, the muscles strong, that it takes me a moment to realize what I've done.

I take my hand away, clearing my throat. "Okay, boys, I know I need to get you cleaned up for dinner, so how about we have our competition now? I'll build a little stage for your art so your parents can see it later."

I can feel James's eyes burning on me, but I don't meet them as I bustle around the room and gather up an even stack of books and a Scrabble board to act as a makeshift stage. Then I take their works and proudly place them on it.

"Who won?" Bjorn asks, coming over and peering at the creations.

"Well, you won scariest creature," I tell him. "And Tor won cutest creature."

Bjorn points at James. "And what did he win?"

Since Bjorn is talking in Norwegian again, James looks perplexed.

"James won an A for effort," I tell them in English.

"Oh, it's just like secondary school all over again," James grumbles under his breath.

All four of us make quick work of tidying the playroom, then I take the boys to their room to get them cleaned up. There was a quiet kind of ease just being with James like that, without too much tension getting in the way. But the more I find myself in situations like that with him, the more I'll actually start liking him again.

And that simply cannot happen.

Eight

. . . .

LAILA

SUNSHINE LIGHTS UP MY DREAMS.

I take a moment to lie in bed, appreciating the way the sun is slicing through the bedroom this morning. It only lasts a short while before the sun moves on, ever closer to the horizon, but after nearly a week of snow, the sun feels good, especially since I'll be heading into Oslo, which always looks so much prettier with the sun reflecting off the harbor.

I have a whole day off, and I get to see my grandmother. I'll stop by Steen & Strøm, the department store, and see if they have any of her favorite cloudberry cake (something she still seems to love), maybe do some shopping for myself, then head on over to her. Afterward I'll get a bite to eat at a wine bar and drink until my heart feels warm, then come back home.

I sigh in quiet contentment, closing my eyes.

Suddenly James's headboard knocks against the wall.

My eyes fly open. I take in a deep, shaking breath through

my nose, willing myself to calm down, my contentment interrupted.

The headboard knocks again.

What the hell is he doing?

I find myself holding my breath and listening now. Any sense of morning peace has vanished.

Wait . . . wait a minute . . .

I close my eyes, as if that will help me hear better.

A moan.

I hear a fucking *moan*.

And not just any moan. A familiar, low, lust-soaked moan.

Oh my god. Does he have someone over? Did he bring a woman back here last night?

My heart pinches, as if I'm jealous, and I'm trying to think, my brain flipping through the files of last night. No. He couldn't have. He stayed in, just as I had.

But while I'm distracting myself with this, he's moaning away in the bedroom next to me. And I'm starting to realize that he's got no one else in there.

He's by himself.

Jacking off.

I smile to myself, feeling all sorts of things I shouldn't be feeling. One is that I'm catching James in the act of something I shouldn't, so yes, I'm feeling a little naughty. Two is that the sounds are bringing me back. Back to when *I* used to make him feel that way. He's always been very vocal, and a dirty talker to boot, and I have to say I sometimes miss the way he let me know how much he enjoyed what I was doing to him.

Three is that James has no idea I'm hearing him right now,

so this could be rather embarrassing information for me to wield.

Except . . . no.

Of course he knows I can hear him right now.

My body reacts, heat pooling between my legs, a tightness in my throat.

I feel a sudden thrill at the knowledge that he's doing this on purpose, knowing I can hear him, knowing how it affects me. It's hot, dirty, and wrong, and I can't help but run my hand down over my shirt, my legs parting slightly.

He whispers *good night* to me through the wall every night—is this his way of saying good morning? He knows I can hear every heated sound that's coming out of his mouth, probably hoping to wake me up.

That bastard. And to think I was this close to touching myself and playing along with him, my nipples already tight against my nightshirt, body feeling flushed with heat.

I get out of bed as quietly as I can, silently seething, and know that the only way to play this is to pretend that I hadn't heard him at all.

I head into the shower and try to forget his asinine attempt . . . at what, even? Turning me on? Reminding me of what I'm missing? As if I didn't know. All I had to do was sleep with him once, and then I was a goner, utterly addicted to him.

I know I sound like some obsessed woman who slept with a guy and let her feelings run away from her, immediately wanting more. I know that's what James thought of me, at one point. But that's not really in my nature.

Before I worked for the Fairfaxes, I was an au pair and a

nanny for a lot of aristocratic and royal-adjacent families around Europe. Back then, my duties were very typical and I always had evenings and weekends off, unless there was a special event. I had all the time in the world to date, but I just . . . didn't. Not to say I never went on dates. I did. They just rarely went anywhere. If I was lucky it ended with a one-night stand, but even the guys who were the best in bed weren't really worth calling the next day. There was no one I wanted to let into my life. No one I wanted to open my heart to. Even friendships were tricky for me as I'm never sure of people's true intentions. You learn to distrust people as a whole when you've been burned before.

Then I got the job for Eddie and Monica, and things changed. Suddenly the freedom I had was gone. I went from being a nobody, gallivanting around London by myself, to being the nanny for the most adored and photographed baby in the entire country, maybe even the entire world. Suddenly everyone knew who I was. They knew every detail about me, from how my parents died when I was eight, to how my grandmother raised me by herself in Todalen, to who I was *not* dating.

It made me a shut-in, and I was already antisocial to begin with. I didn't even want to go out when I had a day off because I knew I'd be photographed. (I know, why would they even bother with a nanny? But the UK media is batshit when it comes to anything to do with the royals.) I stayed in the palace all the time when I could, and my only real friend was Monica, but even that was always precarious because of the boss-employee relationship.

And so . . . there was James.

The minute I first saw him at the Fairfaxes', all tall, with striking dark brows, amazing hair, witty eyes, a panty-dropping Scottish accent, big hands, and a wicked smile—I knew he was trouble.

And then he smirked at me.

It was fleeting, his face quickly going back to neutral. But that smirk did me in. It was another week before we were properly introduced to each other, but even then, in the back of my head, I knew it was just the beginning.

After that, the two of us skirted around each other until James invited me out for dinner in the city with him and his old friends in town, Harrison and Piper. Nothing physical happened between us, but we got closer. A lot closer.

It wasn't just lust either. At times he genuinely seemed interested in me. He seemed to care. It's part of his charm. He would ask about my grandmother a lot, perhaps knowing that part of me often missed my home country and the woman who had raised me.

But after a while, the sexual tension was impossible to ignore. One crisp fall night at three in the morning, the thread of tension snapped.

Next thing I knew, I was getting royally screwed by Prince Eddie's bodyguard. After that, it was all I could think about. It's not just that our chemistry was combustible, but that I found some kind of solace in him, as if he understood me and I understood him through just our bodies.

Or at least I thought I did. The thing about James is that being Prince Eddie's PPO never stopped him from going out and living his life. In fact, he had a bit of a reputation for it. But me? I was blinded by lust and very, very lonely.

Which in the end made me feel vulnerable when he abruptly

broke it off and started acting like I didn't exist. The one time I let myself fall in lust. Lord help me if I ever truly fall in love.

I take an extra-long time in the shower—as if I can wash away the fact that James's skilled hands were ever on my body—then I start getting ready for the day. I put on a thin red sweater that keeps me warm and fits nicely under my coat (also happens to make my boobs look huge), and high-waisted skinny jeans with thick fluffy socks. I blow-dry my hair straight, making a mental note to get more highlights put in at some point, then do a quick coat of makeup. I'm so used to just pulling my hair back and not wearing makeup when I'm here that I almost feel like a different person when I've got lipstick on.

I grab my purse and then step out into the hall.

Nearly colliding with James.

"Hey," he says to me, his eyes taking on a mischievous slant. "How did you sleep?"

Don't give him an inch.

"Just fine," I tell him, offering a quick smile before pushing past him.

And he's right on my tail as I head to the shoe rack by the front door.

"Where are you going?" he asks.

I sit down on the bench, glancing up at him as I grab my boots. "It's my day off." I eye his suit. "Isn't it your day off too?"

He looks down at his suit. "Old habits die hard."

"They certainly do." I'm just glad it's not his new suit that Magnus bought him, because those pants are pretty tight and they leave nothing to the imagination. As in, you can't help but stare at his crotch, and since I happen to know how well-endowed he is, it's an extra tease.

Again, probably done on purpose.

"You're going to visit your grandmother?"

I pull on my boots. "Yup."

"Can I come?"

I pause, eyes widening. "Why? To see my grandmother?"

"Sure, why not?"

Is he serious? "Why not?" I repeat. "Because I don't want you there?"

I don't mean to be so blunt with him, but I can't help it.

"Oh," he says.

Shit. Now I feel bad.

"Look," I say, zipping up my boots and getting to my feet. "It's not a good idea for my grandmother to meet new people. It's overwhelming. She'll probably end up thinking you're her late husband. Sometimes she thinks I'm my mother, and . . . well, that feels like a kick in the chest."

"Totally understandable," he says. "Forget I said anything. Didn't mean any harm by it."

He turns to walk off, and I hate how torn this man is making me feel, how I'm angry at him one second for pleasuring himself loudly enough for me to hear, then guilty the next because it also seems like he's trying to be nice.

"Wait," I call after him, grabbing my coat from the rack.

He looks at me over his shoulder.

"Why don't you come with me? You know, downtown. Olaf drives me. He'd be happy to give you a lift too. We can meet up after."

James faces me with a wary expression. "You sure about that? I don't want to step on any toes."

"I'm sure," I tell him as I zip up the coat. I think.

Then he grins at me, and damn it if I don't get a little winded at the sight of how gorgeous he is. He strides over to me, grabbing his long wool peacoat and slipping on his boots, and we step outside on the porch.

Olaf, ever punctual, is already in the car, the engine running.

"Did you grab any breakfast?" James asks me as we head down the steps and into the sunshine, the snow sparkling so brightly I have to fish my sunglasses out of my purse.

I shake my head, slipping them on. "No. I usually get a cake for my grandmother, so I save myself for that."

I reach for the door, but James is fast and opens it for me.

"After you," he says.

I give him a quick smile, trying not to be fooled by any gallantry, and slide on in. I say hello to Olaf, a super old fellow who has worked for the royal family his whole life. He used to be the king's butler but now is the chauffeur for anyone who needs it. He doesn't hear the best, but he drives well and is always humming to himself happily.

I expect James to get in the front seat with him, but he slides right into the back seat next to me. This is just a black VW, so there's not a lot of room back here, especially when you consider I'm tall and rather large-boned, with wide hips and a big ass, and he's even taller and even larger-boned. Our shoulders are close to touching.

I angle my face away, putting my attention to the window as the car drives off. I hate how the smell of him seems to sink into my bones, so easily igniting the heat between my legs. I close my eyes, and my mind automatically starts playing back the sounds from this morning, that low, rich moan of pleasure.

My eyes snap back open. Nope. Can't think about that.

And now it's too hot in here.

I unzip my coat and try to get the giant puffy thing off me without touching James, but it's impossible.

"Sorry," I say as I elbow him repeatedly, maybe with a few extra jabs in there for good measure, stuck inside my coat until he grabs the ends and pulls me out of it.

"Thanks," I tell him, trying to tame my hair, pushing my sunglasses up to the top of my head. I smoosh the coat between us like a barrier.

I feel his eyes on me for what seems like eternity before I finally turn my head and look his way.

He was just staring at my chest. Like I said, this sweater is extremely flattering (not that my curves need any emphasizing at all, because I have an ample amount). And he makes no apologies for his gaze either. His eyes drift up to mine, the corner of his mouth lifting. "Your hair looks really nice."

I pat my hands over it, for a moment thinking he's being sarcastic. "Thanks," I tell him. "I use Sundays as an excuse to fix myself up."

He looks me up and down, heat simmering as he goes. "You do a good job. That sweater is very . . . *becoming* on you."

I narrow my eyes at him. "If you turn that into a pun, you're getting kicked out of the car."

He grins and looks away.

And then I find myself smiling too.

Not good. This is how it started last time. This is exactly how he got under my skin. That smile and those burning eyes and a rocket full of innuendo ready to launch at a moment's notice.

Suffice to say, the ride into Oslo feels much longer than it should. And hotter. And it feels like there's no air in the car. By the time Olaf drops us both off outside Steen & Strøm, I feel like I've been released from some prison of my own sexual frustration.

"Where you off to?" James asks me, following me as I head into the store, totally prepared to just leave him outside.

"I'm going to get my grandmother a cake from the café," I tell him, stepping out of the way as shoppers come in and out of the store. "Then maybe do a bit of shopping before I see her."

He has this eager, almost hopeful look in his eyes. His puppy dog impression. But I'm not about to invite him along for this. This is the one day of the week that's my time and my time alone. In the name of self-care, I can't have James following me around.

I don't even have to say anything because that hopeful look disappears pretty quickly. "So what time does Olaf pick us up?"

"I'll text Olaf and let him know when we're ready. I usually go for dinner after, so . . ." I pause, rubbing my lips together for a moment, knowing I'll regret this. "So if you wanted to get something to eat when I'm done, I know a nice little wine bar."

His brow creases in surprise. "Really? I'd like that." He walks over to me, and I freeze, not sure what he's about to do.

He holds out his hand.

I stare at it for a moment.

Stare up at his face.

Get overwhelmed at how handsome he is.

And put my hand into his.

He smiles in delight, giving it a squeeze. "Actually I was just wanting your mobile. I wanted to add my number."

Shit.

My cheeks immediately burn, and I try to snatch my hand from his, but he hangs on to it for a few seconds more before I can take it back. I look down and busy myself, searching for my phone in my purse, my skin on fire.

Finally I enter my passcode and give him my phone, avoiding his eyes. Even so, I can tell he's got that cat-got-the-canary smile, and right now I'm one very flushed canary.

He takes the phone and enters his contact information. "Feels kind of silly, doesn't it?" he says as he types. "Considering we're practically sleeping in the same room."

I swallow, trying to calm my flaming cheeks, make my face go neutral. He's baiting me about this morning again. I say nothing.

He hands it back to me. "Text me when you're done. I think I might go check out the Viking museum."

Then he walks out of the store, holding the door open for an elderly woman who gives him the crankiest look. He shoots me another grin over her head and then leaves.

I stare at him for a moment, watching him disappear through the glass doors. If you didn't know he was a professional bodyguard, you'd pick up on it anyway. Yes, he's charming and a little goofy at times, definitely a rascal, but he walks with a sense of purpose and grace, like he can fight to the death and he knows it. His body is a very well-oiled machine, ready to spring into action at a moment's notice, and the man doesn't seem to show any fear. He's all confidence.

And yet, there are times when I've seen his confidence waver. And there was one time when I saw the fear.

It was in bed.

With me.

When I told him I was falling for him.

I didn't think it would be a big deal, not in the moment anyway. It was after a particularly slow and sensual round of sex. I'd just come, hard as hell and in an emotional way, and I was so loved up on endorphins, being held in his arms, feeling his heart beat, that I just blurted it out.

I mean, it wasn't "I love you." I didn't love him. I wasn't in love with him.

I was just falling for him.

That's not the same at all.

But when I said the words . . . James just froze.

Literally froze.

Like I thought he died. He wasn't even breathing.

And the look in his eyes after that was . . . well, it was fear. He was afraid. I opened my mouth and said something I shouldn't have, when I was feeling very open and vulnerable, and I set him off.

So yeah, I've seen him be afraid.

Just sucks that I was the one that scared him.

I shake that out of my head, hating that those old feelings are being conjured up again, the feelings I did my best to forget. Rejection, bitterness, unworthiness. I push them away and then carry on in the department store, looking for cake.

Thankfully they do have cloudberry cake, so I order a small version of it, and then I peruse the makeup section, wondering if a new lipstick in red would be a nice pick-me-up. I find one that's more expensive than it ought to be, but that's Norway's pricing for you.

Then I grab a taxi outside to take me to my grandmother's home.

The care center is just to the north of town and is a bit of a drive. When I finally get there, I take a moment to appreciate the view of Oslo from up here, shining in the sun, then head in to check in with the staff.

Lisbeth, one of my favorite caretakers, is here and greets me with a shaky smile. My heart immediately drops.

"Laila," she says to me. "I'm so glad that you're here."

"What happened?" I ask, hand pressed against my chest.

"Nothing," she says quickly, though her eyes seem worried. "Here, let me take your coat."

She takes my coat from me and hangs it up before taking me down the hall toward the wing where my grandmother resides.

"You seem worried," I tell her, trying to slow my racing heart.

She shakes her head. "It's fine. Helge, well . . . she had a bad scare yesterday."

"What happened? Why didn't you text me?"

"I didn't want to worry you," she says. Believe it or not, since Lisbeth is only a couple of years older than me, we've become friends. Not good friends, but I text her often to ask about my grandmother, and we end up talking about our lives. Or at least her life. My life is pretty damn boring these days, and I'm not really keen to open up about deeper things.

She continues as we walk. "She woke up from her nap and just started screaming. She thought she was young again. In some ways I think she thought I was your mother. Funny how the wires get crossed. We couldn't calm her down, no matter what we did. We ended up having to sedate her."

My heart sinks, the sorrow spreading inside me like ink in water. "You should have told me."

"There's nothing you could have done."

"I could have come here sooner."

She gives me a sympathetic smile. "It wouldn't have made a difference, Laila. You're here now." We pause outside her door. "Just, take it easy on her, and yourself. She most likely won't recognize you."

I stare down at the box of cake in my hands.

"She might not eat either," she says. "She hasn't yet. But maybe that will change. Do you want me to go in with you?"

I shake my head, trying to whip up the courage. How quickly things change. One moment you can't wait to see someone, the next you're so terribly afraid that they won't know who you are and will never remember you again.

The grief has my heart in a chokehold.

"I'll be nearby if you need me," she says before opening the door.

My grandmother is sitting by the window, staring out at the view. I don't know how it's possible, but she seems to have aged several years in a week.

"Grandma?" I call out softly, shutting the door behind me. "Helge?"

She doesn't look at me, but she bundles her shawl closer to her, her gaze fixed outside. The shawl is an old heritage piece that her own mother made, pale blue wool with pink felt flowers. I filled her room here with as many heirlooms and personal items as possible to try to jog her memory, to keep her connected to past and future, but I'm not sure how much pull they have.

I slowly walk in, like I'm afraid she's a wild animal I might spook, and I hate that I have to behave this way. I hate that I can't just run in here, burst into her room like I did as a child, throw my arms around her neck, and ask her to make my favorite cookies. Or stomp into the room, tears in my eyes, crying over a boy at school. She was always able to solve everything.

I carefully sit down on the chair across from her. "Hello," I say. "It's Laila."

She nods but doesn't look my way, and doesn't really seem to hear me either. Her frail hands are speckled with age spots, looking so skinny, the veins thick and raised. Her fingers grasp one another, squeezing and releasing. She's nervous. Afraid.

I feel tears rush to my eyes, and I swallow them down, do everything I can to keep from feeling what I'm feeling. She won't understand why I'm crying.

"I brought you something, in case you get hungry." I hold out the cake and then slowly open the top, trying to keep my hands steady. "Cloudberry cake." I refrain from telling her it's her favorite, because if I wasn't sure of who I was, or when I was, I don't think I'd appreciate hearing things like that. It would make me feel more lost.

She finally steals a glance at the cake and nods. Then looks at me. For a moment I think I see recognition in her blue eyes. Then she frowns and mutters, "No, you aren't her," and looks back to the window.

I take in a deep breath until my lungs feel like they might burst, the pain nearly impossible to ignore.

"We don't have to eat it," I say after a moment. "You can eat it later. Anytime you want. And we don't have to talk. Just know that I'm Laila, and I care for you a lot, and that I'm here."

We sit like that for thirty minutes until she falls asleep in her chair.

The moment I'm outside in the sunshine, I start to cry.

Nine

· · · · · · ·

LAILA

Two years ago

I CAN'T SLEEP.

I've been staring up at the ceiling for hours, doing that annoying thing where I try to make myself feel better for getting only seven hours of sleep, for getting only six hours of sleep, for getting only five hours of sleep, the hours counting down while my mind winds up.

I'm stressed. And it's not just the usual anxiety that comes with being a nanny for a literal princess—it's Grandma I'm worried about. I got a call from my cousin Peter, who lives near her, that put me on edge. Seems she's been acting a little erratic lately, going for walks along the fjord in the night. Strange behavior that frightens me, makes me want to ask for the first available days off so that I can go and check on her.

A shuffling sound breaks me out of my thoughts, and I look

to the open window. Even though it's mid-September and the nights are cool, I can't sleep without fresh air on my face.

I get out of bed and look out the window to see James walking across the path from the back gate to the house. He's wearing a suit as usual, and he doesn't seem overly drunk or anything until he suddenly stops and crouches down, staring at something on the ground.

I watch him for a few moments as he does this, until I feel like a creeper. Then I decide, *To hell with it.* I grab my robe and throw it on over my nightgown. I slide on my slippers and head downstairs, being quiet as I pass by the rooms. In the time I've been working at Primrose Cottage I still feel like I don't know any of the staff. Everyone really keeps to themselves here, and I don't know if it's a British thing, or maybe it's a royal thing, but there's absolutely no camaraderie among the workers. Monica and Eddie are the exceptions to this, the only ones who have really welcomed me.

Aside from James, that is. He's becoming my only friend here, which is scary, especially since my feelings for him over the past few weeks have become less and less friendly and way more . . . sexual. I can't even help it at this point; ever since that dinner, it's like my body has become completely in tune with his. I can feel his presence, his energy, before I even see him, my pulse going wild, my stomach swarming with butterflies, heat between my legs and all that jazz.

I really shouldn't be doing this, heading out to see him in the middle of the night. I'd be better off in bed and staring at the ceiling and worrying myself to death.

You just need to get laid, I think.

And yeah, that's the problem. I do.

And, fuck, I want it to be with James.

But I digress.

I tiptoe down the hallway and peek out the door to see James still crouched down, looking at something on the ground. I quietly step outside and walk over to him.

"What are you looking at?" I whisper.

"It's a frog," he says, slowly looking up at me. He doesn't look surprised to see me out here, but then again, knowing his hearing and instincts, always on alert, he probably knew I was coming.

He points into the grass to the side of the path, and I crouch down next to him to get a better look. Lo and behold there's a frog in the grass, its skin shiny in the lights. It fixes a round eye on me and then hops off.

I watch it go and look at James. "Sorry, I think I interrupted something."

There's something different about him tonight; his eyes are a little glazed, and he seems like he's not really here. Or maybe he's drunk and I've never seen him this way up close. Even when we went to the pub after dinner with Piper and Harrison, the two of us only had one drink each before Charles showed up with the car. And when we sometimes have drinks together in the study, neither of us have very much.

He gives his head a shake, then gazes at me.

"No, it's all right," he says, getting to his feet. "I was getting tired of staring at something that won't talk to me."

"Now you know how I feel with Madeline," I say with a chuckle, reaching out as he begins to lean unsteadily to the right. I grab his forearms, relishing the feel of their strength beneath my fingers.

"Will you talk to me?" he asks, his voice low.

I feel the heat wash over me, my skin prickling, my throat tightening. I have no idea what he's getting at, and I have no idea what to say.

And he's still staring at me, his eyes raking over my body, drinking me in.

"You have no idea what it's like," he continues, his voice hushed to a whisper. "To never be able to just be yourself around anyone."

And before I can even process the words and what to say back—because I do understand what he's saying, very much— his hands are on me.

They slide up my arms and around my back, his hands traveling up and down my spine. He pulls me against him, his mouth crushing mine, his kiss urgent and passionate, our lips and tongues meshing together, making my head spin.

Oh my god.

I moan in his mouth, and I'm vaguely aware of the fact that he's kissing me outside in the middle of the night and that anyone could happen upon us, that we could get caught. But those concerns seem to be far away, like they're in another universe. The only thing that matters right now is that he's kissing me so deeply I feel it in the marrow of my bones.

His hands are on the small of my back, pulling me against him, against the hard length of his cock, which is rigid against his fly. I rock my hips against him, eliciting a groan from him as his lips travel down my neck.

"I've been waiting so long to do this with you," he grinds out as his lips cover mine again, as his hands move to my breasts, cupping them through my nightgown, my robe falling open.

All I can do is gasp.

Then reality hits me.

No! Not here, not where they can see you.

I pull away, breathing so hard that it hurts, and press my hands against his shirt.

"We can't do this here," I say before taking another step backward and doing up my robe. Funny, I had meant to say that we can't do this at all, and yet . . .

He stares at me, nodding slowly. His mouth is wet, his lids are heavy, and the scent of testosterone, pheromones, and lust permeates the night air.

Wordlessly he grabs my hand and pulls me toward the house. Once inside he lets go and slips silently down the hallway with me right behind him. I have exactly ten seconds to decide what to do next, because he's already opening the door to his room and giving me a look that makes my toes curl in anticipation. I could easily go up the stairs and to my room, try to sleep, forget this whole kiss ever happened. But I can't do that now, not when my body has taken the reins, pushing all logic to the side. I know what I want—it's what I've always wanted, and I'm going to get it.

I step inside his room. It's dark and he doesn't turn on the lights, but it looks similar to mine. Same bed, dresser, desk, closet, but his place is much tidier than mine. While I'm taking it in, his eyes are taking me in.

We're silent. There's no use for small talk now. We're both committed. Instead he just stares at me, his eyes moving over my body so hungrily that I feel like I'm on fire.

I kick off my slippers. My fingers tremble as I undo the tie to my robe, and then I let it fall off my shoulders, pooling onto the floor around my feet, leaving me standing before him in just my white silk nightgown. His eyes move down my body, swallowing the sight of me, the muscles in his jaw working. I take another step toward him, closing the space between us, and his hands come up, cupping my face, his fingers pressing into my cheeks. He leans in, his mouth searching mine, his kiss rough, desperate, matching the feeling I have inside me, like all these weeks of pretending I felt nothing for him are finally roaring out of me.

I put my hands on his chest, my body pressed up against his, and he makes a noise in his throat.

"I want you, love," he says against my mouth, trailing kisses down my chin, over my throat, his hands tugging at the straps of my nightgown. I push my fingers into his hair, down his back, tugging him against me hard, kissing him like I'm trying to crawl inside him, to see what it's like to feel his heart beating, his blood rushing through his veins. He pulls my nightgown off in one motion, pulling it over my head and tossing it onto the floor. I'm in just my bra and underwear now, cursing myself for wearing beige granny panties, but as I stand in front of him, his eyes hungry and gleaming in the dark, I don't think he cares.

"Oh Christ," he whispers, his hands on my shoulders, pushing me back onto the bed. He straddles me, his elbows on either side of my head, his fingers sinking into my hair. I shiver beneath him, my hands moving over his shoulders, trying to pull off his jacket. He pulls back and quickly shucks his jacket off, then I push up his white shirt, undoing the buttons so quickly that he laughs. He helps me out and pulls it off, throwing it onto the floor. Then he undoes his pants, pushing them down and kicking them to the side, until he's standing at the foot of the bed in just his boxer briefs.

He is as gorgeous as I have imagined. The planes of his body are coiled and strong, his muscles tense and his eyes burning with need. His skin is pale in the dark, but it shows off each taut line, hard and strong, and I pause when my eyes reach his package, his dick outlined against his gray boxer briefs. His hands go to his waist, and I struggle to breathe as he pushes his boxer briefs down his hips and steps out of them.

Holy hell.

He's hard and thick, his cock jutting out proudly, the tip shining with moisture. I instinctively lick my lips, which brings out an arrogant grin, like he knows just how gorgeous he is. I mean, look at him. Of course he knows it.

He climbs back onto the bed, his cock bumping against my thigh, and I moan, my hands coming up, caressing his shoulders and back as he looms over me. He leans in and kisses me, his mouth taking mine, then he moves down my neck with soft, wet kisses.

I run my fingers over his chest, his muscles tight and flexing. "I've wanted you for weeks, and I didn't know what to do about it . . ." I begin, my voice hoarse.

"Shh," he says, kissing the tip of my nose, then my lips, then my chin. "Shh. You have me now." He brushes his mouth over my jaw, then comes down to my neck and presses his lips against my rapidly beating pulse. He kisses me there, his mouth on my skin making me shiver and arch my back. He travels lower, over my chest, and my breath catches in my throat as he pulls back my bra and takes a nipple into his mouth.

He's sucking it, pressing it between his teeth and flicking his tongue against it, sending electricity through my body. My back bows, the pleasure nearly unbearable, and I moan and whimper as he sucks me, his teeth sinking into my skin, making me gasp. A hand slowly travels over my body, and he pauses as he reaches my stomach, his hand resting on my belly for a second. I look down, watching as his hand trails south, my hips rocking against him. He's touching me, teasing me, his mouth suckling my breast, and then he moves again, his hand going to my hip and sliding beneath my panties. I moan, arching my back, pressing up against his hand, wanting more, wanting his mouth and his fingers to do whatever they want to my body.

He groans, his fingers hooking into my panties, and he pulls them down my legs. I lift one leg up as he takes them off, draped around my ankle, and he slides his hand up my inner thigh. My breath catches in my throat, and I bite my bottom lip until it hurts, my eyes falling closed as a finger brushes against my clit, making me twitch and shudder.

Fuck me. I can't believe he's touching me.

He slides his finger along my wetness, his mouth back on my breast, and my hands clutch at the sheets, pulling back the soft fabric. His mouth travels over my breast, his tongue licking the tender skin, his teeth nipping me, his fingers stroking my clit, and I'm moaning his name, begging him to be inside me, to stop teasing me. I'm whimpering, buried in desire, his hands driving all thought out of my mind.

I feel like I'm spinning out of control. Like I'm tumbling, falling faster than I can handle. His fingers slide over my wetness, his lips pressing kisses over my chest before his mouth returns to mine, kissing me hard and tasting like my heated skin.

His cock presses into my thigh, thick and hard, like I can feel every vein, every ridge, every inch of him. I moan into his mouth, and he lets out a sound, low and desperate, his lips moving to my neck, sucking and kissing and licking, making me whimper, making me writhe beneath him.

He moves lower, down to my breasts, and he covers one with one hand, massaging it, his thumb moving over my nipple, teasing it and making it painfully hard, his fingers pinching and pulling it until I'm moaning, rocking my hips against him.

"Patience, Laila," he whispers against my neck. "Let me taste you."

With his warm, wide hands he spreads my legs. He shifts over me, his mouth moving down my body, over my stomach, tongue sliding over my hip bones. Then he abruptly moves, pushing my legs open wider, his mouth on the sensitive flesh of my inner thigh, kissing and sucking until my eyes roll back in my head. I whimper with need as he pushes my legs farther apart, opening me up for him.

"You have such a beautiful cunt, love," he whispers against my skin, and I nearly come from just the sound of it. "So pink. So wet."

Fire. From my cheeks to my core to my pussy, I am pure molten fire now, flames fanned by his dirty talk.

"I need you inside me," I whisper hoarsely. "Now."

He laughs, his breath hot and wet. "Oh, do you?"

I nod, my eyes falling closed, my head falling back. "Fuck me, James," I whisper.

Two can play the dirty-talking game.

He groans at that, and his fingers slide through my wetness, plunging inside me, making my body arch.

"How about I devour you first, hey, love?" he says, then buries his face into me. I gasp loudly, forgetting to be quiet, as his tongue swirls around my clit and my back bows, my knuckles turning white as I tighten them around his hair. My hips thrust against him, and he laughs against me, at how desperate I am, his fingers plunging deep into me, working me harder and harder. The sound of my wetness fills the room, and I stare down at him, his dark head between my legs, my legs spread wide, my hands in his hair, my hips bucking.

Hottest thing I've ever seen.

Then he pulls his mouth off of me and looks up at me through my legs, his mouth shining and swollen from exertion.

Okay, now it's the hottest thing I've ever seen.

"Get a good look?" he says with a crooked smile before he dips his head again. Only difference is this time he doesn't look away. He keeps his gorgeous dark eyes on me as he begins to eat me out again.

Holy shit, this is intense.

His mouth sucks at me, hard, and his fingers plunge deep, and he starts to work me faster, his eyes never leaving mine. I don't know how long I'm going to last, but no matter what happens, I hope I never forget the sight of this gorgeous man between my legs, my pussy bared to his hungry gaze. My skin is tight and flushed, and I can't breathe as he works me, his tongue playing with my clit, his fingers plunging into me.

"James, oh my god, oh my god," I moan, my back arching, my hips lifting up off the bed. I feel like I'm going to explode from how good it feels. He's not letting up either, his tongue swirling around my clit, his fingers pumping in and out. I'm gasping for breath, my hands in his hair, my hips moving mind-lessly.

I collapse back against the pillow and close my eyes, shud-dering and moaning. I can feel my orgasm building inside, coming for me. I'm tightening around his fingers, and he slides three fingers inside me, and I come with a sharp cry, shudder-ing beneath him, my pussy throbbing.

"Fuck," I hiss, my back arching, my hips pumping against him, my hands pulling his hair. I'm shaking, shaking, shaking, and he doesn't stop. He doesn't let up, and he keeps on fucking me with his fingers, his mouth still sucking at me, his tongue still tracing my wetness, moving up to my clit, my hands dig-ging into his hair. I'm moaning and whimpering, my legs rock-ing against him, my hips jerking.

"Oh my god," I whisper, over and over again. "James, oh my god, oh my god."

I'm spent, ravaged, boneless. I can't move. I can't talk. I can't see. All that I can do is feel, and the feeling is the most intense pleasure I've ever known, better than anything I've ever felt.

I hear him chuckle, pulling his fingers out of me. "Still think you need me to fuck you?"

I open my eyes, and the world is spinning.

"Yes," I tell him, my voice breaking. Because as much as he just rocked me into another world, I want more of him, all of him. I want him inside me, and I want to undo him the way he just undid me.

His eyes glimmer in the light, and then he leans over, his mouth covering mine, my taste on his lips like sweet salt. He kisses me deeply, then pulls away and looks at me with lust-filled eyes.

"Tell me to fuck you again," he says, his voice deep and low, his eyes holding mine, demanding, wanting.

"Fuck me," I say, my voice a weak whisper. My cheeks are hot, as is the rest of my body, and my heart rate hasn't returned to normal yet.

He gives me a wolfish smile, clearly enjoying this. "Again, love."

"Fuck me," I repeat, louder this time, my body on fire with need.

He lets out a greedy growl, then gets up and strides over to his bedside table, rifling through a drawer. He rips a condom open and slips it on, and then he's between my legs again, the thick head of his cock against me.

He grabs my hips with bruising pressure, and his hands dig into my flesh as he pushes inside me.

I let out a startled cry—he's bigger than I expected—and he puts a hand over my mouth, giving me a look that reminds me that we still have to be quiet. Fuck, there's definitely something hot about his hand over my mouth, especially as his cock slides in and out of me.

How is this happening? How is this sex? This is not like anything I've experienced before. I've never let anyone take control like this, given myself over like this.

"I'm going to make you come so hard you forget your own name," he says, his voice deep and raspy, the promise in it sending fire through my body. He removes his hand, and I gasp loudly as he pulls back and thrusts hard inside me, making my body jerk. He grabs my wrists, pinning them to the bed, and then he's pounding into me, giving me what I asked for, deep, hard, unyielding.

"When I'm done with you, you're going to thank me for making you come so hard," he growls, his hips thrusting against mine, hitting me deep, hitting me hard. "You're going to thank me for fucking you so thoroughly that you're ruined for any other man out there."

I moan, and he kisses me, then starts fucking me harder, his hips slamming into mine, his cock moving almost painfully inside me.

He's driving me wild, the way he moves, the way he's fucking me. I don't know how much I can take, but I know I don't want it to stop.

I can feel my orgasm approaching, the edge teasing me, just beyond reach, and he pulls away from my lips, his teeth digging into my shoulder as he bites down, the pain giving to pleasure, his hand squeezing my wrists. He's still fucking me, hard, his hips moving faster, deeper, his cock thrusting into me, hitting me deep.

"Oh my god, James," I moan helplessly, bucking against him, my body rocking beneath his. I am so close, so close, and it's building, building, building, and I moan again, and he slams into me, so hard I gasp.

I'm coming. The orgasm is so strong it's almost painful, my body arching and bucking against him as if it's the only thing that will keep me from floating off into the atmosphere, never to be found again.

He keeps going, and I don't know how he's keeping up the pace, my orgasm taking me away, and he's pounding into me, harder and harder and faster, and then he's coming hard, his cock swelling and pulsing inside me as he comes, groaning, his breath hot and raspy.

"Fucking hell," he whispers, his thumb tracing my lips as he pulls out of me, his eyes burning into mine.

Fucking hell is right.

I can't believe that happened.

I lie there as he relaxes beside me, the sound of our breath competing with the drumming of my heart, and I wait for the shame to hit, for the guilt and regret, that I just had sex with James. He's barely a friend and definitely a colleague, and I know that if anyone found out, I'd probably be fired. Hell, maybe James would be fired too—who knows—especially after Monica warned me.

I should have stayed in my room, I should have tried to fall asleep, but instead I just had the best sex of my life.

And you know what? I don't regret a thing.

As long as it doesn't happen again.

But then James reaches out and gently pushes a strand of hair off my sweaty face, and I know in the deepest part of me . . .

It's going to happen again.

Ten

. . . . . .

JAMES

IT'S NEARLY SIX WHEN LAILA FINALLY RESPONDS TO MY text. For a moment I thought she had left me in Oslo and gone back to the house. I wouldn't have been surprised.

Then again, I was surprised when she invited me to have dinner with her. I can't seem to figure this woman out. But I never really could.

The text just has an address and says to meet her there in twenty minutes.

Luckily I'm back in the city center, after having explored the Viking museum and strolled around the harbor, and the wine bar isn't far.

I hate to admit it, but I'm a bit nervous. I shouldn't be. Thus far I've enjoyed being in Laila's company, even when she's reminding me of how things imploded between us or rolling her eyes when I try to pay her a compliment. But when she's nice, fuck, it's like the sun peeking out of the clouds on those dreary days. You know the sun won't last, but it doesn't stop you from basking in it for a while.

The thing is, I want something from Laila, and I'm not even sure what it is. It's nothing serious—I've learned my lesson there and almost repeated that very same mistake with her. And while a lot of what I feel for her is sexual—my dick has a mind of its own while in her vicinity—there's something else. Friendship, maybe. I just don't know if it's possible to be friends with someone after you've slept with them and want to sleep with them again, let alone after they've decided to hate your guts.

The wine bar is narrow and easy to miss. She's managed to snag the sole window seat looking onto the street, though when I pass by her and give a wave, she can barely muster a smile. It's not that she's mad at me either; there's sadness in her eyes, a look that makes my heart pinch.

I go inside the bar, the warmth and smell of mulled wine and fried fish overtaking me, and hang my coat up on the rack by the small table. It's definitely an intimate spot, two seats beside each other looking out onto the street, and I have to fight the urge to lean down and kiss her on the cheek, like we're out on a date.

I sit down next to her, smelling the jasmine scent of her perfume. "You got the best seat in the house. You charm them with your feminine wiles?"

She lets out a mirthless laugh. "I have no wiles today."

That certainly isn't true. She's wearing a sweater that makes her breasts look stupendous, and I have muscle memory of running my hands and lips and tongue over them, knowing how heavy they feel in my palm, knowing what to do to her nipples so that she's breathing out my name.

God, we had it good, didn't we?

I avert my eyes before she can catch me staring at her chest again. I got away with it in the car, but now things feel different, like we're on rocky ground.

"It was the only seat available," she goes on, flipping over the thin menu. "Got it just in time."

I see what she's saying. She wouldn't have asked to be seated so close to me. Laila is tall for a girl, maybe five ten, and she's all hips and curves. I'm six foot three and have swimmer's shoulders, so a seat like this is a tight fit. Far more intimate than she'd like, but it's perfect for me.

I watch her face for a moment. She's wearing bright red lipstick that shows off her perfect, expressive mouth and full lips, but it can't hide her eyes.

"Did everything with your grandmother go okay?" I ask.

Her jaw goes tense, eyes still glued to the menu, but now I can see they aren't taking anything in. "It was okay."

The waiter comes by, speaking Norwegian, and Laila puts an order in for herself. "I'm getting a glass of the Chiara Condello sangiovese," she tells me. "Plus fried klipfisk. What do you want?"

I would normally get a beer, but the weather and the atmosphere in here (and the fact that it's a wine bar) have me placing the exact same order as hers.

"Do you even know what klipfisk is?" she asks me as the waiter leaves.

I shrug. "No idea. I'm sure I'll find out. It's not like fish eyeballs or something?"

"What if it was?"

"If it's fried, I'm sure I can handle it."

"Quite the stomach you have," she says. "Then again, you're Scottish. You invented haggis."

"We invented a lot of things, lass," I tell her, deepening my brogue. I twist in my seat to try to face her better. "You know, the only problem with sitting this close to you is that I can't get a good look at your beautiful face."

Just as I expected, her cheeks wash with a touch of pink. "Probably for the best. So what did you end up doing today?"

"Went to the museum, walked around the harbor, nearly slipped on ice a few times and went into the sea. Pretty good day as a tourist."

She nods. "There's a lot to see here. I'm sure all your days off will be booked."

"As long as I'm booked with you."

She finally looks over at me, a wry smile spreading on her face. "You're unbelievable, you know that?"

"I know. I believe you've told me that *at least* a few times." I add a wink at the end, so she knows I meant in bed.

Her smile vanishes, her gaze going to the window, watching people pass by on the snowy street. "James . . ."

"What? You going to tell me I'm being inappropriate again?"

She sighs, putting her hands on her face. "What's the point?" she mumbles. Her voice sounds so distraught that I actually don't think she's talking about me.

I place my hand on her back, and she flinches slightly from my contact, which, I have to admit, hurts a little.

"Hey," I say, leaning in. "Are you okay? Do you want to leave?" I'm so close that my lips brush against her hair as I talk.

"I'm okay," she says in a tiny voice. "Today was just rough."

"Can you talk to me about it?"

She gives a slight shake of her head. "You wouldn't understand."

I don't know why, but that bothers me. "Why wouldn't I understand? Just because I never knew my grandmother? Or my parents?"

She takes her hands away and turns her head, her mouth just inches from mine. Her eyes are wet, and they drop to my lips before going up to meet my gaze. "I just mean . . ."

"I know what you meant," I tell her, moving back to give her space.

There's a lot that Laila doesn't know about me, but then there are some things that she does. She knows that my birth mum was a drug addict who overdosed when I was two years old and I was raised by my deadbeat father until I was six, when he decided he couldn't do it anymore. I spent my whole life either being in a home for boys, or being bounced around from house to house. Some of the foster parents were indifferent, some were in it for the government help, others were abusive. Others had family members who were abusive. I barely survived the whole ordeal intact. In fact, I still think that I lost some part of myself then, some part I never got back. But when you're raised among loss, it doesn't matter if something else is taken from you. It leaves you empty all the same.

But while Laila knows the gist of all that, I've never gone into details. I haven't told her about my time in the army, and I barely touched on my divorce. She knows I was married, that is all. She has no idea what that marriage did to me.

Or maybe she does.

Maybe she realizes it's why I acted the way I did with her.

The waiter brings by our wine, and I raise my glass to hers. "Here's to your grandmother," I tell her, leaning back enough.

She does the same, carefully clinking the wineglass against mine.

I swirl the wine around the glass and breathe it in before having a sip. The wine is quite good, but I want to hear Laila talk.

"Listen, love," I say to her, noting how she stiffens when I call her *love*, a pet name I had for her. "I know you think I wouldn't understand about your grandmother, but I can at least try. I know what loss feels like. My father didn't die, but it felt like he did."

Actually, it felt like *I* was the one who died the day he dropped me off at the orphanage.

"That's the thing," she says softly. "My grandmother hasn't died, but . . . it feels like she did. I walked in there today, and I saw her very much alive, and yet I was a stranger to her. And I'm so afraid that means she'll become a stranger to me." She sniffs and has a sip of her wine, swallowing hard. "She's eighty-eight. She's not young. I know the loss is coming. The biggest loss. I've known that since I was young, that she was so much older and that she wouldn't be with me my whole life. I knew that I would lose her just as I lost my parents. I just don't know how to . . ."

"I know," I tell her, placing my hand on her thigh. I meant it out of comfort, but she's giving me the side-eye.

"James, what are you doing?"

"Am I making you uncomfortable?" I ask, hesitating, lifting up my hand. That's the last thing I want, especially after the day she's had.

She closes her eyes and shakes her head. "No," she whispers. "You're not making me feel uncomfortable."

I give her thigh a light squeeze, loving that I can touch her, even if it's just like this, even if she's about to tell me to take my hand away.

"I don't want this to happen." She says it so softly that I have to lean in close.

"Your grandmother?"

"*You*," she says, turning her face toward mine. "I don't want us to go down that same path we went down before."

I know what she's saying. I know why she's saying it. I know I was an asshole to her, and while I had my reasons and excuses, I never even got the chance to tell them to her. Not that it matters now.

But despite knowing why she's saying it, I can't help myself. I'm nothing but impulse.

I reach over and grab her chin lightly with my fingertips, holding her face in place. "What path?" I ask, my voice dropping a register.

She's staring at my lips again. "You know the path." Her nostrils flare as she breathes. "I'm still mad at you."

"I can see that," I tell her.

"You were such a fucking asshole," she says. Her tone is steady, but her eyes, they flash with anger I hadn't counted on.

"I know I was. And I'm sorry."

"You're sorry," she says snidely. "You slept with me and then practically kicked me out of your bed. I couldn't leave fast enough for you. And then after that, you avoided me like I had the plague. You made me feel like shit, James."

Her words are a knife to the stomach. Oh, I know it's all my fault. I know that I acted like a total wanker the moment she told me she was falling for me, the moment the fear of god came alive. I know she deserved better than that, so much better, and that it had nothing to do with her and everything to do with me. I just never told her that. I had the chance, but I chose to be selfish and keep it to myself, because to tell her would mean making myself vulnerable, and I wasn't ready for that.

I'm still not sure that I am. Which is another reason I should stop trying so hard with her, because deep down inside, I'm not even sure I'll be able to handle what I get. People change, but inner demons—well, sometimes those things just *grow*.

But it's as I'm abruptly letting go of her face that my arm comes down and smacks the top of my wineglass. It topples over, splashing the entire glass of sangiovese onto my lap and her chest.

"Fuck!" I swear, trying to scoot back in the seat.

We both get to our feet as a waiter hurries over, shaking his head at the mess. He motions to the bartender for something to clean it up with. Meanwhile the whole bar is watching us.

I give them all a wave to say, *Yes, hello, wine was spilled, carry on*, then both Laila and I head down through the restaurant to the bathroom, with her grumbling the entire way.

Of course, in a tiny place like this, there are only two bathrooms, and one is occupied.

"After you," I say, gesturing to the available one.

She just rolls her eyes and steps in, holding the door open. "Come on."

I step inside with her. The bathroom is the size of a postage stamp. And then I get a good look at the damage.

Yup, looks like I pissed my pants. Thank god they're black and you have to look closely.

On her red sweater, the wine just looks like an artful stain, though her nipples are poking through now. Very, very distracting.

"That was probably the clumsiest thing I've ever seen you do," she says, pulling out wads of paper towel and running them under the tap. "Almost made you seem like a mere mortal."

I can't help but grin. "You're telling me I'm godly?"

She lets out a soft snort and eyes me in the bathroom mirror. "You're something, I'll give you that much. You have the ego of a god, no denying that."

"Pretty sure you called me a god once or twice," I tell her as she dabs the towel on her chest. "You know you might as well take that right off."

"You'd like that, wouldn't you?"

"Yes. I would. It's nothing I haven't seen before, but I wouldn't mind seeing it again."

"I'm good," she says quickly as she shoots me a glare, dabbing again and again until her shirt is pretty much see-through.

Fucking hell, it's a turn-on. My dick is already pressing against my pants, not even caring that they're soaked with wine.

Finally she sighs and then mumbles something to herself in Norwegian.

The sweater comes off, leaving her in just a white lacy bra that looks a little small for her and is stained with red.

"Jesus," I swear. Her breasts are making my mouth water.

She gives me a sharp look, pressing the towel across her chest to cover herself up. "You're making this weird." Then her gaze drops to my very obvious erection. Her mouth parts slightly before she swallows. "Now you're making this really weird."

I'm about to make it weirder. I answer by undoing my belt, letting my pants drop to the floor so that I'm just in my black boxer briefs. I step out of them and gather them in my hands. "Just doing what you did," I tell her. "Easy to wash this way."

I step right up to her at the sink, watching as she gets flustered, cheeks going pink.

"Did I ever tell you how much I love making you blush?" I ask, my voice going low. "Did you blush this morning?"

My question makes her pause, and I know now she heard me this morning for sure.

She glances up at me through her lashes, her eyes simmering with anger and something else. I want to say it's lust, but I can't be sure. There's a good chance she's about to slap me across the face.

"I don't know what you're talking about," she says evenly, before focusing on her sweater.

I can't help but smile because I know she's lying.

I lean in until my mouth is at her ear. "Did you touch yourself?"

She sucks in her breath sharply and turns to face me again, but I'm fast, and once again acting on pure impulse.

I have to kiss her.

My hands cup her face, my fingers pressing into her high cheekbones, and I'm covering her mouth with mine.

She gasps against my lips, her hands going up to my chest, but instead of pushing me away, they rest there. My mouth coaxes hers open, the kiss deepening, widening, letting me in to where she's so soft and warm and wet. It feels familiar and new and freeing at the same time, sending shock waves through my body like lightning strikes.

Her fingers curl around my collar, holding me while I kiss her, hunger freely flowing between us, about to turn into a raging inferno. I'm rock-hard and I'm pressing her against the sink, making sure she can feel every long thick inch of me on her hip.

A breathless little moan escapes her, our mouths moving in tandem, the kiss turning wilder, violent, messy. Fuck, I've needed this. A chance to redeem myself if nothing else.

Then she pulls back, breathing hard, her eyes wild as she takes me in.

"James," she says, taking in a deep breath. "I don't . . . this doesn't erase what you did."

My throat feels pinched, my hands disappearing into her hair, the strands like silk between my fingers. "I know it doesn't. I'm not trying to erase it, I . . ."

Well, fuck. What am I trying to do, then?

I lick my lips, tasting her on them, wanting to kiss her again. I lean in, meeting her eyes, and speak the truth. "I just want to be with you."

"We can't," she says. But when I drive my erection into her farther, her eyes flutter shut. "Fuck, James, you're making this hard."

A laugh catches inside me. "Can't get much harder, love."

I make a fist in her hair, pulling it lightly, remembering how much she loved that.

She drops the paper towels and the sweater into the sink, her neck and back arching for more. My hand goes to her breast, fingers curling around the edges of the lace and pulling it back, exposing her nipple, already pebble-hard. I dip my head, pulling it between my lips until she's moaning loudly, her hands finding their way to my hair now.

Fuck, I want to be inside her, any way I can. I slide my palm down over the curves of her stomach, popping open the button on her jeans, before continuing the dive down below until my fingers dip beneath the soft cotton of her underwear, already a little damp.

"Jesus, Laila," I swear against her breast, licking up over her skin until I'm at her neck, biting gently as my fingers begin to stroke her clit. She's so wet and soft, I think I might just lose my mind if I don't get inside her soon enough.

But first I want to make her come on my hand, right here, right now. I want to watch her as she lets go, feel her around me.

"Tell me you heard me this morning," I murmur below her ear, my fingers rubbing her faster and faster until I ease back and plunge a finger inside her.

She gasps, clenching around me, her grip in my hair growing tight. "I heard you," she whispers, voice choked.

"Did you touch yourself?"

I feel her swallow against my tongue as I lick across her throat, pushing up another finger into her.

"No," she manages to say.

"You wanted to."

"*You* wanted me to," she answers.

I grin, leaving kisses against her jaw, my mouth finding its way to her lips as a third finger is pushed inside her. "I did. But since I'm touching you now, this more than makes up for it. Don't you think?"

She answers with a groan, her legs trying to spread wider in her jeans, but I like how tight it is for my hand as I work at her, my thumb skirting over her clit.

"Oh fuck me," she cries out, fingernails digging into my scalp.

"I'm going to, love," I tell her. "I'm going to bend you over and fuck you so hard the whole restaurant will wish they spilled wine on themselves too."

And then her body begins to seize up, a sharp inhale hitching in her throat, and then she's coming. I keep my eyes glued on her face, loving how beautiful she looks, like she's opening herself to the heavens. I'm the one who makes her look like this, feel like this, like she'd fall to her knees if I wasn't keeping her up.

She continues to shake and squeeze around my fingers, her fingers relaxing in my hair, her breath labored.

KNOCK KNOCK.

And of course there's a knock at the door.

"What?" I snap.

Mumbled Norwegian is the response.

"Oh god," Laila says softly, and I look back to her. Her eyes are glazed, a sweet, satisfied smile curving her lips, yet I know that probably won't last. "Oh god," she says, straightening up, clarity coming back into her eyes.

There she goes.

I quickly remove my hand. "I guess I got you off either way today."

She stares at me for a moment, and that's when I see it.

That wash of regret I knew was coming.

She rubs her lips together, blinking hard, and then quickly does up her jeans. "Fuck," she swears. "They're going to know we were doing something in here."

"So?"

She just shakes her head and pulls her sweater back on. "Come on, we need to go. Get your pants on."

I'm still painfully hard, but I'm deflating pretty fast thanks to the steely look in her eyes, plus the fact that someone is waiting for us outside. I slip on my pants, shivering at how uncomfortable it feels. At least they're black and no one can tell in the dim light.

We step outside to see a young dude in tattoos and ear gauges give us a very appreciative look, then head back into the restaurant. Luckily, for Laila's sake, no one pays us any attention, and we sit back down at our seats.

The fried food is already here.

"Why don't you eat and finish the wine. I'll settle the bill," she says, getting up.

I grab her hand. "Laila. No. Stay."

"My sweater is soaked."

"It's still going to be soaked in an hour too. Let's just finish the wine and the food." I don't let go until she sits back down. "I mean, dear god, I get you off and then you can't wait to leave."

"See," she hisses at me. "Doesn't feel very nice, does it?"

"Listen, we're going to need to move past that," I tell her, spearing the fried klipfisk with a fork. "For both our sakes."

"Regardless, this was a mistake."

"You call an orgasm a mistake? That's sacrilegious."

She points her fork at me, close enough to make me jerk my head back. "We need to get one thing clear. Whatever happened in there was bound to happen. I realize that now. But it can't happen again."

I put my hand on her thigh, dragging it up her jeans. "It could happen right now."

"James," she says sharply. "I'm serious. I had a momentary lapse of judgment in there. But that can't happen again."

"Why not?"

She looks at me like I have two heads. "Why not? For one, there's no way I'm going through what we went through before, okay? To sleep with you, to have you turn into an asshole—no thank you. For two, it's not even allowed."

"That didn't stop us before," I tell her, though Magnus was pretty clear about that on our first day.

"I know. And it should have. Because I like this job, James. Sure, it's harder than I thought, and I guess . . ." She trails off, worrying her lip between her teeth. "I guess it gets a little lonely at times being where we are. But I don't want to lose it. I'm just starting to find my groove. And if we start screwing each other again, one of us is bound to fuck up sooner or later. We'll get caught. And if it's not that, well, then you'll delve right into asshole mode." She closes her eyes. "I'm already regretting everything."

Aye, that hurts. I try to ignore the tight feeling in my chest. "You didn't do anything wrong. I just kissed you. Made you come on my hand. That's it."

"It was enough, James," she says slowly. She looks at me with pleading eyes. "It can't happen again, so please don't even try."

"Your willpower is that weak?" God, please tell me that she finds me as hard to stay away from as I find her.

"It was tonight," she says. Then she nods at my food. "Eat your klipfisk."

I take a tentative bite, reeling from everything.

It's not . . . bad.

"What is this?" *Please don't say it's eyeballs.*

"Dried salted cod," she says. "Like bacalao. It's more popular up north. My grandmother used to make it all the time. She'd even put it on pizza."

And at the mention of her grandmother, her shoulders drop, and it's like watching a candle getting snuffed out.

It's then that I realize what just happened and why. I was thinking too much with my dick to pay attention, but what happened in the restroom wasn't about us succumbing to lust. At least it wasn't for her. It was about Laila trying to process what happened with her grandmother. If I had thought about it for even a moment, I would have realized how vulnerable she was. And I wouldn't have taken advantage of her.

"Hey," I say to her between chews, swallowing it down. I put my hand over hers, giving it a squeeze. "I know what you're saying. And I respect that. I won't try anything anymore, I promise."

She gives me a weak smile. "That includes any funny business through the walls."

"I promise," I tell her again.

I mean it too. I just know keeping that promise isn't going to be easy.

Eleven

. . . .

JAMES

"PACK YOUR BAG, JAMES, WE'RE GOING ON A TRIP!" MAG-
nus announces, hands held high in the air as he appears in the
kitchen doorway.

I put my coffee down, my mind immediately racing to all
the possibilities. Paris? London? Somewhere hot, like the Mal-
dives? I'm usually briefed on Magnus's schedule ahead of time,
and being so close to Christmas, I hadn't seen anything other
than a few public events this week.

"Where to, sir?" I ask, thrilled to be getting out of the house.
Today marks three weeks since I got here, and even though I've
been to Oslo on duty a few times (and of course that fateful last
Sunday with Laila), I've been getting a bit of cabin fever.

"The kikut!" he exclaims, and then walks away.

From beside me, Lady Jane sighs.

I eye her, watching her dejectedly spread butter on her
knäckebröd. "What? Where's kikut? Or *what's* kikut?"

"Kikut is a cabin," she says tiredly. "Up the side of a mountain.

That will no doubt be covered in a load of bloody snow. Magnus loves to drag us all up there around the holidays. Last year he had a New Year's Eve party for all his royal friends up there— King Aksel of Denmark, Prince Viktor of Sweden, and the likes of them. Thankfully that meant I didn't have to go."

"A cabin . . . in Norway?" I'm already disappointed.

"Yes," she says, munching on her bread, trying to keep the crumbs in. "And cabin is a stretch. It's a hut. Thank god they built another addition, but still. There's *no* indoor plumbing. You know what that means? That means having to dig a tunnel through the bloody snow to the outhouse in order to take a whiz."

"And we're all going?" I ask, finishing the dregs of my coffee.

She nods. "Yep. Just for a couple of days. Me, you, Einar, Ottar, the boys, Ella . . . Laila."

I don't appreciate the way she says Laila's name. Or the rather pointed way she's looking at me.

"What?" I ask warily.

"Nothing," she says. "You know I have a theory about you two."

Oh fuck.

"About who?" I ask, feigning ignorance. The blank mask slips on with ease.

"You know who. Laila," she says.

I automatically glance at the hallway, expecting either Magnus or Laila to be there. I haven't seen Laila all that much since I went for dinner with her. Since our little tryst in the wine bar bathroom. I've thought about her a lot. Every damn night as I'm falling asleep, I can't help but try to listen to her. Even when she's snoring. But I've been trying to respect her wishes to keep things professional again.

In some ways it's been easy. She's busy with the boys, and even though I'm their PPO, I go with Magnus everywhere. I never see her at breakfast or lunch, only at dinner, and then we're surrounded by this one big chaotic family. The only time I'm ever alone with her is if one of us is in the library at night having a drink and no one else has shown up yet. But even then, she doesn't stick around.

In other ways, it's been hard because, fuck, I like being around her. I'm still finding my footing with this household, still trying to navigate this royal family and the twists and turns of this job. It should be straightforward, but when it comes to Magnus, *nothing* is straightforward. Laila is the only thing that's grounding me at the moment, a tie to a time when things felt more solid, and reliable. I crave that sense of stability.

And to be honest, I crave her. That taste of her that I had did nothing to get her out of my system. Instead it acted like a drug, the slow-release kind that keeps you coming back for more. She's in my system now, whether she wants to be or not. And I know she doesn't want to be.

"You're rather paranoid, you know that?" Lady Jane muses, wiping her mouth with a napkin.

"It's my *job* to be paranoid," I tell her.

She squints at me. "Perhaps. But don't think I haven't noticed how you look at Ms. Bruset."

"I don't look at her any differently than I look at you," I say, reaching across the table for the French press and pouring myself another cup. I make the gesture to fill up hers, but she briefly puts her hand over her mug, laughing.

"Yes. You do," she says. "And it's not how any other young man, or old man for that matter, would look at her. You're not just seeing her as a beautiful woman, you're seeing her as someone who means something to you."

I swallow. "She's my friend, if that's what you mean."

"You know it's not what I mean," she says, whispering as she leans forward, a gleam in her eyes. "But I won't pry further. Just know that I know."

"Hate to break it to you, Lady Jane, but you don't know anything," I tell her before having a sip of the coffee. This is my third cup this morning. Not sure if this is going to help or hinder my day.

"By the way, when are we supposed to go to the cabin?" I ask her, changing the subject.

She laughs. "If Magnus is telling you to pack your bags now, it means you're leaving now. As in today."

Perhaps this third cup is needed after all.

When I'm done drinking it I head to my room, about to pass by Laila, who is stepping out of hers.

Damn it. I wish I could just give her a nod and move on, but I can't. With her hair pulled back, her striking face, a few freckles showing on her perfect nose, and her long teal sweater and leggings, she manages to be someone worth losing your breath over.

Someone I can't ignore.

"Hey," I say to her, blocking her path. "Did you hear the news?"

She sighs and glances up at me, looking tired. "About the kikut?"

"Yes. What does that word mean, anyway?"

"It's just the name of the cabin."

"It doesn't mean anything in Norwegian, like murder death trap or something?"

I actually make her smile.

"If it did, I wouldn't warn you," she says.

"Have you been there?"

She nods, pressing her lips together. "Yes. Just once, in the summer. It's nice. But it's going to be crowded. Pack warm and bring your earplugs."

"If I can handle your snoring, then I can handle anything." The truth is, I can't wear earplugs. I need to be alert to the smallest sounds. It's a wonder that I've trained myself to sleep deep enough and yet wake up at a moment's notice.

She barks out a laugh, and I grin in response, my chest getting this effervescent champagne feeling at the sound and sight of her. "Oh, you haven't heard Einar yet. You have no idea."

Then she composes herself, as if remembering she's not supposed to laugh or smile around me. "I need to go back to the boys," she says, her face blank, and makes her way past me.

So that's all I get. Just that one moment. Guess it will have to tide me over until the next one.

I go in my room and pack, taking heed of Laila's warning and Lady Jane's talk about snow tunnels. This time, suits won't cut it. I cram sweaters, long johns, socks, thermals, gloves, hats, and scarves all in a duffel bag with the Norwegian Royalty Protection Unit crest on it. When I finally step back into the hall, chaos has taken over.

Bjorn is tearing down the hall and back, dressed in black snow boots and snow pants but no shirt, holding up a toy airplane. He stops when he sees me and aims the plane at me, and I'm afraid he's going to chuck it at my face.

Instead he makes shooting sounds and then yells, "*Du er død!*" which I take to mean that I'm dead or something.

"Bjorn!" Laila yells from the upper floor. She goes down the stairs and runs down the hall in her socks, almost slipping on the floor, looking slightly more mussed up than before. She's holding out a long-sleeved shirt for him, a sweater tucked under her arm.

Bjorn laughs, like the bloody devil, and starts to run away, but I'm quick.

I reach out and grab him by both shoulders, my touch light but firm enough to keep him in place.

He looks up at me over his shoulder and he hisses. Like a snake.

Bloody hell.

"Bjorn," Laila admonishes him again, out of breath. She gives me a sheepish smile, brushing her hair out of her face. "Thanks, James."

Bjorn lets out a bloodcurdling scream, and then there's another scream from the other end of the house. Tor. It's like two caterwauling creatures of the night.

"Need me to hold him?" I ask her, still not letting go, even with Bjorn squirming and screaming. My eardrums feel shot out, and I wonder how Laila hasn't lost her hearing yet.

"Please," she says, and I crouch down to grab Bjorn by the waist while she pulls his shirt and sweater over him. I don't know how she does it—the way he's squirming in my grasp, it's like trying to hit a moving target—but eventually she gets him dressed.

She gives me a look to say I can let go, and I release him.

He runs off, screaming down the hall.

"I don't envy you," I tell her in a low voice, watching as he disappears into their playroom. "I think I'd rather take a bullet."

She snorts. "You wouldn't last a day." Then her eyes go soft. "But really, thank you for that." She pauses. "Being a nanny, you sometimes forget that this should be a two-person operation."

I glance over her shoulder. There's no one else near. "I'm sure Magnus and Ella do a lot."

"They do," she says quickly, eyes wide. "Don't get me wrong. They're tucking them in every night, they're with them as much as they can be. If they lived in Oslo, closer to the king and queen, and were more involved with the public and the limelight, I'm sure we'd see them far less. Remember, I'm officially their first nanny. One of Magnus's sisters was helping them before I came along, and I don't even think she was paid for it."

"Then it's no wonder they hired you," I tell her. "I can tell you think you're not doing a good job, but you are. You're doing a really good job. It's not easy."

She purses her lips thoughtfully. "How did you know that?"

I shrug. "I just know you, that's all. I know how you think." I'm not about to tell her how closely I observe her when I think she's not looking, how even when she tries to pull on a hardened mask, some vulnerability seeps through. I love those glimpses of her, raw and real beneath the surface.

Her brow raises. "I wouldn't be too sure about that."

The screaming suddenly intensifies.

She exhales noisily, shoulders slumped. "I better go check on them."

She walks off toward the terrorizing demons just as Magnus, Ella, and Lady Jane come down the stairs with their bags.

"You're all packed?" Magnus asks. "You know, we're going to be going up into the mountains on four-wheelers. This isn't the place for suits, James."

"I didn't pack any," I assure him, and I'm wearing a heavy-knit sweater-and-jeans combo that would rival any that Chris Evans wore in *Knives Out.*

"You're learning, then." Pause. "You smoke cigars, don't you?"

"Oh, Magnus," Ella says with a roll of her eyes. "Stop trying to get people to join your nonexistent cigar club."

"Nonexistent?" he says, mouth agape. "I'm the Prince of Norway."

"Doesn't mean you have a club," she says.

"Ottar smokes cigars with me."

"Then it's a club of two, and Ottar turns green."

He looks at me, shaking his head like she's lying.

"I do like a good cigar," I tell him.

"There you go, I knew there was a reason I liked you. Okay. Let's round up the kids."

Even with Laila on the job, rounding up Tor and Bjorn takes a team effort, but eventually we're all piling into the cars and heading off into the Norwegian wilderness.

Ottar is at the wheel in the SUV, Einar in the passenger seat, with the prince, princess, and Lady Jane in the back.

I'm in the passenger seat of the VW, absolutely cramped, with Olaf, who drives excruciatingly slow, and Laila and the boys in the back seat. I watch her in the rearview mirror, sitting between them, trying to stop Bjorn from smacking Tor on the head with his mitts.

It's a long drive, made even longer by the stilted conversation with Laila and the kids kicking and yelling the whole way. Olaf doesn't say a word, and I'm starting to think he can't hear much at all. I'm envious.

Finally, after a few hours and several rest stops along the

way, we pull down a long snow-covered road to see the SUV waiting and three rugged ATVs.

"Here we are," Laila says, unbuckling the boys.

"This?" I ask, peering up at a snow-covered mountain, the top obscured by heavy white clouds. There's no cabin in sight. The slope looks steep as hell, covered by forest until it turns alpine. I have no idea how we're going to get up there.

I catch Laila smirking at me in the rearview mirror. "You're from Scotland. Don't you have your Highlands?"

"Aye, but I was born in Glasgow," I tell her. "Let me tell you that at no point did any of my foster families take me on any hiking expeditions up north."

"First time for everything," she says.

We approach the ATVs, where Magnus and Ottar are already securing packs. Ottar takes my bag and brings it to the back of one.

"You know how to drive an ATV, don't you?" he asks me.

I don't, actually, but I can't imagine it's any different from a golf cart. On steroids. "Of course," I tell him, hoping that doesn't bite me in the ass.

"Great. You'll take up Laila, Ella, and the boys. Magnus will ride with Einar up in the front. I'll take the rear with Lady Jane."

At that, Lady Jane bursts out into raucous laughter.

"Oh, grow up," Ottar yells at her, laughing too. He looks at me and shakes his head as if to say, *Women*.

It's not long before we're on our way. The seat is a little small for my frame, but I make it work. Ella sits in the front with Tor on her lap, Laila in the back with Bjorn. I look over my shoulder at her, her arm around Bjorn, trying to hold them both in place.

"Hey, buddy," I say to Bjorn. "This is a dangerous journey we're about to take. Better keep your seat belt on and hold on to Laila so that you don't lose her. I'm counting on you to be the man back there."

I'm hoping that will trick him into behaving.

Bjorn just glares at me.

I look at Ella, hoping I wasn't stepping on any toes. She's staring at me in utter amusement.

"He does know English, right?" I ask her.

She nods, suppressing a smile.

"Yes, I know English!" Bjorn shouts from the back.

Ah, the kid speaks.

I clear my throat, feeling stupid, then start driving.

The first part of the journey is fairly easy, following a trail that was obviously cleared earlier in the day. I have to wonder at how much power Prince Magnus has at his fingertips to just command something like this, clearing half a mountain, on a whim, because that man *only* operates on a whim.

But then the trail gets narrower, the snow higher, and even though driving the ATV is fairly easy to get the hang of, I'm still finding it challenging. I keep glancing at Ella and Laila every minute, asking if they're okay. I think at one point Ella actually wants to take over for me.

Finally we get clear of the pine forest and emerge into the open mountainside, the mountain opening up in front of us, rounded peaks stacked on top of each other, the white sky beyond. Up here the snow is fresh powder, but when it seems like the ATV is about to sink, Magnus and Einar come to a stop.

"We're here," Ella says.

"Yay!" Bjorn yells, and I look behind me to see Bjorn un-buckling and launching himself into the snow. "*Uff da!*"

Everyone laughs, the kid's joy infectious.

Then comes the hard part of the unloading and bringing our stuff up to the cabin, which is still a short walk away. It takes us forever, especially with the snow up to our knees, but eventually we get to the infamous kikut.

It's a quaint little cabin, with a smaller, newer cabin beside it, nestled amid a patch of trees. There's a path of sorts connecting the cabins and the outhouse as well, and though I shudder at the thought of using it in these temperatures, I have to remind myself that if the Crown Prince of Norway can, and does, use it, then I can use it too.

"Don't worry," Magnus says to me, obviously catching my gaze. "We've installed a heater in there. Nicest outhouse you'll ever be in. It used to be over there, hanging off the edge," he says, pointing past the cabins, where the ridge drops away. "You could just shit right out onto the rabbits. It was magical."

Ottar brushes past me, carrying a suitcase. "It was not magical," he whispers to me as he goes.

Magnus, Ella, and the boys end up taking the new addition, so all of the help is in the main cabin.

And when I step inside the cabin, I realize "main" cabin is a bit of a stretch. It's very quaint and homey, smelling of cedar and woodsmoke, but it's very small. I have no idea where we're all going to go.

"Who sleeps where?" I ask, eyeing the lot of us.

"Well," Lady Jane says, "there will be some sharing. Ottar and Einar are up in the loft." She points at the narrow wood ladder leading up. "I'm taking the bedroom. Which leaves you and Laila on the sofa bed."

"Uh," Laila says, raising her hand. "Not to be intrusive, but why can't I share a bed with you?" she asks Lady Jane.

Lady Jane just smiles. "Because I don't like to sleep with someone. I need to sleep alone."

"Well, I don't want to sleep with James."

I manage to hold a million things back. Finally, I say, "You can have the sofa bed, Laila. I'll take the cushions and sleep on the floor."

She seems satisfied with that, even though Lady Jane looks a wee bit disappointed.

With the sleeping arrangements all settled, the royals come back over to the kikut and we start making plans. We're only staying a night, and our plans thus far are just to drink and eat. Einar and I are officially off duty, since there is nary a person in the area for hundreds of miles, so we're told to partake in the festivities.

Even so, I know Einar is keeping his wits about him.

I do the same, knowing that even though this is technically Magnus's home too, I should still be on guard.

But that one beer turns into another beer. And then while the boys are upstairs in the loft, playing Go Fish, the adults start playing drinking games. Prosecco is popped. In the kitchen, Ella whips up Christmas cocktails with cranberries, while Lady Jane makes everyone bangers and mash for dinner. Laila puts on Brian Setzer Orchestra Christmas music. At one point Ottar and Magnus start dancing to "Jingle Bell Rock."

I have to say, it's the most fun I've had in a long time.

It's also the most drunk I've been in a long time. Part of me is still behaving. I'm aware that I'm a protection officer, even if Einar is in charge of the lot of us right now and I'm rightfully inebriated.

I also have to say, it feels good. To shove that part of me that constantly has to be on high alert to the back of my brain. To let things feel free and easy and good for once.

I don't know Magnus and his family very well at this point. I know as a person in my position, gaining trust takes time. It's not just about them trusting me, since Magnus does trust me enough with their lives, but about me trusting them. It was years before I felt that Prince Eddie was someone who had my back, and even then I was always hyperaware of our relationship and our roles. Bodyguards are supposed to slip into the background by nature. We're supposed to remain aloof and mysterious and cold. Devoted to our jobs and our duty. We aren't supposed to form relationships and attachments to the people we are sworn to protect.

And yet sitting here with Magnus telling some outrageous story to Ottar and Einar about a lost goat, Ella giggling with Lady Jane and Laila, it really does feel like I've found something. Not quite family. I'm not sure I'll ever find that (and honestly, I'm not sure I'd ever let myself find that). But it's something that makes me feel included. It's a peculiar, warm feeling that I've never felt before.

Or maybe I'm just drunk.

The party continues until Ella starts yawning and Magnus goes up into the loft to discover the boys have passed right out. He carries them down the ladder, one on each arm like he's in a strongman competition, and then says the family is retiring to bed, leaving the rest of us in the cabin.

Things start to wind down. Einar goes up to the loft to sleep, so it's now Lady Jane, Ottar, Laila, and me talking around the fire, drinking Scotch that will probably add to my hangover. Then Ottar decides to turn in.

Then Lady Jane.

Leaving Laila and me on the couch.

But I'm not feeling the slightest bit sleepy, and I know if we continue to talk, we'll keep everyone up.

"Shall we go for a walk?" I whisper to her.

She gives me a look like, *Are you serious?*

I shrug. "Suit yourself."

I pile on my coat, scarf, hat, and gloves, and then as I'm pulling on my boots, she's doing the same, the bottle of Scotch in her hand.

This is either going to be a great idea or a terrible one.

We step outside into the winter wonderland.

It's freezing cold, our breath white in the air, and yet my blood feels full of fire. The path to the outhouse is worn down by now, and Magnus wasn't kidding when he said it was the nicest outhouse. Fully insulated, with a heater, a lamp, hand sanitizers, a proper toilet seat, even a magazine rack. But there's another small path that leads into an outcropping of thin pines.

"Follow me," Laila says, heading down the path. I follow her. The only sound is our breath and the velvet crunch of our boots on the packed snow.

But as we walk through the pines, the sound of trickling water becomes clearer. The motion lights from the cabin are losing their reach, and before I tell her it's too dark, that we need to turn back, she pulls out a flashlight.

"Where are you taking me?" I ask her. "Is this the murder death trap part of the visit?"

She lets out a soft laugh, sounding like music in the frozen night.

"We'll see."

Well, that's not promising.

"Down there is a waterfall," she says to me. With the moon breaking through the clouds I can see it frozen, suspended in air like magic, with only a thin stream of water pouring through underneath. "That's where the drinking water comes from. In the summer we went swimming and Magnus showed me how they're able to pump the water up to the cabin."

"Very impressive. I'm starting to think you Norwegians can do everything."

"I'm saving the best for last," she says. "You okay to climb up some rocks?"

"Who do you think you're talking to here?" I say. "Just point to the rocks and I'll climb them."

In the light of the moon I see her bite her lip, and it takes everything in me not to hold her face in my hands and do the same to her.

Take it easy, I have to remind myself. The alcohol has a way of making me want to break all my promises.

"Always with something to prove," she says to me, shining the flashlight up a slight incline, the rock half-covered by snow.

"I have nothing to prove," I tell her defensively.

Another coy look from her. She's definitely drunk too, otherwise we wouldn't be about to climb up slippery snow-covered rocks past midnight.

"Here, let me at least go first and help you up," I tell her. I brush past her, hauling myself up before reaching down and pulling her up by her elbows until we're both on the edge of a small, rounded ledge, tall enough to look over the tops of the trees.

And that's when I see it.

It takes my breath away.

Above the mountains, across the fjord, are the northern lights.

Abstract splashes of glowing green and white, like a moving watercolor painting on a canvas of stars.

"Holy shit," I say, my voice coming out in a hush, as if I'm afraid I might scare it away. "This was here the whole time?"

"Mmm-hmm," she says. "Ella told me we might be able to see it tonight, but not so well from the cabin."

"Well, fuck," I say, trying to take in the supernatural magnitude of the display. "This is . . . this is really something."

"I figured you'd never seen them before," she says to me, unscrewing the Scotch bottle with her gloved hand and having a shot straight out of the bottle.

I manage to tear my eyes away from the lights and look at her, and fuck if she isn't even more beautiful than that. "I think I want to kiss you," I tell her. The booze talking.

Her forehead creases with a wry look as she hands me the bottle of Scotch. "You shouldn't."

Shouldn't . . . but not *don't*.

I take the bottle from her, my gaze locked on hers, trying to read her, trying not to get any signals mixed up, even though that seems impossible when it comes to us. All we are is a bunch of mixed signals.

"You mean to tell me, Laila Bruset, that you brought me all

the way here to this prime make-out spot, under the bloody northern lights, and expected me not to get the wrong idea?"

I take back a swig from the bottle, watching her. The Scotch keeps me warm as it burns down my throat.

"When don't you get the wrong idea, James?" she says to me. There's an openness about her expression. An invitation. Something soft like the snow.

I take my chances.

I put my hand on her face, my fingertips resting on her cheekbones, my thumb on her chin. "Forgive me for breaking my promise."

I lean in and kiss her. Her lips offer no resistance; they're yielding to mine, my mouth pressed against hers, feeling the kiss in the darkened depths of me. This kiss feels different from every other one I've shared with her, and I don't know if it's the alcohol, or the thin mountain air, or the beautiful chaotic energy of those lights. But something inside me has switched on, something long left dormant and undisturbed. It's a terrifying feeling, like each pass of my tongue against hers is pushing me closer to this edge that I don't dare fall from again.

And so I pull back, breaking the kiss, leaving us both gasping.

I hold her face tighter, resting my forehead against hers, my nose pressed along the side of her nose, and I'm trying to catch my breath and wrangle my muddied thoughts, and step back, way back from that ledge inside me.

"I'm sorry," I whisper, though I don't know if I'm apologizing to her or to myself.

She pulls back, pressing her hands on each side of my face, staring up at me, eyes searching mine. "What happened?"

I try to shake my head, averting my eyes in case I do something foolish again. "Nothing. I overstepped a line."

"Not my line."

I have to look at her. That softness is still there. For once I didn't chase it away. So why am I so afraid?

"You said . . . ," I begin, licking my lips. "Look, I don't want to mess things up between us."

"That's not it, James," she says. "That's not it at all. You will gladly make things messy between us again. You thrive in it. What is it? What just happened?"

"I don't know," I admit, searching her eyes.

She still won't let go of my face, her gloves warming my skin.

"You told me that what happened before between us can't happen again. I'm trying to be good."

"No," she says, her hands dropping away. "You're not." She reaches for the Scotch bottle and turns her back to me, facing the lights as she has another swig. "Will you answer a question?"

I feel so off-balance, and it's not just where we're standing. "Sure," I say, my voice barely audible.

"Why did you get divorced?"

I widen my stance, because I really do feel like I'm about to go over, my heart pounding against my ribs. "Why do you want to know?"

"Because I want to know all there is to know about you. You think we know each other, but we really don't. And I deserve to know why you behaved the way you did with me."

"You think it has something to do with my divorce?"

She glances at me over her shoulder. "You know it does. So what happened?"

I sigh and reach my hand out for the Scotch. "I need more alcohol for this."

She turns to face me and hands it over, watching me with an expectant look.

I take a drink for courage, knowing she deserves honesty from me, even if it hurts my pride.

"My wife, my *ex*-wife . . . she cheated on me," I tell her. "I was never home. I was always working, always on duty. I could only provide for her, I couldn't give her what she really needed. And some days I think I never could, even if I quit, even if I was there for her all the time. That I just wasn't enough for her, no matter what I did." I pause, raising the bottle halfway, my eyes drifting over the lights, trying to ignore the pang in my chest, the embarrassment, the rejection. "I couldn't blame her either way. I never did. I was used to it. My whole life was just . . . one big rejection. Every time I got close to a family, I was sent away to another. I learned to not get close, to not open myself up. And then I fell in love. I was stupid and young, and I fell in love, and that was the end of me. I should have known it would amount to nothing."

She doesn't say anything for a moment. I dare to glance at her, expecting to see her watching me with pity. But I don't see pity. I see understanding. How rare it is to find someone who understands you. I'm only realizing that now.

"So that was that," I tell her, exhaling before having another drink of Scotch. I swallow, wincing. "She left me for another man, asked for a divorce, and I couldn't . . . I couldn't handle it. It was like the wires in my brain just snapped and whatever had been holding me together was threadbare. I was . . . depressed, to put it mildly. It was hard for me to come to terms with that. Really hard." I pause, gathering courage. "I'm supposed to be strong all the time, inside and out. But I wasn't. I tried, but . . . it was too much. I never realized how much anger I was carrying with me all this time, never knew how close I was to just . . . going over the edge. But I did. I went over, and I lost all sense of self. Lost everything, really. And that's really hard for me to admit."

Laila steps up to me and reaches out for my other hand, holding it in hers, giving it a squeeze. "But you did admit it. And I thank you for that." She gives me a sad smile. "James, I'm so sorry you had to go through all that. I'm not going to tell you the things that you probably already figured out, that you *are* strong, the strongest man I know, from your heart to your muscles to your mind. I'm not going to tell you that what you went through is only natural when you've had the childhood you did. I just want to let you know how much I appreciate being let in. That you've made space for me to hear this." She swallows, blinking fast. "It means a lot to me."

I manage a placating smile and offer the bottle to her.

She shakes her head. "I've had enough."

I sigh, closing my eyes for a moment, bringing myself back to where we are, and the wicked hangover I'm going to have tomorrow. Fuck.

"We should head back," I tell her.

In some ways I want to stay on this rocky ledge, overlooking the dark fjord, the snowy mountains, those dancing lights, and just talk to her the whole night through. Lay everything out, everything I've kept buried inside myself, hoping to ignore. Have an exorcism of sorts.

But I know I have a duty here, and so does she.

So we make our way back down the rocks, taking our time, then to the cabin. When we enter, everyone is asleep, snoring, and we find our places. Laila whispers to me that I'm free to share the sofa bed with her, and while I find that exceedingly tempting—just to have her warm body next to mine, something I haven't had in so fucking long—I know I need to keep my head on straight going forward.

So I lie down on the cushions on the floor, wool blankets pulled up to my chin.

Right before I fall asleep, I whisper good night to her, as I always do.

This time she says it back.

Twelve

· · · · · · · · ·

LAILA

Two years ago

"INSTANT COFFEE?"

I stir my spoon quickly and glance over my shoulder to see James enter the kitchen.

"You got a problem with instant coffee?" I ask, and turn my back to him to hide my smile as I put the spoon in the sink.

"Yes," he says, and I feel him walk into the room. "And it's not just me, it's everyone. I mean, you've got the best espresso machine from Italy right there, and yet . . ."

I turn around to eye him as he's gesturing wildly to the fancy espresso machine, and I lean against the counter, blowing on my mug before taking a careful sip. It's scalding hot, but that's just the way I like it.

He's wearing a suit this morning, as always, but there's something about him that makes me feel a little dizzy, like if I didn't have the edge of the counter behind me I'd slide right onto the floor like a melting ice cream cone. I don't know if it's just how intimately I know his body now, his mannerisms, his way, since we've been sleeping together most nights for the last few months, but I've never felt so connected to someone in all my life. I have to remind myself to act like a human being and not a pile of mush.

"It's still coffee, James. It's not like I'm drinking battery acid," I scoff, straightening up.

"That's up for debate," he says with a roguish grin that makes my heart do backflips in my chest.

"James," Eddie says, suddenly appearing in the doorway. He gives me a friendly nod, then eyes his PPO. "I'm going to head off. Better to get it out of the way."

James's face goes blank. It's amazing to watch how his whole mindset changes when he goes on duty. All that is playful about him is quickly buried by his role as bodyguard. "Aye, sir."

He doesn't even look back at me as the two of them leave the room, bound for London for some event, and I ignore the fact that it bothers me. I know that we have to keep our affair a secret or else we could lose our jobs, and even though I love the idea of having a forbidden romance because there's something so exciting and dangerous about it, it kind of bothers me that we have to hide it. I know it shouldn't, but I can't help feeling like he's ashamed of me. It's probably not true and just residual trauma from past relationships, but even so . . .

Anyway, our whole affair began only as a means to an end, a way to have fun and connect, but somewhere along the way I fell for this man. I don't know how much, or how deeply, just that it's happened. I don't know if it's love—I don't know if I've ever been in love with anyone—but I know that he gets a part of me that I don't give to anyone else. A part of me I try so hard to hide—the me deep down who just wants someone to push through the mire and see me for me.

I don't know when this happened, and it's still not something I'm ready to deal with, but I know that if I don't figure out what I'm going to do with him before it gets any deeper, I might lose him. And I know I can't lose him. I need him.

I'm still standing here, holding my coffee, when I hear the front door open and footsteps on the marble floor. I look to see James walking back into the kitchen, coming toward me and smiling.

I'm grinning like an idiot in response.

"Just grabbing some water for the road," he explains, opening the fridge door and bringing out two bottles of water. He closes it and then quickly leans in close to me.

"See you tonight, aye?" he whispers, his breath hot and smelling of mint.

I feel my cheeks flush at the thought of what we're going to do tonight, and my stomach does a little flip. "Yes," I whisper back, my eyes still closed as I catch his scent again.

And then he's gone, his footsteps echoing on the marble as he goes out the door.

I'm left alone in the kitchen, scared to death that I'm falling in love.

I'm even more scared that I might tell him.

THAT NIGHT, JAMES comes into my room. It's past midnight, and I've been waiting, lying in bed in only my underwear.

The door opens and he steps in, closing it behind him

quietly. I can see the outline of his body in the darkness and I watch as he walks over to the bed, sitting down on the edge.

"You're so beautiful," he whispers, his voice a low rumble in the silence.

I can feel the tears welling up in my eyes, and I'm so grateful that he can't see them in the darkness.

"Laila love," he continues, leaning in to kiss me.

I kiss him back, melting into him as his lips move over mine. His hand is on my cheek, his thumb gently brushing away my tears.

"What's wrong?" he asks with a pause. "Are you crying?"

My heart pounds away in my chest.

"I'm just feeling emotional," I manage to say. "It's nothing."

"Is it your grandma?" he asks, knowing that she's been going downhill lately.

I went to visit her last month, and it was the hardest trip I've ever had to make. She seemed like my beloved bestemor in nearly every way, but every now and then she would get this blank look on her face. She wasn't scared by it, she just wasn't . . . there. And when she came back, it was like it took her a moment to know who I was. My cousin Peter was there, and he told me that it seemed like she was hard of hearing and needed a new aid, but I don't think that's it. She can hear fine . . . I just don't know if she realizes who she's listening to.

Oh god, why is life so fucking hard?

I close my eyes and try to breathe.

"I'm fine," I tell him, not about to get into all the reasons. "I just need you to make me feel better."

"I can do that," he says softly.

He kisses me again, and I let myself sink into him, like I'm letting him carry everything inside, stuff I don't want to carry anymore. I can feel the warmth of his body, the strength of his arms as he holds me. Everything seems to fade away, and for a little while I'm just content to be in his arms.

Eventually, his hands start to wander and I can feel a little bit of the tension start to ebb away.

"Make me feel something," I whisper, feeling like I need him to touch me, to make me feel something other than this weight in my chest.

He moves over me, and I can feel his hardness against my thigh. I reach for him, but he pulls back, teasing me.

"Patience," he whispers, and kisses me again.

He starts to explore my body with his mouth, kissing and licking and nibbling his way down. I arch my back and moan as he reaches my most sensitive spots. My body is a map, and he's tracing and retracing his steps until every path feels like the right one. He takes his time, teasing me, until I'm gasping for air and begging for more. Finally, he slides inside me and I'm lost to him. I don't know what's going on in the world outside this room, but I don't care. Right now, I'm only focused on him, on us.

He moves slowly at first, but then he starts to pick up the pace. I can feel him getting harder, and I match his thrusts, wanting more, needing more.

"Harder," I manage to say, and he obliges, increasing his speed.

"Laila," he groans, and I can feel his muscles tense, like he's fighting off that edge.

I'm so focused on him that I don't realize I'm getting close to the edge myself. I feel my heartbeat start to race, my gasps come quicker, and I know he's almost there. I can feel it just from the sound of his breath and the way he moves. The pressure in my body is coiling, and I try to push it off for even just a few more seconds. I'm so close.

I moan his name, begging him to let me go.

He gives me one final thrust, and I shatter. I can feel the shudders spreading through my body, and I can't hold it in. I cry out softly, doing all I can to stay quiet.

"James!" I say through a rough gasp.

The orgasm pulses through my body and my back arches in ecstasy, feeling so overwhelmed and delirious that I forget where I am for a moment.

Then I hear his breath catch in his throat, the way his body stiffens, the muscles in his neck corded, and I know he's going over the edge.

"Oh, bloody hell, love," he manages to say. "Bloody hell."

We're breathing heavily, and I'm still feeling the aftershocks of our orgasms when he rolls off of me. I roll toward him, using his shoulder as a pillow as I try to catch my breath. He wraps an arm around my body, and we are still for a long moment, trying to calm down. James's ragged breathing is the only sound for a moment as we lie there; the click of the radiator turning on is the only interruption in the silence.

I'm still tingling, still feeling the aftershocks, but now my feelings are crashing over me like a tsunami. My heart is pressing against my rib cage, like it's trying to break free. If I let it loose, I hope it makes a run for it, but I know it won't. I know it thinks it belongs here, with James.

I can feel the tears starting to well up in my eyes, but I keep my face buried in his chest so he can't see. He still has his arm around me, and he gives me a little squeeze.

"You all right, love?" he asks, and I can hear the worry in his voice.

I nod, not trusting myself to speak, and I hold him closer to me in response.

He's there for me. He's right here. And all I want is to stay here with him, in his arms.

"I'm falling for you," I whisper. I regret it instantly. I didn't want to say it. I didn't want him to know how I felt because I know he doesn't feel the same way, that this was just supposed to be a casual thing.

He stiffens beside me, as if shocked, and my heart sinks.

Oh god. What have I done?

I've ruined everything.

Panic floods through me, and I try to pull away, but he holds me tighter.

"Laila," he says, his voice going tender. "Don't."

"I'm sorry," I say, and I really am. I feel like an idiot. I don't know what I was thinking.

"Don't apologize," he tells me, and he's kissing me again, holding me against him. "Just please, don't tell me you're falling for me."

I pause.

"Why not?" I ask, feeling a little angry now.

He runs his fingers through my hair, as if trying to comfort me.

"Because I can't give you what you need," he tells me. "I can't give you what you deserve."

I swallow, trying to get rid of the lump in my throat.

"What if I don't deserve anything?" I ask, my voice catching.

"Don't say that. You deserve the world, Laila, but I can't give that to you."

"Stop saying that," I tell him. "Stop saying you can't give me what I deserve. You're here now."

He doesn't respond to that. He just lies there, holding me, and I can feel his chest rising and falling.

"I'm here now," he finally says, as if thinking about it. "I can give you that, at least for a little while. I can be here for you."

"Then that's all I need," I tell him.

"No," he says. "No, that's not what you need. You deserve so much more."

"I don't want more," I tell him, feeling fucking ridiculous, like I'm bargaining with him to stay in my life, to keep things status quo. "I only want you."

"I'm not sure that's enough," he tells me. "I can't . . . I won't be able to . . . You need so much more than I can give."

I stare at him. How many times have I heard that I'm "too much" for someone?

"Who hurt you?" I ask, suddenly angry. "Who broke your heart so badly you can't even let yourself feel anything for me?"

He blinks at me, surprised at my outrage. I'm surprised myself. I'm in dangerous territory. I try not to let myself get angry often, because when I do it's like the rage blinds me and I say terrible things, things that I might not even mean.

He then gives his head a shake and gets out of bed.

"I'm sorry," I plead, quickly reaching for him, but he's already on his feet. "I didn't mean that."

"You knew that this had to remain this way," he says through a harsh whisper, putting his clothes back on.

"Nothing has changed," I tell him. "Nothing at all. So I told you I'm falling you for you, so what?"

"So what?" he says, an edge to his voice. "So what? I don't

want you to fall for me, Laila, not if I'm going to break your heart."

"Then don't break my heart," I tell him.

He shakes his head again. "This was a mistake."

"It's not a mistake," I cry out, sitting up on my knees. "I'm just . . . I developed feelings and I shouldn't have, but it doesn't have to change anything between us. We can just keep having sex, keep having fun."

He runs his hands over his face, head dropping. "No," he says adamantly. He looks up at me. "We can't. I care about you, Laila, I really do. But I'm not going to string you along like this if I know where your heart is at. I won't do that to you."

"But I don't understand," I say softly, making fists in the sheets, the anger and frustration rising inside me. Frustration at the situation, at how quick he is to call things off, anger at myself for saying anything at all. I hold my tongue because I know if I say anything now my words are going to be harsh and full of venom. I need to be quiet; I need to let him go and not make this worse than it already is.

I feel my eyes filling with tears, and I don't bother to wipe them away. I don't care that I'm crying, I don't care that he sees me like this. He knows how I feel, so he might as well know what I'm going through, the hurt I'm feeling now.

He's watching me, his face unreadable. "I'll miss you," he says quietly. "Miss us."

Hearing him say that just makes my heart sink even more.

"Will you?" I ask softly.

He swallows thickly and nods. "It's always fun until someone gets hurt. If both our jobs weren't on the line, if it wasn't a big deal to be together . . ."

I stare at him through my blurry vision. I know what he's not saying. That it doesn't matter that we could never be. Even if I quit, he still wouldn't want me for anything more than sex. I know it.

The thing is, I'm not asking for anything more.

He opens his mouth to say something but then he closes it again, his features hardening.

"I'm sorry," he says, turning around and heading for the door.

"Don't go," I finally say, voice cracking.

"I have to," he says, looking back at me. "I have to go. For both our sakes."

And then he's gone.

I'm left in bed, heart aching, tears flowing freely from my eyes.

I'm so foolish. I left the door open in my heart, just a crack, and it was enough to lose it all.

Thirteen

. . . .

LAILA

"BJORN, DON'T TOUCH THAT," I WARN. "I FORBID YOU TO touch that."

He stares at me for a moment with his bright blue-green eyes, and I think maybe, just maybe, he's not going to shove his hand into the bowl of freshly mixed cookie dough that I just put on the table.

But then that diabolical grin comes across his face, the one that makes him look like the kid from *The Omen*, and he plunges his hand right into the bowl, laughing as he goes.

"No!" I cry, trying to snatch the dough away from him, but he's a quick little demon and he's already got a handful of it, chocolate chips and all.

"That's for the cookies," I tell him, "not for you to eat."

"But I'm hungry," Bjorn protests.

"You're always hungry," I tell him. "You eat like a horse."

"I do not," Bjorn says indignantly. "I eat like a human being."

I roll my eyes. "Fine, you eat like a human being. But that doesn't mean you get to eat the dough."

Bjorn makes a face. "But it's so good," he says plaintively.

"No, it's not," I tell him. "It's raw. You're not supposed to eat raw cookie dough."

"Why not?" Bjorn asks, shoving more in his mouth. "It's delicious."

"The raw eggs can make you sick," I tell him. "Is that what you want? You want to feel gross and sicky?"

That makes him pause. It's enough for me to grab him and take him over to the sink, kicking the footstool over to us and rinsing his hands off.

"I was about to ask how the Christmas cookies were coming along," Ella says warily.

I look at her over my shoulder. She has Tor beside her, who looks bleary-eyed from his nap. Now that we're back in the palace, I think everyone is still trying to catch up on all the lost sleep from being at the kikut.

"They were coming along great," I tell her.

"I'm going to be sick!" Bjorn says brightly.

"I told him that the raw eggs could make him sick. Apparently he doesn't care."

I dry Bjorn's hands with a clean dishrag and Ella sighs. "Oh Bjorn. Christmas Eve is tomorrow. Do you really want Santa Claus to skip this house because you've been eating cookie dough?"

That gets his attention. He looks crestfallen. "No . . ."

She crosses her arms and puts on her stern-mother face, which I'll admit makes me want to straighten up and fly right.

"Then you need to be on your best behavior now, okay?"

Under her breath she adds, "And after Christmas too would be nice."

"Okay," he says hesitantly, as if he's entering a binding contract with his words.

With Christmas Eve tomorrow, everyone is scrambling to get everything done. Soon the kitchen is going to be packed with Sigrid and Ella making the meal, so I figured now was a good time to get started on the Christmas cookies, which is always a good activity to keep the boys busy and creative at the same time. The chocolate chip cookies aren't traditional for the Norwegian Christmas Eve dinner, but the boys like them, so it's pretty much a batch just for them, and certainly will be now that Bjorn got his hands in it. Later I'll make some proper ones in a shortbread style, and then the boys can help with decorating a few.

"Do you have any Christmas traditions?" I ask Ella.

"Not really. Just the usual things like decorating the tree, making cookies, and opening presents on Christmas morning. I know you do it on Christmas Eve here in Norway, but in Liechtenstein we do a little of both."

Sigrid comes in from the other room with a bag of turnips she must have gotten from the cellar. "Growing up we always made a big batch of lefse for Christmas. My favorite, providing it has enough butter," I tell her.

"I've never had lefse," Ella says. "What is it?"

"It's a flatbread made from potatoes, similar to a crepe. My grandmother used to make it, and I continued the tradition." There were so many holiday mornings where I would join my grandma in the cold kitchen, the fire slowly heating up the room, and help her get started on the lefse. I would roll the sticky dough between my hands into little balls, and she would make them flat and thin with the rolling pin.

"That sounds good. I'll have to try it."

Sigrid gives her a dry look. "Is that a hint for me to add it to the Christmas menu?"

Ella laughs. "I am sure you have enough on your plate."

"I know how to make it," I tell Ella. "It's not hard to make, but it does take a little time."

"Another time," Ella says with a dismissive wave. "Your hands are full with the boys. Speaking of, I'm going to start prepping for tomorrow. Figure out what we're going to wear to church. Do you need a dress?"

I give her an amused look. "Do you really think anything of yours will fit me? Don't worry, I have some church-appropriate pieces."

"Okay, well, if you need a handbag or something, let me know," she says, putting Tor in his chair and leaving the kitchen.

"Do we have to go to church?" Bjorn asks, climbing onto a seat at the table beside his brother.

"You do," I tell him as I grab the bowl of cookie dough and stick a spatula in it, giving it a stir. "It's a special time of year."

"And Santa is watching," Sigrid adds over her shoulder as the turnips roll across the counter.

"Are you coming?" Bjorn asks me.

I nod. "I am. Going to church on Christmas Eve is my tradition too. I used to go with my grandmother to the tiny church we had in our village."

"What other traditions do you have?" Bjorn asks. I'm actually touched that he's asking me questions.

"For Christmas, well, let's see," I muse, taking a baking

sheet and ripping it off before putting it on the table. "Cookies, of course." I place the bowl of dough in front of him. "Now, if you promise not to eat it—that goes for you too, Tor—then you can help make the cookies. Just take a little bit like this and roll it in your hands and press it into the sheet like so." I demonstrate while I tell him, "Actually, my grandmother and I started this tradition the year after . . ."

I trail off, not sure how much of my past to tell the kids. But even Sigrid is looking over her shoulder for me to continue, and I remind myself that sometimes kids can handle death more maturely than adults do.

"When I was eight, my parents died," I say.

Bjorn's eyes go round. "How did they die?"

"They went to a party in another town, and I had stayed with my grandmother. On the way back a landslide came down the mountain and buried them."

Tor and Sigrid are listening intently now too.

"That's awful," Sigrid says.

"It was," I say. I don't talk about it often, and even though it was so long ago, it doesn't stop me from getting a lump in my throat. "The first Christmas after they died, it was so hard. It felt wrong to celebrate it without them. So my grandmother said we should go and buy them gifts anyway. We went to Trondheim together to the department store. I picked out a mug I thought my mother would like, and a tie for my father, and we had them wrapped up. We put them under the tree."

"Did you open them?" Bjorn asks.

I nod. "We opened them for our parents, just as we opened the other gifts we got from each other and friends. Then we put them in a box in a room downstairs. It's filled with presents."

"That is just lovely," Sigrid says with a sniff.

When I look over at her, her back is to me, and she's trying to hide her tears in the turnips.

"Are you getting them presents this year?" Bjorn asks as he mashes the dough onto the baking sheet.

I nod. "They're in my room. I already picked them out. I got my mother a candle and my father some pipe tobacco. I got him a pipe last year, so . . ."

"They must have been nice people," Bjorn says thoughtfully.

I give him a quick smile. "They had many friends," I say. That's the most I can say. They were nice to everyone, and that included me, but that's pretty much where it stopped. They tolerated me, were polite to me, but in general didn't want to have much to do with me. Which makes their death all the more complicated.

"It's a hard time of year," Sigrid says, "for so many people."

"Oooh, what are you making?" Lady Jane says as she steps into the kitchen. "Cookies!"

Even though I shouldn't be crying, even though it's been so long, Sigrid is right in that it's a hard time of year. I feel like if I don't get out of the kitchen, I'm going to burst into tears.

I get up and muster a smile for Lady Jane. "I have to use the toilet," I tell her. "Do you mind watching them?"

"Of course."

I hurry past her and into the hall, the tears now starting to fall, and I'm almost to my bedroom just as James is coming out of his room.

He smiles at me, but it quickly turns to a frown as I try to hide my face and disappear into my room. "Laila?" he calls out.

I shake my head and try to close the door on him, but he pushes into my room and grabs hold of my shoulders.

"What happened? Is it your grandmother?"

I try to pull back. "No. Yes. I don't know, I just . . ."

"Hey," he says softly. "It's okay."

He shuts the door gently behind him, and I put my back to him, burying my face in my hands. I never let myself cry, and I can't tell if I'm crying more because I'm hit with this unexpected wave of grief, or because I'm getting angry and frustrated for crying at all, and especially in front of James.

I try to get myself together, take a deep breath, and straighten my spine.

"Breathe," he says from behind me, his voice soothing. "That's all you need to do. Just breathe."

Then he wraps his arms around me, and I turn around, collapsing against him. Burying my face in the crook of his neck, as if I'm trying to hide from the world.

"It's okay," he says again. "Let it out."

I hug him back, wanting to feel something, anything, other than this ache in my chest and the emptiness in my heart. Why is this happening now? Why can't I seem to keep it together, even after all this time?

He strokes my hair, and I cling to him like he's a life raft.

Talking to Bjorn—a child who is so pure despite his devilish tendencies—made me feel like I was his age again. When all I wanted was for my parents to love me, and then they died before they even got a chance.

I'm not sure how long I hang on to James, but when I finally get myself together, I step back and wipe at my eyes.

"Are you okay?" he asks.

I nod. I'm not sure I'm okay, but I know I'm going to try to be.

"So what happened?" he asks.

"I was so stupid," I say, feeling the tears start again. "I was talking about Christmas and . . ." It's hard to explain it to him, but I try. "I was telling them about how my parents died. Then I told them about what we used to do to remember them, how we used to buy them presents even after they were dead."

"Oh." He sounds like he's not really sure what to say, which is how I feel too. "I'm sorry."

I shake my head. "It's fine."

I pull away and walk over to the window, looking at the snow. The sun set a few moments ago, and twilight has descended already. The trees are barely visible against the darkening blue, and for a scary moment I'm afraid there's a light inside me that's being snuffed out as well.

"You used to buy Christmas presents for your parents?" he asks, and I hear him sit on the edge of my bed.

I roughly wipe at my cheeks. "I still do."

"And your grandmother?"

My throat feels knotted up again. "No. But she did until . . ."

"Are you seeing her soon?" he asks.

I sigh. "I was supposed to go today, but . . ."

Suddenly I hear him get up, and then he's right behind me, touching my elbow. "You didn't go?"

I turn and frown at him, not caring that I'm an ugly mess. "I had to work. It's a busy day in the house if you haven't noticed. Lots of things to do."

"You need to see your grandmother for Christmas."

"She probably doesn't even know it's Christmas." But as I say the words, I feel like I'm being knifed in the heart. I know he's right. I've been beating myself up all day for not going. I even thought about tomorrow, but it's hard when I'm going to be busy all day.

"Why don't we go tonight?" he says.

I stare up at him, sniffing hard. "What? To see my grand-mother?"

He looks at his watch. "It's three. It's early. Ottar can take us. I'll go with you."

I stare at him for a moment, trying to think. "I've got to work . . ."

"No. You don't."

Then he turns and opens the door, leaving the room.

I stand there, dumbfounded for a moment, then walk toward the hall and stop. I can hear him in the kitchen asking Lady Jane if she'll watch Bjorn and Tor until we get back.

"Absolutely I will," Lady Jane says.

I walk out toward the kitchen, and she comes out and gives me a sympathetic look. "Oh, Laila. Sigrid filled me in. I would be happy to watch the boys."

"I'm supposed to make Christmas cookies too," I protest fee-bly. "Proper ones."

She looks aghast, with her hand on her chest. "You think I don't know how to make proper Christmas cookies? Goodness."

James gives me a look like, *See? Easy.*

I open my mouth to tell him that Ella and Magnus are the ones we need to be asking because they'll have to arrange for substitute security with James gone, but he's already going up the stairs two at a time, no doubt to request time off for me.

"He really is a good egg, isn't he?" Lady Jane says, and from her tone I know she's watching me intently.

I finally meet her eyes and try to smile. "He can be," I admit.

Her smile turns coy before it goes sympathetic again, and she puts her hand on my shoulder. "Go and see your grandmother. It's Christmas. I am more than happy to watch the boys." She leans in close and lowers her voice. "Gives me something to do, you see. Not much use for a lady-in-waiting when Ella insists on doing everything herself."

"Grab your things," James says as he runs down the stairs. "I'm going to drive us. Ottar has the night off."

"You?" I say. "Can you even drive on this side of the road?"

"And in snow?" Lady Jane adds.

"Har har," James says, grabbing his coat from the hall and throwing it on.

I walk over to him, feeling nervous for some reason. "Did they really okay it?"

He gives me a funny look. "Of course. Did you really think they wouldn't?"

Actually I know that both Ella and Magnus would have been more than happy to let me see my grandmother before Christmas, but I just didn't want to bring it up. I wanted to be the perfect nanny for them, the one who is always reliable, never pushing things.

I swallow and manage a smile. "Okay."

I go and grab my purse from my room but come to a pause. I walk over to my wardrobe and open the doors. On the top shelf is my plush polar bear, Knut. I grab him and head out the door.

"What's that?" James asks as we head outside.

"It's Knut," I say. "A bear I've had since I was young. My

grandmother gave it to me. I think this Christmas, I want to give it back to her."

James doesn't say anything else to that. Probably thinks I'm a little nuts for hanging on to a stuffed animal, but I don't really care at this point. My grandmother may or may not remember me, but there might be a chance the bear will help. Maybe having something soft to cuddle and hold will give her a sense of love and peace.

Fuck. I'm starting to cry again. This is not how I want to spend my time with her.

We get in the car, and James drives off, the headlights of the SUV bouncing off the snow. Luckily the driveway is shoveled and so is the main road, and for now the sky is clear, little pinpricks of stars appearing above the tops of the trees. We don't talk much on the drive, and I spend most of it with my head against the window, watching the darkened world go past, wringing my hands. I'm nervous, and I don't know why. I guess I'm always a little nervous when I see her, but I'm especially so this time.

Fortunately the department store is open later than normal thanks to last-minute shoppers, so once we get into Oslo we park and brave the crowds. I want to get my grandmother a cloudberry cake, but if there's something Christmassy, like a small version of a kransekake (a towering cake made up of circles stacked on top of each other to resemble a Christmas tree), then I'll get that for her.

The minute we step into the department store it's chaos; people absolutely everywhere in full panic, fretting over their forgotten lists, voices loud. I feel myself taking a step back inside myself and disassociating, but James slides right into bodyguard mode. He steps in front of me, twisted slightly, one hand back to make sure I'm right behind him. His protective instincts are in full swing.

We get to the cake counter, and with all the Christmas stuff gone, I'm lucky to get the last slice of cloudberry cake. I ask for the box to be wrapped with festive ribbons, and then James leans forward and says to the cashier, "Can I have a few extra ribbons?"

She looks surprised but hands them to us along with the cake.

"What is that for?" I ask him as we leave the store.

"I thought if you were giving your bear to your grand-mother, he should have a ribbon or two. I'll make Knut look real dapper."

I give him a grateful smile, trying to ignore the flood of warmth in my veins. I think back to what Lady Jane said, that James is a good egg. I'm starting to think all the good parts of him outweigh the bad.

We leave the city core and drive up the hill, the snow get-ting thicker as we go. It's a real cold snap this winter, and some say the harbor might completely freeze over soon. The roads to the care center are slippery. James handles it with ease, though, and soon we've arrived. I called Lisbeth on the way over so she'd know, and it's not uncommon to have lots of visitors the day and night before Christmas Eve.

Once Lisbeth meets me inside, though, I've forgotten why this visit is different. Her attention immediately goes to James, her eyes sparkling.

"And who is this?"

"Sorry, I forgot to tell you she would have two visitors today, if that's okay."

"I'm James," he says, flashing her a smile that's both solemn and charming while extending his hand. "Friend of Laila's."

Lisbeth shakes it, seemingly lost for words. Sometimes I forget that James has this power over a lot of people, not just me. "Oh, you speak English. You're Scottish."

"Aye. Sorry about that." Now he adds a devilish wink. I have to fight from rolling my eyes.

She gives me a look like, *Wow, where did you find him?* But I ignore it.

We walk down the hall to my grandmother's room while Lisbeth gets her head back on straight, speaking in English so that James can understand. She tells us that my grandmother's health has declined, particularly some heart murmurs and overall weakness, but that mentally she still has her bouts of clarity. For now she seems content, which is all we can really hope for.

"Bestemor?" I say as Lisbeth opens the door and we step into the room.

My grandmother sits by the window as always, even though it's dark outside. There's only her bedside light on, casting her in shadow. I reach for the light switch, but Lisbeth stops me.

"She likes it when it's not so bright. The lights disturb her," she says gently. "I'll leave you two be. Let me know if you need me."

She leaves the room, leaving the door half-open.

My grandmother still hasn't looked at us, and I feel myself crumbling on the spot. James puts his hand on my shoulder and says to me in a low voice, "It's okay. You're here. You have presents. It's Christmas."

He's reminding me of what I have in my shopping bag.

But before I can bring the bear out, my grandmother turns her head slowly to look at us. "Kolbjorn?" she asks, her voice shaking.

I still, my eyes wide. Kolbjorn was her husband. He died before I was born.

James gives me a look like he understands. He nods and slowly walks over to my grandmother. "Helge," he says gently in broken Norwegian. "How are you doing?"

I notice he doesn't correct her and tell her she's wrong, probably because he doesn't know enough Norwegian to do so. I'm grateful, because sometimes she can get scared when she gets confused. He also doesn't say he's Kolbjorn either.

"Oh," she says delicately, fixing her eyes on him. "I am doing better now that you are here. I have been thinking a lot about you lately."

James lowers his frame into the seat across from her. I can only stand where I am, Knut halfway out of the shopping bag, and hold my breath for fear of ruining the moment. The only part of me that moves are the tears running down my face.

"You are loved," he says to her in Norwegian, and be still my heart. He doesn't understand what she's saying, but he can tell from the way she's looking at him that it's coming from a very loving place.

She gives him a genuine smile that shakes a little. There is no mistaking the affection in her eyes. "Do you remember when we would walk to the river and take a swim. That was when the furniture factory was there, do you remember? They would use the water for electricity. We would sneak upriver where no one could see us." She giggles softly at that, pressing a hand to her mouth, as if remembering a scandalous detail, and suddenly I can see her in her prime, swimming with my grandpa, looking so damn beautiful.

James smiles at her, and it's so warm that I swear it lights up the room. "You are loved, Helge," he says, taking her hand in his, his voice adamant yet gentle. "You are beautiful." He's really pulling out all the Norwegian he knows. Well, thankfully not the swears.

My grandmother tilts her head, and I swear even in the dim light she has color on her cheeks. "You are handsome," she says. "I'm glad that Laila has you."

James freezes at the sound of my name. I blink, my heart hammering in my chest.

Did she really just say my name?

James's head swivels toward me in surprise and then back to Helge.

"She is such a good soul, she has been through so much," she says. "I wish I could tell her that."

I'm not sure if my grandmother thinks James is her husband anymore. I know that it can bounce around like that and not match up. Even so, I take a step forward.

"Grandma?" I ask.

She turns her head to look at me. "There you are, Laila. Oh, what do you have with you?"

I break into the widest grin. "This? This is for you. It's Christmas, Grandma. I had to get you a present."

"A present?" she says, looking bashful. "You shouldn't have."

"Actually, I have two."

I come over, and James gets out of the chair. He puts his hand on my shoulder and gives it a squeeze, nodding to the door, to tell me he's going to step outside.

I give him a grateful smile and sit down across from my grandmother, taking out Knut and handing him to her.

"Knut," she says, and I laugh, so delighted she remembers his name. "Oh, he looks so handsome with his ribbons."

"That's for you," I tell her, hoping she doesn't notice the tears in my eyes. "I want you to have him. He will keep you company while you're here."

She blinks, and for a moment I think I've lost her, her face going blank as she stares at him. My chest grows cold. I shouldn't have mentioned the space around her.

But then she frowns and nods. "Of course. I will take good care of him."

I sigh in relief and grin at her, putting the cake on the window ledge. "And in there is cloudberry cake."

"Oh heavens," she says, watching as I open the box to show her. "I haven't had that in years."

I have to force the smile on my face through that one. She doesn't remember all the times I've brought it for her.

"It's a special occasion," I tell her, my voice shaking slightly. "And you deserve it."

"That's very kind of you," she says. "Shall we give some to your grandfather?" She looks around the room, as if looking for James.

I hesitate. On one hand I could bring James back in here, but what if this time she doesn't see him as Kolbjorn but as a stranger. I decide to play it safe. "He'll be right back. He's smoking a cigar outside. Why don't you and I have some cake, okay?"

"Okay," she says with a smile.

I bring the plastic forks out of the bag, and we dig into the cake with the polar bear on her lap.

This might be the best Christmas I've had in a very long time, and I'm eternally grateful to James for suggesting it. No, for actually making it happen. Had he not pushed me, arranged this, I wouldn't be here now with my heart so impossibly full.

I have a piece of cake and watch my grandmother enjoy hers, crumbs falling down on top of Knut's head, but she just brushes it off and laughs.

I laugh too, relishing the love, pushing the sadness of the season away, if just for tonight.

Fourteen

· · · · · · · · · · · ·

LAILA

"LISTEN, I JUST THINK PLAYING SCRABBLE IN NORWEGIAN is highly unfair," James says across from me.

"Don't be a wimp," Lady Jane says from beside him.

He looks at her aghast. "You don't speak any more Norwegian than I do."

"I know the swear words," she says with a gleam in her eyes.

"Everyone knows the bloody swear words," James points out. "Our boss is Magnus, after all."

"Look, we'll play in English," I tell him. "The board is in English anyway. I guess *I'll* just have the disadvantage."

"Oh, come on," James says at the same time that Lady Jane goes, "Phfffft."

"Your English is better than mine," he adds.

"We could always play Twister," Lady Jane says, gesturing to the stack of board games hopefully.

"No," James and I say in unison.

It's the weekend after New Year's, and things are quiet at the estate. With all the festive activities finally over, the three of us decided to stay in, play board games in the parlor, and drink all the bottles of champagne that didn't get used. Ottar suggested putting them in the cellar, but sometimes that man doesn't know fun unless it bites him in the ass. Then again, it could be a product of having to babysit Magnus every day. When you never know if your day will start (or end) with you jumping off a literal cliff, I suppose you're allowed to be the fun police in the rest of your life.

"Laila, you need some more champagne," James says to me as he reaches for the bottle and pours more into my glass.

Lady Jane watches the exchange, her eyes a little too eager. "Trying to get her drunk, James?"

He grins at her. "I don't need to try. I'm just making it easier for her."

Her mouth twists into a knowing smile, but she doesn't say anything to that, for which I'm grateful. That woman is a live wire.

I avoid both their eyes and stare at the bubbles rising in the glass. I don't want either of them to get the wrong idea, even though I don't mind the idea of James getting me drunk—so long as we go our separate ways at the end of the night and retire to our separate rooms.

But as Lady Jane noisily starts rattling the Scrabble tiles in the pouch, my eyes meet James's over the rim of my glass and I nearly choke. To say they're smoldering is an understatement. Where did he learn to look at me like that? It should be illegal.

The corner of his beautiful mouth curves like he knows what I'm thinking. Somewhere in the house a phone rings, but everything seems to zero in on this moment.

Easy, tiger, I think, but I'm warning myself more than him.

"Okay, how do we decide who goes first?" Lady Jane asks.

"Rock, paper, scissors?"

James tears his eyes away from mine. "There are official rules, you know," he chides her.

"Laila," Magnus's voice comes from behind us. The tone is so off, so unlike him, that my heart freezes in my chest.

I twist in my place to see him standing in the doorway to the parlor room, his face grim.

"What?" I ask, my voice barely audible. My heart is beating so hard in my head it's hard to hear anything.

"There's a phone call for you," he says. "It's about your grandmother."

My heart seems to fall straight out of me.

NO.

My glass is shaking so hard that James plucks it from my hand, and I find myself getting up, walking toward Magnus as if shuffling through mud.

Up close I can see the concern in Magnus's eyes. "They tried your mobile, but you weren't answering."

"It's being charged in my room," I say absently as Magnus puts his hand at my lower back and guides me toward his study, where the phone is. I focus on the receiver, how old it looks, and I'm reminded of the one at my grandmother's, and for a split second everything is fine because the old phone is reminding me of my grandma and that's it. There's no other reason to be thinking about her.

But I know. I knew from the moment Magnus said my name that the worst thing in the entire world just happened. That my world shattered while I was about to lose at Scrabble.

I pick up the receiver with shaking hands.

"This is Laila?" I manage to say, everything moving in slow motion.

"Laila?" Lisbeth says, and from the sound of her voice, all my fears are cemented. "I'm so sorry to have to tell you this, but Helge passed away this evening."

She's dead.

My grandmother is dead.

The only person who ever really took care of me, who ever really loved me, who ever really saw me for who I was—she's gone. And maybe she was gone long before this, but there's a difference—there's such a fucking difference—between having someone be alive and having someone be dead.

Lisbeth goes on to tell me more things, how she was fine yesterday and how she died in her sleep and it was peaceful, but I can't take them in. They hit me and dissolve because I've already been shattered from the inside out.

I put the phone down. I'm not sure what I said to her, if anything, not even sure if I've hung up the phone, but I turn around, about to collapse from the sheer weight of infinity, of *gone forever*, and feel myself in Magnus's arms.

He holds me for a moment, a strong and powerful grip, and tells me that they've got me. Not him but *they*, and then I find myself being passed on and I'm in James's arms now. I let out a choked sob and wrap my arms around him, holding on tight, so tight, as it feels like my heart is being ripped out of my throat.

"Laila love," James whispers as he cradles me against him, kissing the top of my head. "I'm so sorry."

I cry, sob, bawl.

And he holds me. He doesn't tell me it will be okay, because he knows it won't be.

But he holds me just the same.

MY GRANDMOTHER'S FUNERAL is being held in Todalen. Other than Lisbeth and me, she knew no one in Oslo, with all her friends, old neighbors, and her nephew Peter up in the village.

So Magnus gave me the week off of work to try to make the funeral arrangements. I don't even know how I did it. I've been so overcome with grief that my brain's operating power has turned to a crawl. One moment I can push through like normal, and in the next I'm hit, going down, like a sledgehammer to the heart.

Somehow, though, with help from Lady Jane and Ottar, I managed to get her casket up there, the funeral being held tomorrow at the local cemetery.

Magnus and Ella wanted to attend the funeral with me. They said I'm like their family, and that my family is part of their family. But I didn't want that. It would attract too much fuss. My grandmother was a simple woman, and she hated attention. She wasn't particularly fond of the Norwegian royalty either, calling it all pomp and circumstance. So as much as I really appreciate that they wanted to come pay their respects, I know a media circus in that small village is the last thing anyone would want. Pretty sure Helge would haunt me if I did that.

So it's just me. Luckily I'm going up by private jet, so I don't have to deal with driving and the train (it's about an eight-hour train ride from Oslo to Trondheim, then a few hours' drive to the village from there). Perks of working for royalty.

I have my bag all packed, ready to go, Olaf waiting outside for me.

I say goodbye to Magnus and Ottar in the foyer (Ella, Lady Jane, and the boys are at the palace in Oslo with the king and queen), a somber affair.

And then James appears.

A duffel bag over his shoulder.

I blink at him, confused. I was hoping he'd see me off since he's been such a support this last week, but I wasn't sure where he was. Now he's here, with a packed bag.

"What are you doing?" I ask him.

"I'm going with you," he says to me.

I stare at him, mouth agape. Then I close it and look at Magnus, raising my brows. "Did you know about this?"

He nods. "I did. James asked. Said you probably needed protection, as well as the support of a friend."

I look at James at the mention of *friend*, wondering if that's what he truly is to me. But all I can feel is gratitude. I know I should tell James not to come, that I can handle it, that I'll be fine.

But the truth is, I feel relief. Relief that I don't have to go through this alone.

I swallow the lump in my throat. "Okay," I say softly.

James gives me a quick smile. "Come on, love. Let's get going."

He takes my bag from me and strides toward the doors.

I look back to Magnus and Ottar as if to say, *You sure this is okay?*

"He'll take good care of you, I promise," Magnus says. He

sounds serious and looks grave, but with him I can never tell if there's some not-so-hidden meaning behind his words.

I take it at face value, thank him profusely, then head off after James.

It's another cloudy day here, with even the snow having lost some of its sheen, yet this is the brightest I've felt in a long time. I know I need to keep my wits about me, that going to Todalen with James might not be the best idea in hindsight, but at the moment I really don't care. I'll take anything that will distract me from the loss I feel inside, that missing piece of me that I don't think will ever be whole again.

I get in the back seat of the VW, surprised to see James sitting beside Olaf. Putting distance between us.

"Thank you," I tell him as the car pulls away and starts down the driveway.

James turns to look at me, an affectionate gleam in his eyes that makes my heart skip a few beats. God, the effect he has on me sometimes makes everything seem extra unfair. "You really thought I'd let you go to your grandmother's funeral alone?"

I shrug, looking out the window. "Yes. I mean, you have your job here."

"I do. But my job is to protect everyone, you included. There might be a nanny snatcher on the loose, and what would happen if I weren't there to protect you?"

I laugh softly at *nanny snatcher.* "That's true."

"Magnus thought it was a good idea too," he goes on. "Not just for protection, but because I'm your friend and you need a friend right now."

I look to him, feeling grateful all over again. "Then I'm glad you're my friend." If I can't have anything more from him, his friendship is still a pretty special thing to have.

The tiny private airfield isn't too far from the estate, and soon we're piling inside the royals' private jet. It's small, but it's swanky, and even though I've been in it a few times, it feels completely different when it's just me, James, the flight attendant, and the pilots. Like we're some rich, jet-setting couple off on a luxurious vacation, not a lowly nanny and a bodyguard off to a funeral.

I sit in a window seat, expecting James to sit next to me. But of course we have the whole plane, and he sits on the other side of the aisle.

I don't like this distance between us. I never have. I've fought for it, I've done what I could to enforce this distance, to keep us in our roles, but deep down, I hate it. I hate that there's that wall separating our rooms.

"James," I say quietly as the plane starts up its engines.

He looks at me. "Yes?"

Suddenly I feel so shy, so vulnerable, like I'm seconds away from crumbling. "Do you . . ." I look down at the empty seat next to me, afraid to ask for what I want.

He nods, recognition flashing in his dark eyes. "Of course."

He undoes his belt and comes over, sitting down next to me and buckling up again. Then he takes my hand in his, his skin so warm against mine, and raises it to his mouth. He places a light kiss on my knuckles as his eyes bore into mine. "I'm right here," he says.

I nearly burst into tears. It wouldn't be unwarranted, but somehow I manage to keep them at bay, blinking fast, looking out the window.

James doesn't let go of my hand the entire flight.

Fifteen

. . . .

LAILA

THE PLANE LANDS IN A PRIVATE AIRFIELD OUTSIDE
Trondheim, and Magnus arranged a rental car for the two of us.
With James behind the wheel of a black Mercedes, we drive
south of the city, through valleys and villages surrounded by
rounded peaks. Everything looks so beautiful and pure, yet there's
an emptiness about it too. Like even these places are touched
by the same loss that I am.

Eventually the road swings through a mountain pass and
the fjord appears before us, the mountains on the other side
towering like overlords.

"Shit," James swears under his breath, trying to keep his
eyes on both the road and the view. "This is incredible. And
you grew up here?"

"I sure did," I tell him as the road winds along the water, the
surface dark and reflecting back the mountains. Eventually we
come to the end of the fjord and the base of the village, which
spreads out into a stunning valley, the patchwork quilt of farms

and houses now covered by unifying snow. All the houses here are in primary colors—red, orange, yellow, white—the same colors they've been since they were built, having been passed down through generations.

Home. This is and always will be home to me. It doesn't matter that I've lived in London or Oslo—this is where my heart feels most at peace. The funny thing is, there's nothing really here for me anymore. My grandmother is gone. I'm friendly with my cousin, but he's literally my only family left now. And I'm friendly with some of the villagers too, but there's nothing keeping me except the sense of belonging. They say you can never go home again, but I hope, deep down, that one day I can.

"So this is the town," James muses as we drive past a handful of stores, rounding the bend of the fjord. "What a journey you've been on, Laila. From fjord farm girl to being employed by royalty. The people here must be very proud of you."

"Turn right up there," I say as we head over a bridge, a frozen river beneath. "And I'm not too sure about them being proud. They're pretty down-to-earth here. I don't think most of them have an opinion either way about the royal family. And anyway, you're the one with the journey. From the foster system of Glasgow to becoming Prince Eddie's and Prince Magnus's bodyguard."

He gives a dismissive shrug. "I suppose we all have our journeys, don't we?"

We continue along the road, now on the other side of the fjord, the street getting narrower as we pass through houses. I point out the different ones to James. "The yellow one belongs to Ernest and Trude Surdal who used to come over for brunch on Sundays. The dark wood one, which has a grass roof during the summer, is where old man Arvid lives. He taught me how to fish when I was young. Then there's the Ragnar family, who I used to play with. Funny how I can't remember their names."

I continue to point out the different houses and people, until finally my grandmother's old house appears. "Pull in here," I tell him, my voice starting to shake as the emotions threaten to overwhelm me, my chest and throat growing tight.

James parks the car and looks at me, reaching for my hand. "It's going to be okay," he says, even though I have no idea how that's possible. How can it ever be okay when you lose the person you love?

I let him hold my hand for a moment, then I steel my nerves, taking in a deep breath through my nose. "I'm okay," I manage to say. I step out of the car.

The neighbors don't seem to be home. I hope they remembered they said I could stay here. Of course, I'll see them at the funeral anyway, but I really don't want to break into the place.

"This is amazing," James says as he gets out of the car, staring up at the house. "Right out of some bloody cottagecore Instagram account."

That manages to make me laugh. He's right. The house is white with black shutters and a black roof peppered with moss, a red door, and big windows looking out across the fjord on the other side of the street. It makes me happy to see the lace curtains in the windows haven't been replaced by anything modern. My grandmother was adamant about not replacing anything unless it broke, and I hope Peter's upkeep of the house kept that in mind.

James grabs the bags while we trudge through the cleared

path toward the door. There's a folded piece of paper resting on top of an upright log, the heavy key on top.

I pick up the key and read the note. It's from Ann and Terre, telling me that the house is all mine, that they've got the logs for the fire ready to go inside, and that they'll be back tomorrow to take me to the funeral.

I swallow and fold the note back up, placing it in my coat pocket as I stick the key in the door.

It's been so long since I've stepped foot inside this house. The cold smell of the dry room, mixed with the pile of wood, brings back so many memories. My father had a workshop down here on the bottom floor that he would always disappear into, and my old playroom is just to the side, though it's used for storage now.

James joins me inside. The heat isn't on down here, so we're quick in taking off our boots and coats and then heading up the narrow flight of stairs to the door at the top where the rest of the house is.

I open the door and step into the kitchen. It's warm, and I'm hit with the smell of waffles, the same ones she would make every Sunday, that have somehow sunk into the bones of the house.

I close my eyes for a moment, just taking it all in.

James comes up behind me and places his strong hands on my shoulders, giving them a comforting squeeze.

"It's lovely," he says. "It feels like a home."

"It really is," I say. "As it always was." Everything looks the same. The table in the middle still has the same lacy tablecloth with red trim, the bench painted a sky blue. There's a fruit bowl in the middle, one that we would always fill with blueberries and cloudberries picked in the late summer on the mountainside right behind the house. Right now it's empty and it reminds me of how empty I feel.

There's another note, this one on the old fridge. I walk over and take it off. It says to open the fridge.

I open it, finding it absolutely packed with food. Tupperware containers, casserole dishes covered in tinfoil, all the meat and fruit one could want. And beer. Tons of beer.

"Oh my god," I exclaim softly. "I feel like the whole town has brought us food."

"Uh, Laila?" James says.

I turn to see him in the doorway to the living room, staring at it. I rush over to him and gasp. It's covered floor to ceiling in balloons, and flowers, and gift baskets.

"Oh my god," I say again, and this time the tears can't be held back.

I break down crying, so painfully raw at the loss, and yet so overjoyed and warmed by the generosity of the townspeople. The people who loved Helge as much as I did.

James puts his arms around me, holding me close to him, his palm pressed against the back of my head. "Hey, it's okay," he says quietly. "You're allowed to feel everything."

I bury my head in his sweater, my hands going behind him and holding on to the strong planes of his back, feeling his strength, hoping he can pass some of that strength on to me.

I don't know how long we stand like that. Time doesn't seem to matter much. It passes with each beat of his heart that I can hear from his chest, each long and steady breath he takes. His grip on me remains firm, keeping me up, and I think I'm losing myself to the comfort he brings me, his touch and affection.

Why do I keep losing myself to the very man who broke my heart and will no doubt do it again?

Finally, I calm down, even though everything inside me feels more wild and chaotic than ever, feelings I don't even have names for that want to take me for a ride.

I lift my head and look up at him, studying the sharp line of his jaw, the black stubble over his chin with the deep dimple, his strong aquiline nose, the faded scar on his cheek. His dark eyes are what give me the most trouble, after that smile. Right now they're brimming with intensity, the kind that leads to trouble. And right now, I'm welcoming that trouble with open arms.

I clear my throat, aware of how close we are. "I should show you to your room."

I pull away from him and walk back through the kitchen and to the staircase leading up. The stairs are steep and narrow, and I'm very conscious of my ass being in his face, but then again, he's always complimented me on my "arse."

We get to the second level, and I take him straight to my bedroom, which overlooks the garden at the back of the house and the hill that rises directly behind it, all the brambles and blueberry bushes hidden as lumps of snow.

Just as downstairs, it looks exactly the same. Like nothing was touched.

"You can sleep here," I tell him as he puts his duffel bag on the bed, leaving my suitcase in the doorway. He walks around the room, taking in the green wallpaper, the framed photos on the walls, the row of horseback-riding ribbons from when I was a teenager, the bookcase full of well-loved books.

"Is this your old room?" he asks, enthralled by each and every photo.

"Yup. And it looks exactly the same as it always did."

He nods, eyeing the queen-size bed with a wooden frame painted the same green as the walls, the pale blue and pink bedspread.

"Where are you sleeping?" he asks.

I suck on my lip for a moment, meeting his eyes. "Here." I walk over to him, stopping a foot away. "With you."

He cocks a brow in surprise.

"I don't want to be alone tonight," I add. Or any night, really.

His black brows knit together. "Are you sure?"

I reach up, holding the back of his neck with my hand, feeling how hot and soft his skin is beneath my palm. "Yes." My gaze flutters down to his lips. "Kiss me."

He hesitates for a moment. Then lightning flashes in his eyes.

He moves fast, his lips pressing against mine, soft and tentative at first as my grip on his neck tightens. Then our mouths widen, the kiss deepens, and we are moving against each other in an easy rhythm that grows hungrier by the second.

I break away briefly, my hands going down to the hem of his sweater, pulling it upward.

"You sure?" he whispers again, though I can see the lust has already overtaken his eyes.

"Yes," I tell him. He raises his arms and I pull his T-shirt and sweater off, throwing them to the floor.

He's now bare-chested in front of me, and I take a moment to marvel at him, to run my fingers over his impossibly broad shoulders, his hard pecs, the carved abs of his hard-earned six-pack that he works for in the estate gym. I spent so many nights with this body in the past, and yet to see it like this again, to feel him beneath my touch, feels like I'm with him for the first time.

I glance up at him, about to tell him how beautiful he is, but he's on me like wildfire, grabbing my face roughly between his hands as he pushes me back on the bed, climbing on top of me.

And I let go.

Sixteen

· · · · · · · · · · ·

LAILA

I SETTLE BACK INTO THE PINK-AND-BLUE-STRIPED BED-spread, raising my arms above me as James reaches down and pulls up the hem of my sweater, removing it and my bra. Cool air flows across my breasts as I'm bare and exposed, and I shiver, more from anticipation than anything else. His strong hands begin to play over the soft skin of my belly, his fingers dance across my rib cage until they reach my breasts.

He pauses for a beat, and I look up at him, raw desire in his eyes.

"Please," I breathe, and he doesn't need to be asked twice.

He kisses me. A soft yet hard kiss, his mouth covering mine with sweet urgency. His tongue enters my mouth, and he's exploring me, touching me, tasting me even as I taste him. We can't seem to get enough of each other, and I'm losing my breath as I lose myself to this kiss, to the feeling of being so delicately devoured. My hand reaches up to his face and I hold him, pull him closer to me, both of us savoring the feeling of the other.

Then he breaks away, already out of breath, his eyes searching mine in a wild haze of lust before he leans down, his mouth covering my breast, and I arch my back, offering myself up to him. His tongue swirls around my nipple, and I moan, my fingers tangling in his hair. I can feel his smile against my skin, and then his teeth scrape gently over my nipple, making me gasp.

The sensations are overwhelming, and I writhe beneath him, wanting more, needing him closer. I want to drown in him; I want him to erase all the pain inside me, the hurt I've buried deep down since I was a child, all of which has risen to the surface, threatening to shatter me into a million pieces. If I'm going to collapse, if I'm going to feel obliterated to my core, then I want James to be the one to do it. I want him to fuck the soul out of me until I feel nothing but him.

"Laila love," he whispers to me, bringing his mouth up to my neck, causing lightning strikes along my spine. "Tell me what you need from me."

"I need to feel," I manage to say. "I need to feel you and only you. Nothing else."

"Then I will make you feel me," he says roughly. He kisses me, his mouth claiming mine in a brutal, desperate kiss that leaves me breathless. He pulls away, his forehead resting against mine, and I'm panting and bereft, my body aching for him. His eyes search mine, and he whispers thickly, "I will make you feel everything. I'm going to make you come so hard you'll see stars."

I believe him.

I reach down and unzip my jeans, and he helps me wriggle out of them and my underwear until I'm totally naked. If it were any other time I might have felt insecure about being with him like this—I've gained quite a bit of weight since we were last together—but right now I don't care much about anything. To be worried about something like belly rolls or cellulite seems trivial and pointless when you realize how little it matters in the grand scheme of life.

With an appreciative, molten look in his eyes as he appraises my naked body, his hand slides down my belly, his fingers slipping between my legs, and then he kisses me deep again, his tongue sliding against mine, and I moan into his mouth as his fingers enter me. I'm wet and ready, and he sinks into me easily, his fingers moving in and out of me as his thumb circles my clit. I cry out, the pleasure intense and instantaneous. I arch my back, my hands fisted in the sheets as he increases the pressure, and I feel myself spiraling out of control. I'm so close, so goddamn close to losing myself to him, and then he slides two fingers inside me and I shatter, the orgasm ripping through me with quick and brutal force. I cry out, my body writhing beneath his, and he doesn't let up, prolonging my pleasure until I'm a quivering mess. There's a locked box of emotions just below the surface, and I'm scared that he might just have the key.

"I know that wasn't enough," he says, and he starts moving down my body, wet kisses trailing over my stomach. I manage to raise my head to meet his eyes as they glint with hunger. His mouth moves lower, never breaking eye contact, and he parts my legs wider with his large hands. A wicked grin curls his lips, and he lowers his head. I moan loudly as his lips brush against my clit, my head going back. I'm so sensitive after my orgasm that it only takes a few strokes of his tongue before I'm moaning and begging for more. There's always so much begging with him.

"Does that feel good, love?" he asks hoarsely, placing a kiss on my inner thigh, his breath hot. "Should I keep going?"

I can't answer, I'm too lost in the pleasure, but he doesn't need an answer. He knows what I want. He knows me so well. His tongue swirls around my clit, and I shatter again, crying out as the pleasure washes over me in waves. I'm trembling, my body weak and pliant as he keeps licking me, savoring me with lips and mouth and tongue, until I feel close to coming, the tension coiling up inside me like a snake. I'm crying out, unable to control myself, and then he plunges two fingers inside me and I come apart, the pleasure so intense I nearly black out.

"Jesus, James," I manage to say, my voice hoarse and raw. "Oh god."

The orgasm flows through me, a golden fire licking through my veins. My eyes are closed, but I can see bright colors behind my eyelids like a rainbow. I'm moaning and crying out his name, and it's both beautiful and torturous.

James is still between my legs, his mouth latched on to my clit, drawing on it with lips and teeth, his big hands cupping my ass, lifting me up to his sucking mouth until I nearly beg for him to stop.

Finally he pulls back. He doesn't say a word, he just brings his fingers out of me and shoves them into his mouth, savoring me, and I can't help but stare, my breath catching. He's staring at me, his gaze hot and dangerous, and I feel myself growing wet again.

He moves up to kiss me, his lips seeking mine out so that I can taste myself.

"You're so beautiful, Laila," he murmurs, his fingers tracing over my cheek. "So bloody beautiful."

He kisses me again, and I can feel his smile against my lips. I'm boneless, completely spent, and I can only lie there and let him kiss me and touch me. I'm in danger of falling for him, and

I know I should be scared, but I can't bring myself to care. I'm safe with him. I know I am.

"Come on," he says, moving over me. He slips an arm underneath my waist and flips me over so I'm on my stomach. I try to roll over, wanting to see him as he fucks me, but he pins me to the bed, laughter in his voice. "I'm not done with you yet." He rests a hand on my waist, tilting my hips up so I'm on my knees and my ass exposed to him.

He lines up behind me, and then I feel the head of his cock pressing against me and I moan, arching my back, but he doesn't enter me yet.

"Tell me what you want, Laila." He leans forward and breathes into my ear.

"I want you," I say, my body aching with need. I'm still trembling from the orgasms he's given me, but I still want him inside me. I want him to pleasure me again and again and again. Put me out of my mind.

He teases me, rubbing the tip of his cock along my entrance, and I cry out.

"Please, James."

"Tell me what you want, Laila."

"Fuck me. Make me forget."

"I'm going to fuck you," he agrees. "I'm going to fuck you until you can't think, can't feel anything but me."

The blunt tip of his cock presses against my entrance, and I wriggle my ass toward him, wanting him so badly.

But then he pulls back. "Just a minute," he whispers, and I know he's looking for a condom. I keep myself spread for him as he kneels up and slips one on, watching him over my shoulder, my mouth parted.

I feel him move back over me, and then he sinks into me, a deep groan escaping his lips as he fills me up, taking his time pushing inside me in a long, slow slide. I gasp and then moan, the sensation of his cock filling me up, stretching me out and making me feel complete. It's so overwhelming that I close my eyes, reveling in it, feeling his muscles bunch against me as he pulls back and thrusts forward again, slamming back into me, and I gasp, my head falling, the pleasure so sharp and sweet it makes me gasp. His hands are on my hips, holding me in place as he pumps into me, his cock hitting just the right spot, sending shock waves of pleasure through me.

"Jesus, Laila," he says, his voice strained. "You feel so good."

My legs are trembling, my ass pushed up in the air as he fucks me, and I can't stop thinking about how much I want him. I want him to ruin me, to destroy me, to make me completely his.

"Look at me," he whispers, his hand cupping my cheek, turning my chin to the side so I can see him. His shaft moves in and out of me so slowly, his eyes burning into mine. "Look at me, Laila."

I open my eyes, my lips parting as he continues to fuck me. His eyes never leave mine, and I feel his cock moving inside me, claiming me as his. I'm helpless beneath him, and the more he fucks me, the more I want him. The pleasure is so acute, so sharp, that it hurts, and I know we'll never go back to what we were before. All these weeks have been leading up to this moment, to where we finally give in to each other. It was always inevitable.

We were always inevitable.

He picks up his pace, his cock pounding into me, his grip on my hips punishing. I'm crying out, my head falling forward, and he leans down so I can feel his hot breath on my neck as he fucks me.

"You're going to come for me again, aren't you, love?" he whispers, his lips moving over my skin, his fingers slipping between my legs until they find my clit.

"Please," I whimper. "Please, James."

He growls and slams into me, one big hand tight on my hips.

"That's it, love," he murmurs, kissing my neck. "Give it all to me."

I am. I'm giving it all to him. Everything I have right now is his to take, and I can only hope I can trust him with it this time.

"Oh god," he says through a groan, thrusting up deeper, his skin slapping against me. "You feel so good wrapped around me."

"Yes," I moan, my vision going blurry, my body on fire. It's too much, too intense. "Fuck."

"Come on, love. Come on my cock."

He's fucking me faster now, his hips slamming into mine, his cock so deep inside me I'm sure I'll feel him tomorrow.

He brings his mouth to my ear, his breath hot against my skin as he whispers, "Come for me, Laila."

He knows all the right things to say.

I can feel his cock rubbing against my G-spot, and with a couple of hard thrusts, I'm done for. Pleasure rips through me, a firestorm of heat and light, and I can't stop myself from coming, the orgasm ripping through me like a hurricane hell-bent on destroying everything in its path.

I hear him cry out my name, and the knowledge that he's coming for me sends me over the edge again, pleasure pulsing through me, my pussy clenching around his cock, my body shaking, unraveling, his name like a prayer on my lips.

He's still inside me, his cock twitching, when he falls on top of me, and I can feel his heart pounding against my back. He wraps his arms around me, kissing my neck, his lips moving over my skin, and I'm lost in a sea of pleasure while he pulls out, leaving me shaking and bereft.

I collapse onto my stomach and look at him. He's lying on his side, his chest heaving as he tries to catch his breath. He looks at me, and I see the satiety fade from his eyes, quickly replaced with concern.

"Are you okay?" he whispers, reaching forward to cup my face, his palm damp and warm with sweat.

I try to swallow, tears springing to my eyes, my heart sinking deeper and deeper until I'm not sure how I'll ever rescue it again. "I don't think I'll ever be okay again," I whisper, my eyes closing, my tears spilling over my cheeks. "I am so broken."

He doesn't say anything, just gathers me into his arms and holds me close, letting me cry until I have nothing left. And then he kisses me, his lips soft and gentle on mine, and I know that even though I'm broken, I'm not alone.

At least not at this moment.

"Laila love," he whispers to me, stroking my hair. "You're not broken. You're just a little bruised. We all are."

"It hurts more than I can bear," I manage to say, closing my eyes. "I thought because I've been through this before, when I lost my parents, that I would know what to expect. I thought because my grandmother was old, that she had dementia and we knew this end would one day come, that it would make all of this easier. That I could handle it. But I can't. I can't handle it at all," I sob into him. "It hurts so much."

He holds me even tighter. Time passes, but whether it's passing fast or slowly, I don't know. I feel the world has condensed itself into this room and there's nothing else out there for me.

Just James.

Someone I'm falling for, the man I'm letting in past all the guards and walls, into my inner courtyard where the real me resides. The irony that he's the last person I trust isn't lost on me.

I've almost fallen asleep when I hear him say faintly, "I'm so sorry."

I open my eyes, my vision blurry from tears and my eyes sore from crying, not sure what he could be sorry for. After all, it's not like he lost his grandmother.

"I'm sorry," he repeats, pulling back to look at me with those intense eyes. "I'm so sorry."

My breath catches in my throat. "What are you sorry for?"

He doesn't answer me, just keeps stroking my hair, his eyes never leaving mine. What am I supposed to think after he says something like that? He looks away from me, and I reach out, taking his chin in my hand, his stubble rough against my skin.

"James," I say, my voice trembling. "What are you sorry for?"

He looks me in the eye and says the words I've been waiting for since the day he came back.

"I'm sorry for hurting you."

"Oh," I whisper, feeling my heart swell a little. It doesn't change things, but I'll take what he's giving me because I've learned that sometimes things need to be broken down into pieces if they're going to be rebuilt.

If it's even worth rebuilding. I'm still not sure on that. I'm not sure about anything in this world anymore.

"I didn't want to hurt you. I never wanted to hurt you," he says again, a look of anguish on his face.

"I know," I say, cupping his cheek in my hand. "I know you didn't. You were a mess; I was a mess . . ."

"I'm still a mess, Laila."

I can't tell if he's warning me or not, but I nod. "I know that too."

He sighs and kisses my palm before moving off the bed and pulling back the bedspread, both of us shuffling under it, a cold draft coming in from the thin windowpanes now that our body temperatures have returned to normal. "We better get some sleep," he says. "Tomorrow is going to be hard."

A lump builds in my throat as I rest on his chest and his arm goes around me. "I know."

He kisses my forehead. "And even though it's going to be hard, I'm going to be here with you, every step of the way."

I give him a quick smile, appreciating the hell out of him.

He's going to be by my side for now.

That's going to have to be enough.

Seventeen

· · · · · · · · · · · ·

JAMES

HELGE'S FUNERAL WAS BEAUTIFUL, HELD AT A WHITE church in the middle of town. It felt like everyone in the town showed up. There must have been at least sixty people or more, some even standing outside the low stone walls of the graveyard and watching from afar.

She was buried next to her husband, Kolbjorn, and next to her children, Hedda and Erik.

I held Laila's hand the entire time. I wanted to be her wall, the thing that could shield her from the world and everything bad in it. But I could not shield her from her grief, and that was a hard thing to come to terms with. Each tear that fell, each sob that escaped her lips . . . I wanted to take it all from her, free her from her pain.

But I couldn't. I could only be there and try to be a source of comfort.

I wasn't the only one doing that, of course. Laila had an endless stream of love from the villagers, neighbors, and friends.

I met her cousin Peter, someone she doesn't speak of very often but who I understand is her only family left, and it was touching to see them together. He's a very quiet, stoic fellow in his late sixties, with a wife and a daughter who live in Canada. He promised Laila that though the house is hers now, he will take care of it for as long as she needs him to, which she seemed so touched by. The house is special and should be passed on through the generations, but at the moment, with her job in Oslo, it doesn't seem like she'll be able to use it anytime soon.

"That was nice of your cousin," I tell her on the walk back to the house. We were given a ride to the funeral by the neighbors, Ann and Terre (they insisted, practically snatched the rental car keys from my hand), but Laila wanted to get some exercise and process everything by walking back. She said it's only a half-hour walk, but the roads aren't fully plowed, so it makes it a rather slow stroll through the snow.

"Yeah," she says with a sniff, wiping at her eyes with her mitten. "He's always kept to himself, you know. Growing up I didn't see Peter's daughter, Ingrid, very much. I think they, like so many people my age in this town, weren't sure what to do with me."

"What do you mean?"

She shrugs. "I was a strange kid. I mean, I still am, but . . . yeah. I listened to dark music—you know, Norwegian metal, that type—I dyed my hair black. Did everything except tattoos and piercings, and that's only because I'm a wimp when it comes to pain."

I can't imagine Laila with black hair. "But everyone goes through that phase growing up, and I'm sure you weren't the only metalhead."

She gives her head a shake. "I didn't have very good control of my emotions back then. It all felt too much. I liked to do things that maybe seemed young for my age. I started reading more, spending more time online. That's where I could be real, in fandoms and chat rooms and all that. I could just let myself be free."

"Do you feel you can do that now?"

She lets out an acidic laugh. "Are you kidding me? No."

"Not even with me?" I have to say, I feel a little insulted.

An apologetic smile plays on her lips. She doesn't have to answer.

She's going through something, and you lost her trust long ago, I remind myself. *Don't make this about you.*

I decide to change the subject. "And so what is your plan for the future?"

She frowns. "What do you mean?"

I gesture to the wide frozen fields that lead out to the dark fjord, the mountains towering above, the red, yellow, and white houses dotted across the landscape. We're walking in a damn painting.

"Will you ever make this your home again?"

She rubs her lips together in thought, and I'm astounded by how beautiful she is, as tends to happen when I'm with her. It always hits like lightning.

"I want to, one day," she says. "With Peter taking care of it and the neighbors keeping an eye on it, I know it's in good hands. I can just focus on my life in Oslo, working, and then maybe if I have enough money saved, I'll come up here. Or, hell, maybe I'll get a job somewhere in town. Do something online. Start a business. I don't know."

Even though I know it's good she's feeling optimistic about the future, that there are possibilities, it bothers me that I'm not in any of those scenarios.

"I think that's smart," I tell her. "To know you'll come back, sooner rather than later." I clear my throat. "So you don't see yourself working for royals forever?"

"Nah," she says. "It's been fun. I've enjoyed my jobs. I enjoy being with kids. But now everything seems turned on its head. The life plan I thought I had, however feeble it was—I feel like there's been a major course correction. Which is scary, but . . . I'm realizing how important home is. I don't want to realize it too late."

"Makes sense."

"And you?" she asks.

"Me, what? My plan?"

"Could you see yourself living somewhere like this?"

"*Somewhere* like this? Or this place in particular?"

What exactly are you asking me, Laila?

"Okay. Somewhere like this."

Hmmm. Can't help but feel a little disappointed that she wasn't talking about this town. Guess I was getting ahead of myself.

"It depends," I say. "Am I here alone? Am I here with someone special? Am I here because I'm hoping to catch the eye of a pretty blond girl with the world's loudest laugh?"

She nearly laughs at that but clamps her lips shut. "Right," she eventually says.

"I don't know," I say. "I never thought about it until now."

"Because you're a city boy through and through."

"That's true. I have been. But we don't always remain the

same through life, do we? And since I started working for Magnus, I've actually gotten used to living in the middle of nowhere. I've come to peace with it. In fact I think it actually *brings* me peace, believe it or not. And if you had told me that last year, I would have said you were crazy."

Laila is actually looking at me like I'm crazy right now. "Call me shocked."

I shrug. "I don't know what to say. I think . . ." I look around, taking in the amazing scenery, feeling like I'm actually one with the wilderness. Maybe I have some secret Norwegian blood in me after all. "I think I could thrive in a place like this. As long as I could thrive *with* someone."

I want to be direct. I usually am. But with Laila it can be so hard to know where you stand, and the last thing I want is to seem like I'm coming on too strong, especially on a walk back from her grandmother's funeral.

But when we finally get to the house, faces red from the cold, all worries about coming on too strong are quickly pushed aside. Laila grabs my hand and takes me up the narrow, steep steps to her bedroom, pulling me inside.

I'm already hard just from the anticipation of sex. Last night was amazing, but I never assumed it would happen again. I thought Laila would have chalked it up to a mistake, a bad idea, and it would have been put past us. But now . . .

"James," she says as she puts a hand behind my back and pulls me against her. There's desperation in her voice, the way her jaw tenses as her hands slip down over my cock, giving me a hard squeeze through my pants that makes me moan.

"I want you," she says, her eyes searching mine.

She wants to escape from everything. She wants to forget.

She wants to feel something other than the deepest and darkest pain.

I will do everything I can to help. I want to forget too. I want to pretend that our past never happened and there's only our future.

Even though it scares the fuck out of me.

I grab her face and kiss her hard and then bring a hand down to the hem of her dress and pull it up while sliding my fingers down the waistband of her leggings and underwear.

Damn, she's soaked.

I let my fingers explore, and it brings out a moan from her mouth. It's as if she's starving for me. When my fingers slip between her cunt and her hips buck, I let my middle finger slip inside her tightness and begin to fuck her slowly with it, taking my time. I know that what's happening between us here is only meant to be *here*. I know this, I feel it . . . she doesn't even have to say it. And so I want to savor this, every moment that my fingers touch her body, every moment that I feel her, touch her, because I know that we might not have another chance after this.

"James," she says in a throaty whisper and her head goes back. I kiss her neck, slipping another finger inside her as we both stand at the foot of the bed. She feels like she's offering herself to me, and I know I have to be careful in how I handle her. Not in a physical way—she likes it rough and she can be pretty wild herself—but emotionally. She has been letting me in bit by bit, like the leaves of a rosebud opening to the sunshine, as if I don't bring rain. But maybe this time I don't have to be what ruins her. Maybe I won't make a mistake this time. Maybe I won't get cold feet and run if she lets me into her heart again.

"Am I making you feel good?" I whisper to her, my fingers working her harder now.

"Yes," she pants, her hands gripping my shoulders now. "God, James. Yes."

I'll never tire of hearing my name said like a fervent prayer.

I grin and press my thumb against her clit as I fuck her with my fingers, and she cries out, her whole body quivering, her legs shaking like they're about to give out from under her at any minute.

I put my hand at the back of her head and bring her head forward, our eyes meeting each other for one electric moment before I kiss her, my mouth seeking hers out. As our tongues touch and dance, I slip a third finger inside her. She moans and writhes against me, and I can feel her getting close. I can feel her orgasm building, and I increase the pace, wanting her to come hard, for her to let loose and come undone in all directions.

"Oh god!" she says through a choked cry.

She comes apart, crying out and gripping my fingers tightly as she comes. I keep fucking her until she's finished, and then I pull my fingers out of her and kiss her softly while she staggers slightly.

"Thank you," she whispers, her eyes shining as she takes me in, lids heavy, eyes still red from crying.

"Thank you," I say, kissing her again. "For trusting me."

She swallows at that, perhaps taking in what I said. Because it's true, because she is trusting me right now, and I feel I've worked long and hard for this trust. It's not lost on me that it's something I don't even deserve.

She doesn't say anything in response.

Instead she drops to her knees.

I'm taken aback at first, completely unprepared for what she's doing. But then I get it, and I undo my belt and push my jeans and boxers down, giving her free access. I've been hard as hell from the moment we stepped into the bedroom.

She looks up at me, her eyes bright green and wanton, and takes me in her pretty, full mouth.

I moan, a long and low sound that rattles in my chest, as she starts to suck me off. She knows what she's doing, knows how to work her tongue and lips around me, and I can feel myself getting harder by the second until there's no place for me to go, my cock throbbing and begging for more.

She doesn't disappoint, picking up the pace and sucking me harder until I feel like she's sucking my brains out. I reach down and run my fingers through her hair, gripping it tightly as she brings me closer and closer to the edge.

"Oh, sweet Jesus, Laila," I whisper roughly. "I'm going to come if you keep going."

She acts as if she doesn't hear me, twisting her hands at the base until my eyes roll back in my head.

Finally I can't take it anymore. I pull away from her and grip her arms, pulling her up to me. I kiss her, tasting myself on her, then quickly step out of my clothes while she wrestles out of hers.

Then I'm pushing her back onto the bed, taking in the soft, exquisite beauty of her body, the way her curves flow into pure feminine energy.

"You're a goddess," I tell her in awe, and I mean it. "I wish I could sculpt you."

I decide to do so with my hands. I kneel on the bed, looming over her, and start tracing the lines of her body with my fingers, traveling to no destination in particular. My dick is still throbbing and hard as hell, pressed against the soft flesh of her hip, but I'm enjoying the torture.

I touch her neck, the crook of her shoulder, over her collarbones, down between her breasts, her skin especially soft there. Then under her breasts, feeling the curve and the lush weight of them.

I cup them and squeeze gently, and she moans, her breath coming in quick gasps now. I don't linger too long, instead trailing down to her ribs, then along the smooth skin of her stomach. She feels like a dream.

Then I'm moving between her legs, parting them with my hands as I kneel before her. Her cunt is glistening with wetness, and she's whimpering softly as I gaze at it hungrily.

I can smell the heady scent of sex in the air, and all I want to do is devour her. But for now, all I allow myself is one long swipe of my tongue up from her entrance to just below her clit.

She cries out and bucks against me, pushing herself closer to my mouth so that I have no choice but to continue licking and sucking at her soft flesh until she's writhing in pleasure under me while begging me wordlessly never to stop.

I could do this all day. All night. Just this slow, teasing consumption of her, taking in every single ripe inch of her.

"James," she says through a heady whisper. "I want you inside me."

I look up at her then; the hunger in my eyes must match the hunger that I see in hers. I want to be inside her too, but not before I get one last taste of her sweetness.

So I lean down, burying my face between her thighs and

licking and sucking at that deliciously wet cunt until she's sobbing with pleasure and begging me for more.

And when she can't take it anymore, when she's screaming my name as I bring her over the edge, only then do I finally allow myself to sink into her warm depths. She feels like heaven around me as we move together slowly at first and then faster, harder, until nothing else exists but us and our primal need for each other.

In that moment there is nothing sweeter than being with this woman. Nothing more exhilarating or satisfying or right than feeling the force of our bodies colliding in wild abandon while we come together.

There is sadness and grief and pain, but there's also hope. Hope that this doesn't have to end here, that it doesn't have to stay hidden, that perhaps we can continue like this together in some way. I have my doubts; I don't see how Magnus would ever be okay with the two of us together, and with the way that Laila is sometimes, the way she closes up, I can't tell if that's something she'd want. I fear that if I ever threw it all away for her—my job, my reputation—she would ghost me sooner or later. I just never know where I stand.

Focus, I tell myself. It's not the time to worry, not when I'm so deep inside her. It's like the two of us are moving as one.

And so I focus on the way her nails are digging into my back, the way she's moving underneath me, the way she's moaning my name like it's a prayer.

My orgasm comes for me with no warning, and I feel her tense around me and shudder, and that's enough to push me over the edge the rest of the way, my grip tightening, a hoarse cry escaping my mouth. I come inside her, feeling her roll her hips against me, wanting to take all of me in, wanting it all.

"Oh god," I whisper into her ear as we settle, tingles of bliss still shooting up and down my legs. "I could stay inside you forever."

She laughs a little, a breathy sound compared to her usually boisterous one.

I kiss her neck tenderly, feeling overcome by things I don't even want to unpack.

"I'm serious, Laila," I say, wondering if she'll ever take me seriously. "I never want to let you go."

She doesn't say anything, just stares at me with those big green eyes.

Those eyes suddenly go wide. "We didn't . . . a condom."

Oh fuck. The thought hadn't even entered my mind.

"I'm clean," I tell her. "Clean bill of health before I came here. It's part of the job. And I haven't been with anyone but you."

She exhales through her nose in relief, as if she really believed I was gallivanting around Oslo.

"I'm on the pill," she says. "Was actually thinking of switching up to an IUD at some point. But yeah."

I smile at her and kiss her forehead. It's early enough in the day still that we could go for a hike like she suggested, but right now I could easily drift off to sleep in her arms. Before I can finish another thought, I'm out.

Eighteen

. . . .

LAILA

I WAKE UP TO KNOCKING AT MY DOOR. I'M STILL UNDER the covers, wondering for a moment where I am, then throw them back, squinting at the window where gray light comes in through the bottom of the curtains. Did I sleep in?

The knocking continues. Sounds more like pounding from tiny fists, halfway down the door. I grab my phone and peer at the time. I slept in a little but not that much.

"Bjorn," I hear Ella's hushed and annoyed voice on the other side of the door, and the knocking stops. Oh boy. Kid woke up full of beans.

I sigh and decide to get out of bed anyway. Even though everyone usually sleeps in here, I should be getting up earlier. It's funny, just a week away in Todalen and my body has already adjusted to that schedule. In fact, it adjusted to that schedule a little too well. Sex, crying, sex, hiking, sex, drinking, sex . . . on repeat.

I go to the sink and splash water on my face, hoping that will wake me up and stop my daydreaming. But I can't help it.

Even though last week was the hardest time of my life—saying goodbye to my grandmother like that—it was also the happiest time of my life. It's so odd to feel that way, so *wrong*, and the guilt is strong. I want to just drown in my grief because it really is the most overpowering thing, like it's changing every single molecule in my body.

But that's not the only change that's happening to me. While the sorrow rewrites me, something else is setting another course.

I think I'm falling in love with James.

How can I grieve the loss of the greatest and closest person to me, the one who has been there since the day I was born, while falling in love with him? How does the heart hold that kind of space? How can two opposites exist inside each other like this? Many times over I've heard that grief is love, that we grieve because we have all this love and nowhere for it to go. And yet that doesn't seem to encompass what grief is. It is love, but it's also fathomless pain. It's a complex, nebulous thing that makes a home in your chest, and it stays there, letting itself be known every waking second of every day. The loss cuts you so deep that the grief is rooted in the wound.

But then there's love. And that too has roots. That too slowly takes over your life until it also wants to be known every second of every day. Grief and love; sorrow and hope. They're both turning my world upside down.

I exhale heavily, patting my face dry with a towel and slathering on moisturizer, my skin flaky from the cold. All I know is that everything is so damn complicated right now.

That's your own fault for having sex with him again, I tell myself in the mirror.

And again and again. My god, it was like the moment I had James's body on top of mine, the moment he was inside me, the moment he was drowning me in pleasure, I became addicted to him. I know it's a cliché thing to say, but it's true. It was like, for once, I felt myself just giving all my fears and insecurities away. I was letting the walls down and letting him in. Maybe not all the way, but enough to let me feel. To feel what it's like if I just exhale around him.

The ridiculous part of all this is that I've been here before. I've fallen for him before.

I brush my teeth slowly, feeling the emotions creep up through me again. The tears come, and I let them. I'm learning not to push the sadness away. I did that as a child, and it only fucked me up.

I cry for a few moments, ugly sobs that I keep quiet, and then it's over and I feel drained, like I could crawl back into bed. I know Ella and Magnus have been giving me sympathetic looks and winces since I got back. They told me I can have time off, but I just want to get back to work. Thank god my job doesn't involve anything like writing or important administrative work, because the brain fog is no joke. Half the time I have a hard time remembering my name.

When I glance back in the mirror, my eyes are red, puffy, full of deep sadness, and there are new fine lines around my mouth and eyes. Great. So grief ages you too. *Thanks, Grandma.*

I reapply my moisturizer, put on some heavy concealer and mascara, then get dressed. Bjorn is up and at them, and I'm sure Ella needs the help.

I step outside my room, hearing Bjorn in the kitchen, with Ella talking to him in hushed tones, the smell of coffee and baked goods wafting out. I poke my head around the door.

"I'm so sorry," Ella says when she sees me, sitting at the table with a cup of coffee and looking as tired as I feel. "I didn't mean for him to wake you."

"It's okay," I say, watching Bjorn happily eating a banana.

"I made the mistake of telling the boys last night that today you would finally take them to the Fram Museum, and Bjorn barely slept at all."

"You wanted me to take them today?" I ask.

She frowns unhappily. "Oh, I'm sorry. I should have consulted with you first. It's just that I promised them at Christmas we would go, and they've been asking ever since. I have some work for my environmental society to do all week long, to prepare for the unveiling of the new boat we got, otherwise I would go with you."

I raise my hand. "Honestly I would be happy to take them." I give Bjorn a smile. "When I was little, all I wanted to do was come down to Oslo and go to the museum."

"You never went?" he asks between mouthfuls of banana.

"I couldn't. It was just my grandmother taking care of me, and Oslo was so far." And my own parents never took me anywhere. I never got to do anything fun like go to amusement parks or visit museums or toboggan hills or take pony rides, the stuff that all the kids I went to school with would do. Once my childhood friend Sinova took me along with her family to a play center in Trondheim out of pity, and she avoided me after that.

"Well, it has that new exhibition," Ella explains. "With the boat inside the museum, all interactive."

"Polar bears!" Bjorn roars, making claws with his hands.

Ella laughs. "And yes, polar bears. It looks amazing. We just haven't gone yet."

"First time for everyone, then," I say, making my way over to the kettle to put it on for my instant coffee. I've wanted to see the new exhibition too. I heard you can explore all the parts of the old ship to see what a polar vessel was like back in the day. It will at least be a welcome distraction.

"Of course James will go with you," Ella adds.

I freeze for a moment, then grab my coffee mug. "Does he know that?"

"He will," she says, sounding pleased.

I force myself to play it cool. Since we've been back from Todalen, we haven't quite been avoiding each other, but there's this unspoken agreement—I think—that what happened there can't happen here. I mean, it just can't. We can't do the Fairfaxes sneaking-around thing all over again.

It's just damn hard.

When James eventually gets up, he looks surprised to hear his job for the day. Surprised and a little excited, if I'm being honest. I don't blame him. Since he took on the role as Ella and the kids' PPO, he's been with Magnus most of the time, since neither Ella nor the kids go out very much. There was the trip to the kikut, of course, then our visit to the church in Oslo for the Christmas Eve procession (which was with the rest of the royal family as well, and I finally met the king, queen, and all his sisters, save for one who is in Spain; they're all lovely, although the king seems quite frail). That went fine, and even Bjorn was on his best behavior.

But this would be the first outing with just James and me. I have no idea how the kids are going to be. Tor is calm now, but he might cry the whole time (let's be honest, I might too), and Bjorn, well . . . no comment.

While James and I are in the hall putting on our coats and scarves, our eyes meet above Ella's head as she's crouching down and dressing the boys. He raises his brows as if to say, *This is going to be interesting.*

I give him the same look in return, hoping I don't look like a lovesick sap since there are a few butterflies loose in my chest.

We go outside, Ottar tasked with driving us, and pile into the car. Ottar talks on and on about the museum's history, better than any tour, I'm sure, and it only gets the kids more excited.

I have to admit, it feels like a family outing. As if James and I are the parents and Bjorn and Tor are our children, and our friend is dropping us off. It's a nice feeling. Don't get me wrong, not nice enough for me to suddenly want kids, but it's comforting all the same.

The museum is just outside the city center, and by the time Ottar pulls up, the kids are raring to go. Ottar tells us he'll be in the city and can come get us at any time, so we get out of the car and I take both of the kids' hands while James effortlessly steps into bodyguard duty.

"How do we do this?" I whisper to James as Ottar drives off. To be honest, during the Christmas event, there were so many PPOs swarming around the church it was hard to keep track.

"I'll stay behind you," he says in a low voice, and damn if that isn't a turn-on the way he says it. "That way I can spot any potential threats."

My blood runs cold at that. I know it's his job to protect the boys—and me, I guess—but it's hard to imagine how anyone would want to hurt them.

"Don't worry," he adds. "We're here to have fun. Right, boys?"

"Yeah!" Bjorn yelps, pulling away to run toward the building. My grip is strong, though, and I hold him back. This isn't going to be easy.

We enter the museum, which is this gigantic A-frame building, and we're automatically immersed in the experience, even while we're at the cashier. I pay for our tickets, and the museum worker seems to recognize the boys, but she doesn't say much. She also seems to recognize James and can't stop giving him shy glances. She's gotta be sixteen or something, so it's pretty cute.

It's a Saturday, so the place is packed with kids and tourists alike. With the weather being unseasonably cold lately, and with huge dumps of snow, wandering inside the museum seems like a nice, warm way to spend the day.

But also, chaotic as hell, and we're only adding to the chaos.

"I hate crowds," I grumble under my breath as we walk over to the ship.

"Me too," James says, even though he must be so used to them with his job.

The middle of the museum is this three- or four-story space where a giant polar ship, the *Fram*, sits. It is huge, taking up the entire length and height of the museum. On all sides of it are more exhibitions, such as ice caves and igloos, and realistic polar bear and seal statues, all showcasing what it was like to travel through the Arctic back in the day. At the very top of the building, above the deck of the ship, is a huge wraparound screen that mimics the waves and the weather, so when you're on the top deck of the ship you can pretend you're out in the Arctic Ocean.

"Oh, I want to go up on the top deck," I say, not meaning to say it out loud.

"Look at you," James says in a low voice from behind me. "You're loving this."

I am. I suddenly wish I didn't have the kids with me so I could explore the whole museum on my own, pretend to be a kid again myself. But being the nanny, and also an adult, I have to live it through Bjorn's and Tor's eyes.

And Bjorn wants to see the polar bears and go through the ice.

And Tor very much does not want to see any bears.

"Nooooo!" he screeches as Bjorn tries to pull us in that direction.

"Bjorn," I warn him, pulling him back. "Your brother doesn't want to see the bears right now."

"But I do! He can stay with James."

"That's not how this works," I tell him. "There's only me here taking care of you. We have to compromise."

From the look on Bjorn's face, I don't think he's ever compromised before.

I sigh. "Look. We will go through the ice caves, and you can take a quick peek at the bears."

"I don't think that's a good idea," James says, looking out for Tor.

I glance at him over my shoulder. His jaw is firm, eyes sharp, posture straighter than it's ever been. It takes a lot to keep from swooning. What an inappropriate time to want to jump someone.

"We'll see how it goes," I tell him quietly. I just want to calm Bjorn and Tor down for now.

So we head off toward the sides of the museum where the interactive exhibitions are, going up the steps to the first floor and marveling at the ship as we walk down the length. I also want to read about the history in each exhibit along the wall, but Bjorn is so headstrong I don't have the time.

"Don't you want to go on the top deck?" I ask him, but he won't have it. He pouts and shakes his head vigorously, and I know this usually leads to a meltdown. He knows this too.

"I want to go on the boat," Tor says in a small voice.

Finally I have to put my foot down. I stop, James nearly running into the back of me, and pull Bjorn toward me, putting my hands on his shoulders. "Bjorn, wait. We can't only do what you want to do. We will see the bears, but the rest of us, myself included, would like to go on the top deck and go through the boat."

He's not looking me in the eye, and his face is going red, but he nods.

Phew.

We walk up another flight of stairs until we can access the top deck of the ship, just as ominous music fills the air. We step on board, the lights dim, and the screen that takes up the top of the building comes to life with images of glaciers.

It's crowded on the deck of the ship, but we manage to find a bench to sit on to watch the show. Bjorn keeps getting up, unable to sit still, so I let him fidget around me, while Tor is entranced. James isn't watching the screen, but he is watching around us, always on alert.

Then the museum gets dark, and the waves start to build until it feels like we're in the middle of a storm. It is a bit intense, so Tor starts to cry, just as a group of tourists straight off a tour bus gathers around us, speaking loudly in a foreign language.

"Okay, let's go," I tell Tor, getting to my feet. But when I go to grab Bjorn's hand, he's not there.

Oh my god.

"Bjorn!" I yell, which makes James flip around, his focus having been on the push of the crowd.

"Where did he go?" James says.

"I don't know, I had him right here." Wasn't I holding his hand? But then Tor started crying and I just kind of forgot. This fucking brain of mine.

And now Bjorn's gone.

I pick up Tor and start calling for him, but the tourists are everywhere and I can't see him.

James is fast, though. He's parting the crowd, eyes like a hawk searching every inch, and then he suddenly starts running off the ship.

Oh my god. Oh my god, Bjorn has been taken. Someone took him, stole him. I'll never see him again. I'm responsible.

Now I'm crying along with Tor. I can't help it.

I watch as James runs along the edge of the third floor, away from the exit, and that's when I see him.

Bjorn.

He's attempting to climb on top of the taxidermy polar bears that are posed at the end of the museum, on a ledge a few feet off the ground. James appears just in time, snatching Bjorn up before he reaches for the bear to pull himself up. Had Bjorn actually climbed up, the chances of him falling would have been high.

I breathe out the biggest sigh of relief, but my heart is still thundering in my chest and I feel sick.

I manage to work my way through the tourists—no one paying me much attention, thank god—and reach James, who has Bjorn in his arms . . . Bjorn, who is kicking and screaming and calling so much attention to himself. That's when I notice a few people taking pictures or video, and I am so scared that someone actually got a photo of Bjorn climbing up on the polar bear. Oh my god, I'm going to get fired.

"I think it's time to go," James says.

I don't even feel disappointed about not seeing much of the museum. We need to go right away, get far from prying eyes, and figure out what the hell happened.

I nod, and James doesn't let go of Bjorn or pass him to me. He just carries him out while pulling his phone out of his pocket and calling Ottar.

"He'll be right here," he tells me as we step outside the building.

It's starting to snow lightly, but I don't want to wait inside for the car. I know that people are starting to talk, and soon they'll start hounding us for pictures and the paparazzi will arrive.

I must be going into dissociative shock because James says gently, "Hey. It's okay."

I blink at him just as the car pulls up.

"What happened?" Ottar asks, coming around and looking concerned and out of breath. "You sounded serious."

"I wanted to see the bears!" Bjorn yells through angry tears as we shuffle him into the car. "They wouldn't let me, so I went on my own!"

Ottar gives us a look like, *Oh boy.*

That's an understatement.

WHEN WE GET back to the estate, we have to explain the whole thing to Magnus and Ella. We all sit down in the living room, and James takes the lead. I'm so grateful for that; all I can do is feel awful inside, shrinking smaller and smaller inside myself, wringing my hands together.

"So how did this happen?" Magnus says, looking strikingly serious.

Not that I blame him. I can't imagine how it must feel for him and Ella to think that their child could end up the subject of tabloid news.

"I messed up," James says.

"No," I interject. "You didn't. I messed up."

"Laila," he warns. "I'm the PPO. My job is to have eyes on the boys at all times." He looks at Magnus. "Please forgive me. I didn't happen to have my eyes on him in that moment. I won't make any excuses."

"I will!" I say, looking at Magnus and Ella imploringly. "My head . . . I've been so out of it with this brain fog, and Bjorn . . . he really wanted to see the polar bears, but Tor didn't want to, so I wanted him to compromise by getting us to go on the deck of the ship. We sat down to watch the screens, but Bjorn was so restless, he couldn't sit still. Then the storm part came and Tor got scared, just as all these tourists came from out of nowhere, crowding around us. I guess I was caught up in calming Tor—when I looked up, Bjorn was gone."

"I should have been watching him," James says with his chin raised. "It's on me. I was scanning the tourists for a threat instead."

"Which is your job, you know," Magnus says. "Your job is to protect Ella, Laila, and the boys. Not to watch them. It's not your job; that's Laila's job."

Oh fuck.

"And, Laila," Magnus says, his eyes kind, voice becoming gentler. "I know you. I know you love these boys, and I know they are hard to handle. Very hard sometimes. Mistakes happen. Don't beat yourself up over it. The issue isn't so much that you weren't paying full attention, and in your current state I can't blame you at all. It's that . . ." He sighs, running his hand over his face and looking to Bjorn. "Bjornsy. Why did you do that?"

"I wanted to see the bears," he says, crossing his arms in a huff.

"But not everything is about what you want," Magnus explains.

"Yes it is. I'm a prince," he says.

"Oh, there it is," Ella says with a sigh, sitting back on the couch. "I knew this day would come."

Magnus gets up and kneels in front of Bjorn. "I'm a prince too, Bjorn. But I still have to follow the rules. I still have to listen to people. I used to be like you, you know. I did what I wanted, all the time, not caring. And in the end all it did was hurt people. And when I realized that I hurt people, that ended up hurting me. I had to change. Look, I know it's busy up in that brain of yours." He reaches out and gently taps Bjorn's temple. "It's the same up in mine. I know you have a million thoughts going on at once that never turn off. I know it channels itself into this endless energy that makes you itch, you know? Like all over your body from the inside out, and that you want to run around and scream because it's the only way to let it out."

Bjorn stares at him, shifting back and forth in his seat. "You feel that way too?"

Magnus nods. "I used to feel it more. When I was your age. It changes as you get older, but the thoughts? Those stay the same. Look, son, we don't blame you for doing things that are wrong sometimes. We aren't mad at you. But what you did today . . . it was very dangerous. You could have hurt yourself, or even worse. And, Laila, she cares about you very much and only wants what's best for you, and you frightened her half to death. Same goes for James. For Tor. And same goes for me and your mother."

Bjorn nods. "I'm sorry," he says, staring down at his feet that are swinging against the couch.

"I am too," Magnus says, kissing the top of his forehead. He gets up and looks at me. "Laila, you've done an amazing job. But I'm ordering you to take the rest of the day off and get some rest."

I shake my head. "I'm fine."

"You're not, and that's okay," he says. "I'm not trying to punish you. You're like family to me now, and therefore I just want you well. Okay?"

I nod, feeling I don't have much choice.

But even though I retire to my room while Magnus and Ella take care of the kids, it feels wrong to be alone. My thoughts are so jumbled over the scare at the museum, over my feelings for James, over the loss of my grandmother, that I have a hard time sitting still with them.

This must be what it's like in Bjorn's and Magnus's brains, I think. The constant chatter, the thoughts that won't stop bouncing, the need to move and make it go away.

So I put down the book that I spent twenty minutes trying to read and get up, heading back down the hall. I hear the kids and Ella in the playroom and pause in the doorway.

"Is everything okay?" Ella asks as she tries to make a puzzle of a woodland scene while Bjorn races a car into whatever Tor is building with blocks.

I nod. "Yes. I'm fine. Just turns out I don't take orders very well. Do you mind if I . . . ?" I gesture to the room.

"Of course not," Ella says, patting the floor beside her. "You can help me finish this puzzle before Bjorn destroys it."

I sit down and help Ella, and it's not long before Bjorn runs his toy car over the puzzle. To be fair, he was saying, "Beep beep, beep beep," for a good minute before the collision.

After that I tell Ella I'm fine to take care of the kids, and I end up in there with them for most of the night, building a fort in the corner with sheets and pillows.

"Laila," Bjorn says to me as the three of us sit in the fort, finding a moment of calm.

"Yes, Bjorn?"

He looks at me with his big eyes. "Are you mad at me?"

The sincerity in his voice breaks my heart. "What? No, sweetie. Not even a little."

He looks down at his paint-stained hands. "You sounded so mad at me."

"Only worried," I tell him. "Sometimes it sounds the same because our emotions are heightened and get the best of us. But it all comes from a place of love."

He nods at that, worrying his lip between his teeth. "I'm going to try to be good," he says after a moment, announcing it like a New Year's resolution.

I have doubts it will last long, but I still tell him I appreciate it.

"Bjorn, Tor, come here, please," Magnus's voice rings out through the house. Bjorn gives me a worried look, like he's still in trouble, and he and Tor scramble out of the fort, running out of the room.

I sigh and lean back against one of the cushions, the top of the fort sagging toward the middle, just as I see a pair of legs standing outside the entrance.

"Permission to enter the fort," James says in his serious bodyguard voice, and a second later I see his face as he bends down.

I raise my brow. "Are we talking this actual fort, or is this sexual innuendo?"

"Both," he says, getting down on his knees and crawling inside. His hulking frame barely fits, and his head snags the sagging sheet ceiling, causing it to collapse.

"Oh no," he says dryly as he sits beside me, the sheet falling between our faces. "It's a cave-in."

He goes to lift up the sheet, but I reach out and grab it, keeping it in place.

"I think it's best I don't see your face," I tell him.

"Ouch."

"I'm feeling a little emotionally vulnerable," I admit against my better judgment. I drop my hand, and James continues to raise the sheet, holding it up so he can look at me.

He's too handsome for his own good and far too close to me in a setting that's a little too private.

"You're right," he says, swallowing thickly as his eyes get that heavy-lidded, lustful look. "It was easier when I couldn't see you."

Then he leans in and cups my face in his hands and kisses me.

I let out a soft whine, a startled noise, my mouth opening to his for just a moment, one sweet moment where his tongue slides against mine, and I'm ready to throw it all away again, the sheet falling down on our heads. If anyone were to come in here there would be no doubt what we were doing.

I break off before we get carried away, placing my hand on his chest to keep him back. I can feel the quick beat of his heart under my palm.

"I'm having a bloody awful time trying to stay away from you," he says, but I keep my hand pressed on his hard chest.

"Me too," I admit quietly. "Whose silly idea was it to leave all the sex behind in Todalen?"

"Your silly idea," he says, taking my hand in his and raising it to his lips. "But feel free to negate it at any time."

I give him a quick smile and take my hand back, putting distance between us. "I think we should probably vacate the fort."

He sighs and looks around. "Are you sure? There's something comforting about this. Maybe it's because I didn't really get to do this as a wee lad, but I feel safe in here. Safer than I should, considering we're sitting ducks."

I agree with him. While sitting alone in my bedroom felt empty and cold, sitting in the fort felt comforting, like being sheltered by strong, warm arms, even before James came in.

But now that he's here, that feeling of comfort skyrockets.

And that's a dangerous thing.

He stares at me for a moment before he crawls back out, and I see the want and longing in his gaze, and I feel it too, because I want him the exact same way and I can't have him.

I can only have stolen kisses and pretend that's enough to sustain me.

Nineteen

. . . .

LAILA

"YOU KNOW WHAT YOUR PROBLEM IS?" LADY JANE ASKS. I look up from my book to find her pointing at me with an accusatory carrot.

Even if I don't say anything, she's going to tell me what my problem is. I slide the bookmark inside the pages and close it, putting it on the table. I was having a quiet lunch to myself here in the kitchen, just me and my book, a mug of tea, and some cheese and crackers, but then Lady Jane showed up, on some carrot stick diet, and hasn't stopped talking since.

"What is my problem?" I ask her.

"You need to get laid."

Thank god I don't have a mouthful of tea, or I would have spit it out.

"Excuse me?"

Her smile curves around the carrot she's eating. "You heard me. You need to get laid."

I attempt to swallow, willing my cheeks not to go pink, but they feel a little hot already. "Why do you say that?" I say after a moment.

"Because," she says, gesturing to the kitchen. "Look at where you are. It's Sunday afternoon, your one day off, and you're here. In this bloody kitchen. Reading a book!"

I roll my eyes. "I happen to like my book."

"You should be out there." She jabs her carrot toward the window. "Downtown. In the bars. Meeting men. Or women. Anyone. Hooking up, having fun."

I give her a steady look. "I'm quite happy the way I am."

"Nah," she says dismissively. "You're becoming one complicated Norsewoman."

"What?"

"I know this is a tough job, I really do, but you're cracking a little under pressure."

I open my mouth to say something, but sympathy flashes in her eyes and she quickly carries on.

"I know you just lost your grandmother. I know how hard that is. That's why I worry about you, darling. I don't think it's healthy for a woman your age to have no friends, to be cooped up in this house all alone."

"I'm not alone," I protest. "You're here."

"I'm an old woman," she cries out, laughing. "You need friends your age. Or maybe a man who can show you a good time."

I know what she's getting at. The problem is, I'm too tired to try to deflect. Because she's right. I do need a friend. I need someone to talk to. And Lady Jane is that friend.

I push back my chair and stand up. "I'm going for a walk. Care to come along?"

She frowns at me, her brows tangling with her bangs. I've never gone for a walk with Lady Jane before.

"Sure," she says, putting her carrot sticks back in the glass container. "Let's go."

It's not long before we've got our boots and coats on and are stepping out into the snow. It's sunny today, and I wish I'd brought my sunglasses.

We walk off down the driveaway and toward the road. It's been quiet here the last few weeks now that the holidays are over. Magnus went into Oslo with Einar and Ottar for fun, and even though it's James's day off, he went along with them anyway. Ella and the boys are somewhere in the house.

"So what's on your mind?" Lady Jane asks me. She has short legs compared to me and has to move them twice as fast to keep up. "Are you about to confide some secret in me? Because I know I have a reputation as a bigmouth, but I promise I can keep it in the vault. Believe it or not, I have many people's secrets there."

"Good to know," I tell her, giving her a stern look. "Because what I'm about to tell you, you can't tell anyone."

"I promise," she says, making the sign of the cross over her heart. "Swear to it."

I take in a deep breath, trying to figure out how to say it when there is so damn much to say. "I'm in love with James," I blurt out.

Well, shit. I definitely didn't mean it to come out like that.

Lady Jane stops dead in her tracks, an incredulous look coming over her face. "You what? You're in love with him?"

I press my lips together and nod, afraid of what else I'm going to say. I mean, I don't even think I knew I was in love with him for certain, just that I was falling for him. And yet it just came tumbling out. "I think, anyway."

"No, you are," she says. "Oh, I see it now, darling. I see it. I really thought you were just going to tell me you were sleeping with him, though."

"I'm doing that too. Or I was. We keep . . . I keep trying to break things off."

"What for? You have a man like that giving you some loving, you hang on to that."

"It's complicated," I try to explain. "For one, it's not allowed."

She shrugs. "I can see how it would be frowned upon, but it's not like there is a bloody rule book of dos and don'ts . . ." She trails off. "Actually, maybe there is."

"Pretty sure there is," I tell her as we head down a path through the trees, snow falling off the branches around us like icing sugar. "There is protocol. Ella mentioned it to me when I got hired, just as an aside. The king and queen are especially sensitive about scandals since Prince Magnus is a reformed bad boy with the sex tape and all the gossip from before he met Ella."

"Does it say anything about shagging the bodyguards?" she asks. "Because I've got my eye on Einar." She wags her brows.

I burst out laughing. "I don't think so. But even so, I know I would get in trouble."

"Right," she says thoughtfully, brushing her bangs out of her eyes. "So I suppose that's something to worry about."

"Yeah. It is. I mean, we got away with it once. I don't think we'll get away with it again," I say.

"You what? Where? Oh my god. You were shagging up at the Fairfaxes', weren't you?"

I bite back a smile, trying not to look proud, but the last few weeks of *shagging* must be visible on my face.

"You harlot," she cries out, smacking me on the arm. "I knew it! I called it the day he arrived, didn't I?"

"You did."

"So why are you telling me now?"

I shrug. "I guess I trust you. And honestly, back then, I didn't want anything to happen. Things had ended badly between us. I wanted him to stay as far away as possible."

"What happened?"

I run my hand over my face and sigh, looking down at the snow between us. "I did a dumb thing and blurted out how I was feeling, much like I just did with you. I told him I was falling for him, and he just freaked the fuck out and wouldn't talk to me after that."

"James did that?" she asks with an air of disbelief and disappointment. "Fucking men, huh?"

"Yeah. So you can see why I wasn't happy to find out he'd be working alongside me again."

"But now you're sleeping together," she says.

"That's right."

"And you're not just falling for him this time, but you're properly in love with the Scottish bastard?"

"I guess so."

"Hmm," she muses. "I can see why you needed to confide in someone. That's a tough thing to deal with. On the one hand, you're getting all the sex you want, if you want it. On the other, you're in love with him, and if you tell him, he might end up running again."

"Exactly. I'm fucked."

She nods. "Yes, it appears you might be. But do you have any idea of how he feels?"

I shake my head and stop walking, looking at the snowy clearing, the tall pines around us. I take in a deep breath. "No clue."

"Well, is he any different now with you than he was then?"

"Yes," I say, and I don't even have to think about it. "He's very different. He's more open, more vulnerable, more affectionate, more . . . involved. Tender. Like he doesn't just want my body; like he wants all of me. Maybe my heart and my soul, I don't know. It's too much to ask for when it comes to him because I still see that fear inside him, the fear of getting hurt, of losing himself again."

She lets out a long exhale, giving me a sympathetic look. "Well, that may be your answer there. You were falling for him before, now you're in love with him. Isn't it possible that this time it's different for him too? You're not going to know unless you tell him."

I shake my head, my heart feeling constricted. "No. I can't do that. I can't go through that again."

"Then it looks like you're going to have to find out how he feels, one way or another," she says. "Why not pull him aside one night and see?"

I smile. "You know that pulling him aside will only lead to sex."

"So then at least you're getting something out of it. Come

on, let's go back and make some tea. My toes are frozen. I'm not made for this bloody weather."

DESPITE THE PEP talk with Lady Jane about James, I don't actually work up the nerve to pull him aside and talk to him about how I feel. It's been a week now, and I've done nothing to deal with it, my love for him turning into a festering mess inside me, until I must be bleeding out through my pores. Every time I see him now I feel like I can't breathe and my gut churns and my heart beats wildly, as if to remind me that it's still here and it wants what it wants. I'm lovesick, and it sucks, and I don't think James has any idea.

But today we're going out with the family to Holmenkollen, the ski jump in Oslo where one of Ella's environmental charities is holding a competition, and I'm looking forward to being out of the house and around civilization. The more distance I can put between James and me, the better, if I'm going to be a wreck around him. And once he's in bodyguard mode, he becomes even more untouchable.

We ride to the event in two separate cars, but because I'm with the boys, James is with me. Even being in the close confines of a car with him makes my blood run hot, despite the fact that Bjorn and Tor are yelling and bouncing around in their seats at the excitement of seeing some ski jumping.

"Ah, field trips," James says as we get out of the car, breathing in deeply as he looks around. Holmenkollen is located at the top of the five-hundred-meter mountain that overlooks Oslo, giving stupendous views of the city and harbor. Up here the snow is deeper, the sun brighter, and the air fresh and cold. There's a large black wooden chapel up here as well, which we went to for the Christmas ceremony, and next to it the Royal Lodge where the king and queen spend a lot of their holidays.

James gives me a small smile before he slips on his sunglasses, then his face turns into a mask, and I know he won't say another word to me until we're back in the car going home.

I bring my attention to the boys and do what I can to keep them in the background and out of the way as we follow Magnus and Ella through the crowd toward the podium, where an even larger crowd has gathered. We Norwegians love everything to do with skiing, and this sort of event is no exception, especially at Holmenkollen, which is serviced by the Oslo Metro line, making it easy for anyone to come and visit.

To be honest, the crowds are making me a little uneasy. The distraction from James feels good at first, but after a while there are just too many people and too much to focus on. I don't know if it's because I've gotten used to the isolation at the estate, but today seems especially overwhelming.

And I'm not the only one who feels it. Bjorn is starting to get anxious, and even sweet Tor is getting fussy and squirmy. I hold on to both of them with an iron grip, keeping them far behind their parents as Ella starts to make her speech about what the charity did for the Norwegian environment last year and the new goals for this year. The whole event is basically an excuse to get the public reinterested in Ella and Norway's environmental initiative. Despite being a country funded mainly by oil and gas, Norway already has some hearty subsidies when it comes to electric cars, making it the country with the most electric cars per capita in the world. The number of Teslas on the street rivals California.

"I want to go on the ski jump," Bjorn cries out, tugging me in that direction.

"Bjorn," I say, bending down to whisper to him. "You know you have to be quiet while your mother is talking. Remember last week when you said you would behave."

He grumbles something under his breath, and I do not want to know what it is, but at least he calms down for a moment. I take the reprieve to glance around. James is standing just to the side of us and behind while Einar is at the side of Magnus and Ella. Both of them seem especially cagey today, their heads constantly swiveling. There are so many people here, and it's only now that I've noticed a few protesters being held back by police, members of the oil and gas industry who aren't happy with all the new environmental policy, no thanks to Princess Ella.

Ella pays them no mind and continues with her speech. When it's over, Magnus leans in to the microphone and announces that the ski-jumping competition has officially begun, and everyone starts clapping.

"The boring bit is over now," Bjorn says, tugging at my hand, and I have to bite back a laugh at that.

I put a hand on Bjorn's shoulder and start guiding him away from the crowd, with him in front of me. "Okay, let's go see the ski jump."

I squeeze Tor's hand to get him to follow, and as I do so, I glance over my shoulder at James. It's so hard not to look at him, and I don't expect him to be looking my way.

But he *is* looking my way. I can't tell exactly what he's

looking at under his sunglasses, but he's facing me, and his brows start to come together like he's about to be upset or yell or something.

Instinctively I whirl around, looking at the crowd, just in time to see a tall, skinny man with a scarred face approaching me. He's coming fast, his strides assured, and in his eyes I see only malice and a frenzied mind.

He means us harm, I think absently, fear numbing my brain.

He's coming straight for us, not slowing down, and I see in his hand the glint of a knife.

I grip Bjorn's shoulder hard enough for him to cry out, and I quickly shove him behind me, putting myself between the man and the boys. I hear someone in the crowd shout, "He's got a knife!" Or maybe it's me who says it. All I know is that I can't let any harm come to my kids, even if it means I'm about to be stabbed.

The man opens his mouth in a garbled scream, spittle flying, the knife raised, and while everyone seems to be moving around us, no one seems fast enough to prevent the man from stabbing me right in the heart.

Except for James.

Suddenly he's all I see, his big strong body in his fine tailored suit throwing himself in front of me and taking the brunt of the attacker.

I scream, stumbling backward, terrified that the man just stabbed James, and there are hands behind me, holding me up. The boys are screaming and Magnus and Ella are yelling as Einar swoops in to hustle them away from danger.

And all I can think of is James, my James, and I watch as he wrestles the attacker to the ground, bending the man's arms so that the knife is dropped. James makes quick work of him, pinning the man down with his knee, holding his hands above his head, and for one horribly inappropriate moment I imagine James using that move in the bedroom, before the harsh reality of what's actually happening slams back in.

"Laila," Ottar says from behind me, grabbing my shoulders and pulling me and the boys away, but I'm fighting against him, trying to see if James is okay.

"James," I cry out, a choked sound. "Is he okay?"

"I'm sure he's fine," Ottar says. "Please come with me. That's an order."

I've never had Ottar order me around before, and the gravity in his voice makes me listen. Lady Jane then swoops in and takes Bjorn and Tor, who are bawling uncontrollably, absolutely terrified.

We're quickly shuffled away into the car, doors locked and guarded, waiting for the news about James and the attacker. Eventually Bjorn and Tor calm down a little, thanks to Lady Jane trying to tell them a story. I'm absolutely useless until I know what has happened to James. If he was stabbed, if he was hurt in any way, I don't know what I'd do with myself. I'm suddenly filled with remorse over not having told him my true feelings earlier.

Finally, I see Einar, with Magnus and Ella behind him, walking toward the car, and behind them I see James.

He looks the same as before, his jacket a little rumpled, but no signs of blood or injury. The only difference is the hard set of his jaw and the flexing of a hand at his side, no doubt a product of all the adrenaline that's running through him.

I exhale audibly, relief flooding my body as the doors open

and Magnus and Ella enter the car, reuniting tearfully with the boys and fawning over me. Magnus tells me the man was part of an extremist group and that he meant to kidnap one of the boys in protest of Ella's environmental initiative. James was able to disarm him without incident, and the man is now in police custody.

But though no physical harm came to James, it's when he climbs into the front seat and slides his sunglasses off that I see how affected he is. It's in the way his eyes meet mine and how the man I see staring back at me is full of nothing but fear.

Twenty

LAILA

I CAN'T SLEEP. DESPITE GOING TO BED EARLY AFTER SUCH a traumatizing and exhausting day, I'm lying in bed and going over every single thing that happened, replaying it in my mind like a movie. But instead of just dwelling on the events like a normal person, my mind is creating new events that never even happened.

What if I hadn't put Bjorn behind me in time? What if he had gotten stabbed?

What if James hadn't been fast enough or there was another attacker?

What if the attacker ended up stabbing James fatally?

What if I lost him before I had a chance to tell him I love him?

It does me no good to entertain the what-ifs, yet I can't get my mind to stop. After we got back to the estate, everyone was on edge and wired, and I never got a chance to talk to James afterward, never got a chance to thank him for saving my life, and now I crave his company, his body, like a balm on a wound.

It's much later, past midnight, when I finally hear James getting into his bed, the headboard knocking slightly against the wall. He's been good at trying to be quiet lately and probably doesn't realize I'm still awake.

"James?" I whisper toward the wall.

His throat clears. "Yes?" he asks, sounding surprised.

I press my lips together for a moment, scared. Then I whisper, "Can you come over here?"

A pause. "Yes."

I hear the bed move again, then his door quietly open, the creak of the hardwood floors outside the room, and then the door to my room opens. A crack of light from the hall shows his tall silhouette, then the door closes.

I reach over and flick on the light at my bedside.

He's wearing only thin pajama pants, the dim light casting flattering shadows on his muscles. He stops at the side of the bed and stares down at me, searching my face, brows furrowed. "What's wrong?"

I sit up, staring down at my hands, so damn scared. I don't want to tell him how I'm feeling, but at the same time I need to know how he feels. If it's even possible for him to fall in love with me. I'll hang everything on just the possibility.

"I don't feel like being alone tonight," I manage to say. "Not after what happened."

"Sure," he says softly.

I stare up at him, a strand of hair coming across my eyes, and he reaches out and brushes it away. "You saved my life," I whisper.

He swallows audibly, pain brimming in his eyes, that same pain I saw in the car afterward. Something about this pain scares me. "It's my job," he says, his voice strained.

"I know, but—"

"I don't want to talk about it," he says roughly. "Please."

I understand that. I nod. "Okay."

Then he gets on top of the bed, prowling over me, his knees bracketing me in.

I lean back against the pillow and the headboard as he braces himself up with one hand, the other cupping my cheek. He kisses me, his tongue sliding across my lower lip, taking his time.

I could kiss this man for hours. Just sink into his mouth, let him lead the way. Sparks and joy and desire rush through me, crackling down my spine as the kiss deepens, making my toes curl.

We start off strong, but we quickly grow messy, and aside from the stolen kiss the other week, it's been a lot of avoiding each other, of pretending that we don't want each other, *need* each other, and it's coming to a head. Our lips turn from soft to violent, teeth clashing, a voracious beast inside me wanting to claw its way out.

I want him, I need him.

I love him.

My nightgown is pulled over my head as he hastily tugs off his pants, fully commando. He throws back the covers and then slides his knee between my legs, his fingers curling over the hem of my underwear, yanking them down over my legs quickly, like they're on fire.

Every inch of my skin is alight, my breaths feel short and

feverish, like I can't get enough air and the air that I do get is burning away. I need to have him inside me, need his hands over every part of my body, to put out the flames or kindle them. He makes quick work of me tonight, and for that I'm grateful. He positions himself and pushes into me with a long, hard thrust and I'm gasping again, the air expelled.

"Fuck," I whisper, breath catching. My nails scratch down his back, feeling every inch of him, how warm he is too, and growing warmer by the second as he starts pumping inside me.

His mouth goes to my neck, rough stubble tickling me as he licks and sucks at my skin, every touch and sensation combining the feeling of him hot and hard inside me, making me feel dizzy and elated and alive.

I grab his face, forcing him to look at me. He's been so good at eye contact, but not tonight, not when I want to see him.

There's an awareness in his eyes now, mixing with the determination to get me off, to come. It's like he's seeing me, really seeing me, and I wonder if he knows now. If he knows I love him. I wonder if I don't have to say a word.

He stares at me, a million emotions passing through his eyes, and I'm trying to grab hold and examine each and every one of them, like trying to pluck shooting stars out of the sky. Then he kisses me, the spell broken, groaning breathlessly into my neck as he moves so deep, in and out, hips pumping in expert circles.

I'm so close to coming as it is, but when he reaches between our hot, slick-with-sweat bodies and touches me, I know I don't have a lot of time.

"Fuck, James," I cry out, feeling it come for me, the way my limbs tighten, the pressure building to that sweet and scary point of no return. I just hope I keep my mouth shut.

"Oh god!" I dig my nails into his shoulders, holding on as every other part of me lets go, and then I'm just light and starshine and opening, opening, opening.

My back arches as the orgasm rips through me, my eyes looking up at him just as he starts to come.

The look on his face startles me.

The intensity turns from desire to pleasure to fear as he comes inside me, grunting loudly before his eyes pinch shut, his neck going back. He stiffens, thrusting harder and harder until he stops and shudders, his whole body shaking the bed. He lowers himself on top of me, his face in my neck.

And I know something has changed already.

I can feel it.

The air in the room has become electric, like before a storm.

He knows.

He fucking knows how I feel.

I didn't have to say a word.

"James," I whisper. "Are you okay?"

Please be okay. Please be okay with this.

He doesn't say anything. I can hear him breathing heavily, feel his heart beating fast against mine.

"James," I say again.

He finally lifts his head to look at me, and that look in his eyes is the bearer of bad news. My heart automatically drops.

I try to smile. "Are you okay?" I ask again.

But the fear in his expression doesn't go away. I know that expression so well. I saw it in my head for far too long afterward.

His jaw shuts, the muscles tense, like he's not letting himself say something. He swallows thickly, and then I see the worst look of all cloud his features.

Regret.

He pulls out of me and then gets off the bed, pulling his pajama pants back on. I pull the sheets up to cover myself and then I grab his wrist, holding him in place before he can walk away.

"What is it?" I eke out.

"Laila," he says to me. He blinks, unsure of how to proceed. But this time I don't want to be left in the dark.

"No," I say, shaking my head violently, panic clawing up through my chest, my hands gripping the edge of the sheets. "Don't do this, James. Not now. Not when we're finally figuring this out."

God, *are* we figuring it out? Was it all in my head, this feeling that we were heading in the right direction together, that it was only a matter of time before we decided to take the plunge and be together?

Was I delusional this whole time, just as I had been before?

"I almost lost you today," he says, his tone turning sharp and hard though his eyes hold all the pain. "I almost lost you. What was I thinking? What was I thinking that I could be with you, be with the very woman I have to protect?"

"You're not supposed to protect me. You're there for—"

"For you!" he exclaims, eyes flashing. "For the boys, for Ella, and for you. I saw that man come at you with the knife and all I could think about was you. For a moment it wasn't about the kids and it wasn't about the royals and it wasn't about anyone or anything but you. How can I do my job properly when all I care about is you?"

I'm not sure what to say to that. I press my lips together, my heart pounding wildly, trying to think, trying to figure out how to talk him off this ledge he's on.

"It doesn't matter—"

"It does matter. This is my job, this is my purpose."

"Can't you have both? Can't I be your purpose too?" I ask softly.

"You are my purpose," he says adamantly, running his hands down his face. "And that's the problem. I should have noticed that man well before he reached you. But instead of focusing on the bloody people I was hired to protect—people who feel like friends, who feel like family—I'm losing myself to you. It's unlocked a new level of fear, and I don't think I can go through that. Everything is so messy and complicated now."

"James, I like it messy and complicated. I like what we have." God, I hate the pathetic tone of my voice, like I'm almost begging him to reconsider. I'm having déjà vu, and it's making me sick.

"I just can't risk you getting hurt," he says with a shake of his head. "Everyone I've ever cared for has left me. I almost lost you today, and I already feel like my heart is being torn apart, like I'm splintering. I don't think I can go through this, having you so close if it means putting you in harm's way."

"I'm not asking to get married to you, James, or have your babies. I'm not even asking you to be my boyfriend. I'm just . . ."

"What?" he asks, looking wild. "You're just what? What do you want, then? What do you want from me?"

My chin starts to tremble, and I know that if I lay out the truth, if I tell him how I truly feel, it won't change anything. He's already afraid, so afraid, and it will only give him a reason to push me further away.

It's what he wants.

It's his default.

He gets close to me and then gives in to the fear. The fear of losing me permanently, the fear of compromising his job . . . it's still the same outcome.

"I just want you to care for me the same way I care for you," I finally say.

"And how do you care for me?" he whispers, words broken. "How do you feel about me?"

But I can't answer him honestly anymore. That ship has sailed. My words, my heart—they're not safe with him. Not when it won't change a thing.

So I lie. "I care about you as a friend," I tell him. "We're just two friends having fun. That's all."

It's *such* a lie that I don't think he'll even buy it.

But he takes it. He pretends to buy it. He'll use it as a way out.

"I see." He clears his throat, eyes drifting down to the pattern on the duvet. "Then I think maybe it's for the best that we go back to just being friends again. Colleagues. While we still can."

Even though I knew that was coming, even though I enabled it by lying, it still stings. "Sure. That's fine with me."

But I can't look at him anymore. I close my eyes, trying to keep it together.

"Laila?" he asks gently. I feel his fingertips at my cheek.

The nerve of him. To say all this shit and then to still show me this kind of soft touch, this kind of affection.

When I open my eyes to look at him, I know he sees my anger.

That we won't even go back to being friends now.

That we're right back at square one, when he waltzed into this fucking place and turned my whole life upside down again.

"You hate me," he says, his voice cracking with emotion.

I harden my heart against his words. "I don't care about you enough to hate you, James."

He flinches like I slapped him across the face.

Eyes going dark.

He nods, getting to his feet and striding quickly toward the door.

He closes it behind him, and I hear him go down the hall, open the door to his own room. Hear the headboard knock against the wall as he climbs into bed.

I can't handle it.

I get up and go into the washroom, sitting down on the toilet.

The only place I can cry without him hearing me.

Twenty-One

JAMES

I FUCKED UP.

I fucked up *big-time*.

I fucked up big-time before with Laila, but this time, this is such a monumentally huge fuckup that it's blown past the boundaries of the solar system. I'm talking a fuckup of galactic proportions, one that I will take to my grave as my biggest regret.

"James?"

"Huh?" I turn to see Magnus staring at me quizzically. I guess I am standing in the hallway outside Laila's room, just staring at her door like a fucking stalker. Since I fucked shit up last night, I've been trying to apologize for how I acted, but she won't give me the time of day, and I can't exactly grovel in public here with her. So I've been standing outside her door in hopes that I'll catch her for a moment. It's after dinner, and I know she's in there with a book or perhaps sticking her pins in a Scotsman-shaped voodoo doll.

"You look rough, man," Magnus says, slapping his hand on my back. "I mean it. You need to come with me."

"Go with you where?" I ask, pivoting to watch him throw on his coat.

"Well, me and Einar. We're taking you out. You haven't had a night out in a long time."

I give my head a shake. "I'm fine."

"It's an order, James," Magnus says. "From the Crown Prince of Norway."

I sigh and grab my coat. I hate it when he pulls that out. Frankly it's no different from when Bjorn did the same after the fiasco at the ship museum (which, thankfully, didn't result in any news articles about bad boy Bjorn).

Einar drives us into the city, and it's no surprise where we end up—Harold's, the dive bar that Magnus took me to before.

Einar enters the bar, and when he deems it secure, waves us in; meanwhile I'm watching behind us for any threats. But the street is dark and quiet, the sounds muffled by the falling snow, and with the way the temperature is, people aren't walking around much. Yes, it's even too cold for the locals.

I step inside the bar behind Magnus, and he immediately turns around and gives me a look. "You're off duty. Stop that."

"Stop what?"

"Being a bodyguard."

"I am your bodyguard," I tell him. I've been especially on edge ever since the attack.

"Not right now. You're here tonight as a friend. And as a friend, I'm getting you drunk."

"I told you, I don't like to drink in public if—"

"I'll fire you if you don't do a shot with me."

I stare at Magnus. His eyes are glinting, and it's hard to tell if he's serious or not. He very well could be, as unpredictable as he is.

"All right," I concede under my breath.

He lets out a devilish laugh, and I definitely see how Bjorn is his son. "You made the right choice. Come on."

We go over to the bar while Einar stands by the front door. Magnus says hello to the regulars, none of whose names I can remember, except for Slender Man, for obvious reasons.

Harold pours us both a shot of aquavit—not my first choice, but I down it to appease Magnus. Maybe he'll just stop at one.

But that's just wishful thinking. Because he orders another shot for both of us along with beers to take back to our booth in the corner.

"Okay, let's try this again," he says, raising his shot glass once we've sat down. "Let's skål to you, James. To your happiness."

I frown. "Okay . . ."

I lift my shot glass and clink it against his. The second time it goes down feels a lot better than the first, but I'm grateful for the beer as a chaser.

Except the beer happens to be dark as sin and strong as hell.

"Whoa," I say after a sip. I'm used to the low-alcohol beers that you find in every grocery store. "Now that's a beer."

"I knew you'd appreciate it," Magnus says.

Do I ever. I end up drinking the beer rather fast, and when I'm done, I'm pleased at how even-keeled I feel. Definitely on the way to drunk.

Magnus doesn't hesitate in getting us another, and when I'm halfway through that one and feeling rather defenseless, he tilts his head and gives me an expectant look.

"So what happened with you and Laila?" he says, point-blank.

Even drunk, I know to keep my facial expressions controlled.

"What do you mean?" I ask carefully, though my pitch sounds funny.

"You know what I mean," he says earnestly. From the way he's staring at me, I'm not sure if he actually knows something or if he's suspicious and trying to ensnare me into admitting it.

Fuck.

I open my mouth to speak, then decide to drink some more of my beer instead. Good ol' beer, always saving the day when things get awkward.

"I know you're sleeping together," he says.

Oh fuck.

"What was that?" I ask, blinking, hoping he buys my look of shock and confusion.

Magnus gives me a tired sigh. "I said I know you're sleeping together. You don't have to play ignorant."

I have two choices here. I could continue to deny this and call his bluff. Or I can admit it. If I admit it, I could be fired. In fact I most likely will be. I wasn't hired to sleep with the nanny, and admitting that I've been with Laila means that he might look back on other instances, such as what happened in the ship museum, and think that I lost my nerve because I was distracted by Laila (which wasn't the case).

Maybe you should be fired, a voice inside my head says. This voice doesn't sound drunk at all. It sounds sober. *Maybe you deserve it. Laila opened herself up to you, and you shut her down because you were scared. For the second time. Maybe you should admit what happened and give up your job because Laila deserves to be in that house, but you certainly do not, especially if you're afraid your feelings for her complicate your job.*

But if I admit it, that means Laila might get fired too.

Only one thing left to do.

"I think I should quit," I tell Magnus.

His eyes bug out. "What?" he exclaims.

I hate it. I hate that I'm saying this, and maybe if I were sober there would be some other way, but I'm saying it anyway. "I quit. I quit the job. I shouldn't be working for your family anymore."

Magnus looks around, as if to check if anyone is listening, then looks back to me and shakes his head. "No. James. No. You aren't quitting."

"You can't tell me what to do if I quit. You're literally not the boss of me."

Okay, now I sound like a bloody child.

"Then I think I'm allowed to know why you're quitting," he says. "You owe me that much."

"I don't think I'm a good fit," I tell him. "I think . . . there's someone better equipped for your family."

He stares at me for a moment, then slowly shakes his head. "You're really willing to let go of your job for her?" he asks in awe.

"What?"

He rolls his eyes to the ceiling. "James. You must think I'm an idiot. And I don't blame you for thinking that because most of the time I am an idiot. I'm the first to admit it. But I did my due diligence when I hired you. Which meant I was very thorough in asking Eddie questions. And wouldn't you like to know a surprising piece of info that Eddie told me?"

Oh no. Bloody hell.

"What?" I ask, the word barely audible.

"He told me that you had an affair with their nanny."

Jesus Christ.

Eddie knew? He *knew*?!

Magnus continues, eyes dancing like he's delighting in blowing my mind. "And that their nanny was of course Laila. So, naturally, I had to hire you."

I do a hard blink. "What? *That's* why you hired me?"

He lifts a shoulder in a half shrug. "Well, I knew that you were good at your job and that's what really mattered. Eddie told me that you might not appreciate being out in the countryside, and that you really wouldn't appreciate working with Laila again, but you see, I like a little chaos in my life, if you haven't noticed. I thought it would be amusing. And it has been."

Holy fuck.

"You're sick in the head," I tell him, half joking.

He grins at me. "I know that. And honestly, Eddie thought it was a brilliant idea too. I guess he thought you needed to grow up or something."

"Grow up?!" I exclaim, fingers pressed into the table. A few people in the bar turn to look, then go back to their drinking.

"You don't agree with that assessment?" he asks, taking a casual sip of beer.

My mouth opens, closes, and I'm hit with that sad realization that he's right. I did need to grow up. And, obviously, I haven't.

"So what happened with you and Laila?" he goes on. "Why did the both of you go from staring into each other's eyes like Kate and Leo on the *Titanic*, to her telling you she'd never let go and pushing you off the floating door?"

"That's quite the analogy."

"I watched the movie last night. Anyway, did you break her heart again?"

Even though I deserve that and I know it's true, my hackles go up. "What makes you think I did in the first place?"

"Just what Eddie told me. Well, Monica was more astute to that. Heartbreak is pretty obvious if you know what to look for."

I look down at my beer, feeling a rush of shame.

"So you did," Magnus muses. "May I ask what happened? Because Ella and I have a bet going on."

"Ella knows?" Oh god, please don't tell me that Lady Jane does too.

"She does. We talk about the two of you all the time. Lady Jane does as well, but that's only because Laila confided in her."

I run my hand down my face and make an anguished noise. "I can't believe this." How does everyone know? How is this possible? "What did Laila say to Lady Jane? Do you know?"

"Yeah, she said she was in love with you."

The noise gets louder.

"Oh, bloody hell," I cry out softly.

"Here, finish your beer and I'll get you another," Magnus says, pushing my glass under my face. He goes to the bar, and I stay where I am, stewing in the enormity of what he said while finishing the rest of the beer, as if it will drown my feelings.

Laila told Lady Jane that she loved me.

When? Before I nearly lost her, lost my balls, and fucked everything up? Or did she tell her afterward? Like, is it possible she still feels that way about me, even after all I did?

Magnus comes back with the beers and sits back down, sliding mine toward me.

"When did Laila tell Lady Jane?" I ask.

"I'm not sure."

"Was it before or after . . ."

He raises a brow. "Before or after what, James?" he asks dryly.

"Before I fucked shit up with her for the second time."

"And so what happened?" He gestures for me to continue. "How exactly did you fuck shit up this time?"

I exhale heavily and lean back in my seat, wiggling the tension out of my jaw. "I don't know. I was just . . . it was the same as the time before. We had sex and it was emotional and . . . I freaked the fuck out."

"And why did you freak the fuck out?"

"Because I almost lost her," I tell him. "When that man tried to attack her. I saw my whole life flash in front of my eyes, but it was a life without her in it. I realized I can't be close to her and do my job. I can't be with someone who's in the line of danger."

"But as a member of the royal household she has always been a target."

"I know," I tell him. "But it didn't really register until that day on the mountain."

"And now you're scared." He pauses. "But that doesn't change the fact that she's in love with you . . . for some reason," he adds under his breath.

"I'm not deserving of her love," I practically snipe. "I'm a mess. I'm flawed. I'm . . . not a person that people stick around for. Not my parents, not my first wife. People leave me. And they should. I mean, look at how I treated her. If she loves me, then . . . I'm only going to hurt her."

Magnus's eyes are sympathetic as he gives me a half smile. "I see. So it goes deeper than just the fear of losing her. Do you think you're protecting her, or are you protecting yourself?"

I hesitate, needing to mull that over. I thought I was protecting her from myself. But maybe I'm actually protecting myself from her.

"I don't know," I admit. "Maybe both. But in the end, I hurt her. I pretty much stonewalled her again, and this whole time, this whole fucking time we were together, that was my worst fear. That I'd hurt her."

"And you did," he says simply.

I close my eyes. My chest feels like it's getting knifed between the ribs.

"You know what a dritsekk is in English, James?" Magnus asks.

"A shitbag?" I say, looking at him.

"Yes. You are a shitbag, James."

My shoulders sink, and I have a gulp of beer. "I know."

"So what is the solution here, then?" Magnus says. "You can't quit because of this. Don't make us suffer because you can't handle your emotions properly."

That's rich coming from Magnus, but I bite my tongue.

"The thing is," he goes on, "love is always going to be a risk. I should know, I'm the king of risks."

"More like the prince of risks," I point out. It's not lost on me that we're talking about love now. Because that is what I'm feeling for Laila. It's love. There's no question about it.

"James," he says gravely, and I have no choice but to shut up and listen. "I've done many scary, outrageous fucking things in my life, but falling in love with Ella was by far the most terrifying.

No one who loves truly and freely does so without being scared, because the loss of love is a world-ender. If I lost Ella, my world would simply cease to be. But we accept the risk and take a leap of faith, because if—*when*—it works out, there's nothing greater. You just have to accept the risk and take the leap and have some damn faith that things will work out the way they're supposed to. You're a brave man, James, I know that. If you can dive in front of a bullet, you can give your heart to Laila."

I stare down my drink, humbled by his words.

"But there's really no point in thinking about such things since you won't have a relationship until you make things up with Laila," he continues. "But the question is, what is your end game? Do you just want her to accept your apology and not be mad at you anymore? Or do you want something more from her?"

I rub my lips together hard, trying to find the truth. I don't have to look too hard. "It's possible."

"Possible and likely?"

I palm my beer, turning it around on the table. "Possible and very likely," I say, feeling my heart sink.

"Well, then, shitbag, you only have one course of action," he says. "You must try to win her back."

I give him the most withering look. "That will be impossible at this point."

"But does that mean you're not going to try? Don't you think Laila is worth the effort?"

Magnus looks so sincere I almost laugh.

"You know you could have been a therapist in another life."

He grins at that. "A Viking and a therapist. A most noble occupation."

By the time we get back to the estate I am pleasantly drunk

and bolstered by Magnus's confidence in me. There's something freeing now about the fact that he knows—nay, the whole entire house knows—that there's something going on between Laila and me. Of course the biggest bloody issue is that there isn't anything going on between us—not anymore.

But if I can make it up to her somehow, if I can perfect the art of groveling, then perhaps I can change that. If I explain to her how I truly feel and how I'm going to try to work through what I'm afraid of, whether that's with her or with a therapist, then that's what I'm going to do.

"James," Magnus says to me in the hallway as I'm about to walk off to Laila's room. He puts his hand on my shoulder, keeping me in place, and I sway a little. "Tell me you're going to bed right now. Your own bed."

I give him a sheepish look. "I was hoping to maybe do a bit of groveling."

"It's almost midnight and you're wasted," he whispers roughly.

"I believe you said you'd fire me if I stayed sober," I point out.

"Do your groveling some other time," he says, giving me a hearty shake that makes the hall spin. "Let the dear nanny rest."

I sigh and he lets go of me, and I nearly stumble into the wall. I make my way to my door and open it, glancing over my shoulder to see Magnus staring at me with his arms crossed, like a father making sure his child is really going to bed. I've never felt more like Bjorn.

I go inside my room and close the door behind me before flopping down on the bed in my suit.

I lie there for a moment, trying to gather up the strength and courage to go out and see Laila anyway. Then I hear her bed creak from her room. I move myself up on the bed until my head is pressed against the wall.

"Laila?" I say. "Are you up?"

No answer.

"Laila?" I say a little louder.

I push my ear harder against the wall.

"I want to talk to you," I go on, trying not to slur my words. "I need to talk to you. Can I come over?"

Silence.

Then, "No."

I shouldn't be surprised at the rejection, but my drunk little heart feels the pinch.

I open my mouth to protest, to say something, anything to convince her, but I hear her sigh loudly. A sigh filled with sadness and longing.

"Go to sleep, James."

And so I do.

Twenty-Two

. . . .

JAMES

"BLOODY HELL, IT'S FREEZING," I MUMBLE AS I STEP OUT of the house.

"Not going to lie," Magnus says, closing the door behind him, "I'm actually getting sick of this weather. Coldest January in a decade. I'm counting down the days to Morocco."

"So am I," I admit. Next month the family is going to Morocco, and because the kids are going, that means I get to go. I've been craving sunshine like nothing else, and a week in the heat will do me a lot of good.

Unfortunately, it means that Laila will be going too.

Being around her now has become unbearable, and of course I have only myself to blame.

It's been two weeks since I did the stupid thing where I didn't reciprocate her feelings and said things in order to push her away, partly because I was protecting her and partly because I was protecting myself. In that time, and since Magnus let me know that the family is totally wise to our affair, I've been doing all I can to tell Laila both that I'm sorry and how I feel. I know laying out an "actually I love you too, and that's what scared me the most because I realized how far gone I was" isn't going to get me anywhere, but neither is a good old-fashioned apology. Laila refuses to be alone with me, and when we have to interact with each other there's a fake pleasantness. No one in the house is buying it, which makes things extra awkward because everyone knows why Laila is acting that way, but of course no one is saying anything.

So whenever I'm around her, I feel like I'm being punished over and over again. Something I totally deserve, yes, but quietly devastating all the same. I just want to make her smile, hear her laugh, see that light in her eyes again. I want to be the person who puts that light there, who opens her doors and climbs over the walls, and sees the precious person she hides from me. I want her in every way possible, but I can't get much more than an icy stare and a cold hello.

My world is very cold now in every way possible.

The SUV pulls up with Einar behind the wheel. Ella, Lady Jane, Laila, and the kids come out of the house, with Lady Jane and Magnus getting in the SUV and the rest of us waiting for the other car to come around.

"Okay, let's go," Ella says, and we all pile into Ottar's car. This is the first time I've been in an enclosed space with Laila since everything went to shit, but since I'm in the front beside Ottar, I don't have to deal with the icy vibes.

"You must be excited," Laila says to Ella as the car starts down the driveway.

"I am. A little nervous. You know, considering the last time we were in public."

And there goes that spike of fear again. I can't pretend that I'm not already on edge over this, though we have extra police presence now, and no one is allowed to get within spitting distance of the royal family without having been thoroughly vetted beforehand.

It doesn't help that Ella is doing an unveiling of her newest expedition boat for her charity, the Ocean Crusaders, in Oslo harbor, and all the press are invited too. The only good thing about the attack is that it put the focus back on environmental issues in the country, which in turn is giving Ella's charity more attention.

Of course, there won't be another attack. I'll make sure of that. Aside from the extra police, we have a few PPOs taken from the king and queen's service who will provide extra protection at the scene, and I'm not letting my guard down for a second.

"So what's the name of the boat this time?" Ottar asks. "Don't tell me Magnus named it again." Magnus got the first boat for Ella's organization, which meant he got to name it. He called it *Princess Planet*, after his nickname for her. Let's hope this boat isn't *Princess Planet 2*.

"It's a surprise," Ella says coyly, and I eye her in the rearview mirror. Oh, she has something up her sleeve.

While I'm looking in the mirror, though, I also catch Laila's eyes. And for a split second, I swear I see a flash of warmth in them, like the deep freeze has thawed. It makes my heart skip a damn beat.

Then she hardens and looks away and the moment is lost, as so many of them are these days.

I force that out of my head, though. I have a job to do, and it's an important one.

Once we get to Oslo and the harbor, we trudge through snow and slippery paths toward the docks where a crowd of people have gathered. There are news cameras and lookie-loos, all hoping to get a glimpse of their beloved royal family, and security has already roped off an area where Magnus stands, Einar behind him. I don't know how on earth they got here so far ahead of us, but sometimes I think Magnus makes Einar drive at the speed of light. Or maybe Einar does it for fun. He probably used to be a rally driver.

People and security part for us and I bring up the back, knowing they're protected from the front. Ella goes to Magnus and waves to the crowd—it is her moment, after all—while Laila guides the boys behind Ella and Magnus. We're close to the end of the dock but not close enough to fall off, with the boat covered in a big tarp, ready for the unveiling. I stand on one side of the boys with Laila bookending the other, and I keep an eye out for anything unusual.

Ella talks to the crowd—in English, since there are media from all over—all about how Ocean Crusaders did a lot last year and they're hoping to do much more with their second boat and the big group of organizers, activists, and volunteers that they have. But I'm not listening much. I'm glad to see her in her element—even though she says she doesn't like the spotlight, she really comes alive when she's talking about her organization—but I'm paying attention to everyone in the crowd, memorizing every face, reading body language. So far, everything seems fine and people seem really interested in the cause (okay, there are some protesters with signs in the background, calling out the government for killing a friendly walrus that visited the harbor a few years back, but that's to be expected).

Finally we get to the unveiling. I back the boys up a little bit, standing behind them now, as Ella and Magnus grab the ends of the tarp and lift it off with aplomb.

"Introducing our newest research vessel, the *Dame Jane!*" Ella announces.

I hear Jane gasp from the crowd. Yes, Ella named the boat after Lady Jane. I shake my head.

"Maybe in ten years there will be a boat called *The James,*" I say to Laila, forgetting for a moment that she hates me.

She turns her head to scowl at me, and then her eyes widen because a seagull has decided to dive-bomb us.

Which causes Tor to yelp and cling to Laila.

Which causes Bjorn to laugh, twist around on his heel, and chase after the bird.

I reach out to stop him, missing him by an inch, yelling his name, but he's running off down the dock.

"Bjorn, stop!" Laila screams.

And to his credit, he does listen, his eyes going wide at the sound of Laila's scream.

But he stops so fast he slips on the dock and goes sliding off the edge.

Onto a piece of ice on the water, where he slides farther along.

I'm already running for him, hoping to grab him from the ice before he falls into the water.

"I've got you!" I yell, reaching for the hood of his coat.

But I'm a second too slow.

He slides, crying out now, and then goes into the water, fully submerged.

Ella lets out a bloodcurdling scream, and I can hear Magnus

running as fast as he can behind me, but I'm already launching myself onto the ice. I'm not the size of Bjorn and it immediately breaks underneath me.

I sink down into the water, it goes over my head, and it's so cold, so cold, that I'm sure my heart has stopped and that I'm going to die here. I can't think, the air is frozen in my lungs, and I open my eyes to near darkness, this inky, deep gray blue surrounded by bubbles.

I could let myself go. I could just let myself sink. There's a part of me that wants to, that thinks I should, that maybe this is what I deserve. How would the world change without me in it? It wouldn't even notice. It would probably be better off. My parents seemed to think so. My father certainly thought so. My ex-wife thought so too. They all probably wished I would just disappear into the ocean one day and never return.

But as tempting as it is to just sink, I know I can't.

Because the world would notice if I was gone.

Because an innocent little boy would be taken with me.

Bjorn! I yell inside my head, and I'm frantically splashing around, trying to get feeling in my limbs while I'm running out of air, and then I see him, his eyes open and staring at me, alive but drowning.

I grab him and I kick, and in seconds we burst through the surface.

I've got you, I try to tell him, but I can't speak. I can't even take in any more air. I use all the strength I have to swim toward the end of the dock where Magnus is reaching down. I'm sinking as I try to hold Bjorn above water.

Magnus grasps Bjorn by the arms and pulls him out of the water, and I push through the surface again, the current taking me a few inches away from Magnus. He quickly hands Bjorn to Ella, then lies down on the edge and tries to reach for me.

"Come on, James," he says as I'm about to sink again. "Kick, you shitbag. Just a few more inches."

I'm starting to feel myself slip away. It's so cold that I can't even think, the ice affecting my brain, my will.

I'm starting not to care.

I did my duty.

"James, please!" Laila yells at me as the water starts to go over my head, her voice becoming muffled. "James! Come on, please!"

The sound of her pain . . .

Somehow I muster up all the strength that I have and kick as hard as I can until I break through the surface and am closer to the dock.

Magnus grabs the top of my coat, pulling me closer, then grabs me by the arms and hauls me up onto the dock.

"Ambulance is on the way," I hear Lady Jane say, as I'm turned over on my side and I cough out water.

"He's in shock," Laila says. "Where are the blankets?" Her arms go around me, trying to hold me to her, as if to give me her warmth. It's not working, and yet I don't ever want her to let go.

"They're coming," Magnus says grimly, and I feel him smack my arm. "You're going to pull through, James, just know that. Just stay with us, okay?"

My teeth are chattering so hard I can hardly hear him, and I think I've already cracked a tooth. "B-Bjorn?" I try to say.

"He's fine," Magnus says. "He's got blankets on him—he's okay. You saved him." He looks over his shoulder. "Look, we have blankets for you now."

"The ambulance is here," I hear Einar say.

Suddenly blankets appear and Laila is wrapping one around me, tears streaming down her face.

"There you go again," she says to me, her voice shaking though she's attempting a smile through her tears. "Always saving someone."

"It's . . ." I try to speak but I can't form the words. I can't stop shaking.

It's my job, I finish in my head.

And that's when I realize that no matter what happens, no matter how I feel about Laila and how she feels about me, I'll always be able to do my job. I will always be here to protect someone. It's in my DNA, in the very fabric of my being.

But for once, with Laila holding me close, the blanket wrapped around me, everyone staring at me with encouraging if not tear-filled smiles, urging me to stay awake, I know that even though it's my job to protect these people, it's nice to know they want to protect me too.

Twenty-Three

. . . .

LAILA

"LAILA?" MAGNUS SAYS, APPEARING AT THE END OF THE row of chairs that are lined up outside James's hospital room. I glance up from my fingers, which are bleeding from where I've torn the skin while waiting.

But his eyes are bright, his smile kind. "Did you want to see him?" he asks.

I get to my feet, moving on instinct toward him. "Is he okay?"

"He's fine," Magnus says, placing a hand on my shoulder and giving it a light squeeze. "Just a bit of hypothermia. They'll keep him here for a few more hours, but then he's coming back with us." He leans in; his dark eyes have a knowing look in them. "Take it easy on the boy, okay?"

Then he strides off toward Einar, who is standing at the end of the hall, the entire wing blocked off for the royal treatment, so to speak.

I pause outside the door, trying to compose my thoughts, trying to get my emotions together. I'm afraid that the moment

I see him, the moment I'm alone with him, I'll lose all my resolve. It's been like that under the best of circumstances, let alone when he's been close to death.

I swallow hard, take in a deep breath, and open the door.

James is in the room, the bed raised to a sitting position. He's wearing no shirt, and the fact that I can see his bare, hard chest and muscles is more distracting than the IV lines going into his arms.

He gives me a lopsided grin, and that alone nearly buckles my knees.

"Shouldn't you be wearing a shirt?" I manage to ask, coming over to the end of the bed and stopping there, my hands on the railing, afraid to get any closer.

He shrugs lightly. "I've been bundled in a variety of things for the last few hours. I guess the nurse just wanted to see what I was made of."

I give him a shy smile at that. "How are you feeling?"

Another shrug, one shoulder now. "Out of sorts, to say the least."

I stare at him like he might disappear before me if I don't. He stares right back at me, pinning me in place, and I can feel a million different things in his eyes, but I don't know which one is true. He opens his mouth and exhales, his chest sinking. Then he licks his lips and the intensity in his gaze fades, a moment having come and gone. "How is Bjorn?"

"He's fine," I tell him. "Thanks to you he was only in the water for a few seconds. Doctors looked him over, and he's the same as he ever was. Well, almost. That fall struck the fear of god into him. Would you believe me if I said he's a changed boy?"

He laughs, the sound making my heart bloom in my chest.

"I wouldn't believe you. Bjorn will be Bjorn until, well, until he turns into Magnus, I guess."

"I'm not sure how my country is going to fare having King Bjorn follow King Magnus," I admit. "Complete chaos."

"Ah, but chaos is what makes things fun," he comments.

"You sound like you've been hanging around Magnus for too long."

"Perhaps," he muses. Then his gaze darkens. "Laila . . . I have some things I need to say to you."

I raise my hand, looking down at the foot of the bed. "You don't need to say anything to me, James."

"I do," he says, his voice strained. "I do. Look at me."

I obey, lifting my chin so my eyes meet his. He's staring at me with so much anguish that it causes cracks to form in my heart. "I have everything to say to you. I am so bloody sorry, Laila. So damn sorry for acting the way I did with you. I shouldn't have gotten so scared again. I shouldn't have pushed you away. I shouldn't have let the fear of losing you make me lose you for good."

"It's fine," I say, but I have to drop his gaze.

"It's not. I know it's not. You put your trust in me after I worked so hard to earn it again, and I broke it again. You put it in my hands, expecting me to keep it safe, and I fucking broke it."

"Yeah," I whisper, closing my eyes. "You broke it."

Tears burn and build but never fall, and inside I just feel hollow and tired and sad.

"Forgive me, please," he says, his voice breaking.

I nod, running my tongue over my teeth, swallowing the pain down. "I forgive you."

Because I do. I do forgive him. I know he's being sincere, and I know he knows he fucked up. I had a talk with Magnus and Ella the other day that told me as much. I was furious with Lady Jane for breaking my confidence in her, but I suppose her duty was always to Ella first. What I didn't expect was for the two of them to know about our relationship ahead of time, about what happened in London.

I also didn't expect them to fully support it. I thought for sure one of us would get the boot, but instead both Ella and Magnus were thoroughly invested in us as a couple. Unfortunately for them, there's no way that James and I will come together now. I can forgive him because it's the right thing to do, because he almost just died saving Bjorn's life, just as he came close when he saved mine, and I can forgive him because it's too much to carry that burden with me. I don't want to work with him and hate him. I don't want to be in that house avoiding his gaze, letting something hard build inside me, covering everything that was once soft.

"Do you mean it?" James asks, and I look at him to see the desperation on his brow. "Do you forgive me?"

I nod. "Of course I do."

He gives me a sad smile. "You say that as if it's a given. You don't owe me anything, Laila, but I'm still asking for it." He holds out his hand. "And maybe you can give me your hand too."

That feels like one ask too many. I hesitate, my heart thumping awkwardly in my chest. I can forgive him for being scared and pushing me away, but the idea of him touching me again makes me feel like I'll do more than forgive him.

"Please," he says.

And I can't say no to his request.

I come around the bed and place my hand in his. He grasps it tightly, and my blood fizzes where his skin presses against mine, a lightly calloused and utterly familiar grip.

It feels like he hasn't touched me like this in so long, and it takes everything in me to keep all of that inside me, to bury the gasp my lungs yearn to make.

"You were a brave man," I manage to say.

His grip tightens. "You make me brave, Laila." He takes in a deep breath, his gaze consuming, like it's taking up all the oxygen in the room. "You made me so fucking scared. And then, only then, did you make me want to be so damn brave. It's all for you, love. I'm sitting here for you, because of *you*." His voice cracks on the last word, his grip on my hand taking my breath away.

"James," I whisper, trying to find the words, but there are no words that will appease him. They don't appease me either. That's what's so awful about all of this.

"I am so sorry I hurt you," he goes on hoarsely. "I turned into my worst fears."

"You did," I say softly.

"And I had you, didn't I? I had you and I lost you."

I close my eyes and exhale a shaking breath. "You did," I say, and those words cement the truth but, god, how I hate the truth.

His fingers loosen at that, and his hand slips away, and I feel him slip away. I feel *us* slip away. And I want to just crawl onto that bed and kiss him, hold him, tell him that I love him and I don't care if he hurt me and I don't care if my heart isn't safe in his hands.

But self-preservation is an animal we don't really think about.

It lives within us and rears its head when it thinks we might step straight into harm. Right now, it feels like James is harmful, that he'll hurt me again, so all the dark and hidden places inside me are putting on the brakes. I'm protecting my own heart from being shattered again, even though I've barely begun to put together the pieces.

"I don't want to hate you, James," I whisper. I dare to open my eyes, but his head is turned, brows furrowed in pain, staring out the window and at nothing at all. "I want to go back to being friends. I like being around you as a colleague, as a housemate. I know it's hard, but . . ."

He nods slowly, rubbing his lips together. "It's hard, but it's for the best."

"I don't have any hard feelings for you," I add feebly. It pains me to see him like this, so vulnerable, physically and emotionally. I wish he'd been this vulnerable from the start.

"Do you have any soft feelings?" he asks. He moves his head back to look at me, his expression strangely hopeful.

I give him a weak smile. I can't lie. "I do. They're all soft for you, James." I pause. "But that's why I need to protect them."

He gives me an equally weak smile in return. "I think that's smart," he says, clearing his throat. "I can protect you from everything but myself."

Oh. God.

How painfully true that is.

It's a knife to my stomach.

I straighten my shoulders, taking a step back from the bed. I'm shaking inside, sick and terrified that I might forget everything I just told him.

"They said you can leave soon," I say, my voice sounding unnaturally loud and high-pitched.

"I heard," he says. "I was hoping I could turn the hospital stay into a little bit of a vacation, but I guess not."

"I'm sure Magnus will put you on bed rest for a week," I tell him.

He laughs. "Bloody hell, I hope not. I can just see Lady Jane trying to force me to eat chicken soup by the spoonful."

I can't help but laugh too, even though my heart still burns in my chest and my laugh rings hollow.

"Laila?" Ella's voice comes from behind us, and I turn to see her standing in the doorway, trepidation on her face, her hands clasped in front of her. "Sorry to interrupt."

"No, it's fine," I say, walking toward her. "I'm done with him."

At that I hear James's sharp inhale, like my words cut him, and I force myself not to turn around and look at his face. Of course I didn't mean it the way it came out, but if I try to take it back, I'll just make things worse.

Ella's looking over my shoulder at James sympathetically, and to my surprise that look doesn't change when she meets my eyes. "I'm heading back to Skaugum with the boys. Did you want to come now or come with Magnus and James later?"

I feel James behind me, the pull to him, the urge to tell her that I'll come back with him. But I know that's not what I'm going to choose.

I'm going to play it safe instead. As safe as I can when I'm going back to the same damn place that James is, where only a thin wall separates his bed from mine.

"I'll go back with you now," I tell her.

"Okay," she says, giving James a smile. "I'll see you later."

James doesn't say anything. Maybe he's waving his hand goodbye, maybe he's nodding.

I don't turn around to see.

Twenty-Four

. . . .

LAILA

I DREAMED OF MY GRANDMOTHER LAST NIGHT.

This is the first time I've seen her in my dreams since she died.

We were in a meadow, high in the mountains, above the clouds, and the meadow had orange and purple flowers everywhere, like poppies. Suddenly I was sitting in the middle of this field, as if having a picnic, and my grandmother was standing in front of me.

At first I didn't know what to say. The feelings were too overwhelming, and I didn't know how to get it all out.

But she calmly raised her hand and said, "There is no need to tell me, Laila. I already know everything you want to say. I have been with you every step of the way, listening and watching. Sometimes I try to give you a sign, but you don't notice. It's not your fault. The world is made to keep you grounded, so that you don't spend so much time thinking about this one."

"You've been watching me?" I asked.

She nodded. "Hearing your thoughts if they pertain to me. I know how much you've missed me. And while I know your grief is love, I want so badly for you to be happy too. Life is for living, every second of it, and I don't want my death to hold you back. You must live with your chest out and heart open. It's the only way you'll learn why you took the journey to earth, what it was that your spirit wanted to learn."

It was like I understood everything at once at that moment. Like it hit me, dawned on me with frightening clarity, what it all meant.

Of course, lying here in my bed this morning, I don't remember any of that. I just remember what she said. And what she said afterward.

She said, "I saw what happened to James. I saw your heartbreak. His spirit was very close to joining his other spirit on this side. You pulled him back, Laila. It was your love that brought him back. He chose you. No matter what you do going forward, you have to accept that he chose you."

And as much as my grandmother's message of love—the knowledge that she wasn't really gone—meant the world to me, it was hearing her talk about James that made everything feel real.

Because I know I was close to losing him.

But when he was in the hospital, I chose to lose him again.

Why? Because I'm fucking stubborn, that's why. Because he hurt me, and I wanted him to hurt too. Because I'm scared to death that if we can somehow work past our complicated history, if we could learn to be open and vulnerable with each other, then maybe both of us would fall so deeply in love that there would be no way out. That we would make the choice to be with each other for the rest of our lives.

And, whew, that's something I never thought about. How love isn't just about the here and now but about the forever. That we might become to each other the things we've always lacked, and that once again, our lives would change.

But it would change for the better, part of me thinks. *It would change for the better.*

I sigh and slowly get up. I stayed up late last night with Lady Jane and Ella in Lady Jane's room, having too much wine. It was nice to have a girls' night and everything, but my body is paying for it this morning.

I take a shower, trying to remember the bits from my dream until all that's left is just the feeling, a most wonderful calm feeling, one that I know won't erase my grief but will give me some sort of comfort. I think about why my grandmother would tell me that about James (and if it were truly just a product of my mind, why is my mind telling me that?). And I wonder if I'm going to do anything about it. It's so hard to change, and I've spent most of my life harboring grudges and pulling away from people, it's going to be tempting to stay mad at James for eternity. I get dressed, ready to face another day.

Luckily the day goes by easily. The boys are quiet—Bjorn really is trying to be more in control, and at his age that's something to be commended—and we spend the day going for a walk, building snowmen, watching a cartoon, then coloring.

We're sitting in the playroom, about to break out the watercolor paints, when Ella comes in the room.

"Laila, can I speak with you for a moment?"

Oh shit. What did I do now?

I get to my feet, wondering if this is retroactive firing for sleeping with James, and walk over to her. "Yes?" I ask warily.

"Oh goodness, Laila," she says with a laugh. "You should see your face. This is nothing bad. It's good. I was thinking of taking you out for dinner tonight."

Hmmm. This is a surprise. "Just me?"

"The boys and Magnus won't be going."

"Oh," I say with a shrug. "Well, sure. Of course. That would be nice."

"Good," she says. "Lady Jane will watch the boys, if you want to go get ready now. I'm taking you to Oslo."

Wow. That's even better. "Is it fancy?"

She purses her lips in thought. "Kind of. Just wear something nice."

I wave goodbye to the kids and then go off to my room, half expecting to see James on the way, but I don't. In fact I haven't seen him all day, which is for the best.

I go through my closet and select a simple black dress that shows off my curves but not in an obnoxious way. I'm tempted to put on my boots, but because I don't know where we're going, I opt for a pair of low heels. Not the best for winter, but I'll walk carefully.

I pull my hair back into a messy bun on top of my head, pop in some amethyst earrings my grandmother once gave me for my birthday, some quick makeup, and then I'm ready.

To my surprise, Ella hasn't changed at all, but I guess she's a princess and can do whatever she likes. Not that she looks bad in her wool sweater and skinny jeans.

"Am I overdressed?" I ask her as I get in the car, surprised to see Einar at the wheel and not James.

"Not at all," she says.

"Where is James?" I ask. He is her bodyguard after all.

"He's busy," she says. "Einar will be taking us."

"Oh."

We drive off and Ella makes small talk, but there's something about her energy that's confusing. It's not that she's nervous, but she's excited about something. I mean, maybe it's just that she's going out for dinner without her kids or something, I don't know. I know moms should be making as much time for themselves as possible.

But when we should start heading toward the city core, the car veers to the left of the harbor.

"Where is the restaurant?"

"By the water," she says. "You've been there before."

I try to think, but I have no idea what she's talking about. The wine bar with James? No, that couldn't be it.

Then everything starts to look familiar, even in the dark, and as we pass the Viking ship museum, I realize where she's taking me.

The car stops right outside the Fram Museum.

"What's going on?" I ask.

Einar comes around and opens the door for me, helping me out onto the shoveled sidewalk. I look behind me at Ella for explanation, but she's only slid over to my seat, staring up at me with a mischievous look. "Are we supposed to go into the museum? Is that where we are eating?"

"It's where *you're* eating," she says.

I don't understand. "What about you?"

She shakes her head. "I have plans with my husband. I'll see you later."

Then she reaches over and shuts the door just as Einar goes back to the driver's seat.

"Wait, Einar, you can't leave me here alone," I call after him.

He gives me the rarest of smirks and nods at the museum. "You're not alone."

I turn to look at the museum again, and this time I see James, dressed in a tuxedo, standing at the front door with a bouquet of flowers in his hand.

Oh my god.

What is happening?

Before I can ask Einar, the car drives off and I'm alone at the museum with James.

"Why don't you come inside where it's warm?" he shouts from the door. "You can call a cab from here to take you back if you'd like."

He's got a point there, though part of me just wants to stand where I am and stare at him. Let my heart keep tripping over itself.

I walk a step, and then my heels wobble on the slick path.

In seconds James is by my side, holding me by the crook of my elbow to support me, and gently guiding me toward the museum.

I stare at him, at his freshly shaven face, at the way his eyes glow blue under the lampposts, at his tuxedo that definitely pushes him into the James Bond category.

Then I stare down at the flowers in his hand. A bouquet of daisies, orange on the outside and purple in the middle. The colors from my dream.

"These are for you," he says, handing them to me. "You never struck me as a roses kind of girl."

"You're right," I manage to say as I take them. I like roses and all, but they always felt too stuffy and adult for me. Daisies are actually my favorite, but I don't want to tell him that. In fact, what I should do is turn around, call a cab from my phone, and wait in the cold. That's what I would have done in the past, when my anger was its most potent.

But I don't have the strength to do that.

I don't want to turn from James anymore, even though he hurt me.

I don't want to hate him either.

I just want to love him and for him to be okay with that.

He opens the door to the museum, and we step inside. All the main lights are off, with a few mood lights here and there, and alongside the ship is a table lit by candles. Behind it, in the distance, are a couple of waiters dressed in black tie.

"What is this?" I ask, looking around in amazement.

"This is for you," he says, pulling back a seat for me.

"I don't understand."

"This is me telling you I'm sorry."

He comes over to me, taking the flowers from my hands and placing them on the table, before reaching out and cupping my face, his strong, warm fingers pressed into my cold skin.

"This is me begging you to trust me again," he says, his voice lower now, his eyes watering with emotion as he stares at me. "This is me telling you that it was your love that made me swim to the surface, Laila, and I will spend the rest of my life trying to prove to you, and to myself, that I am worthy of it."

I open my mouth to say something, but no words come out.

I don't know what to say.

I don't know what to feel.

He runs his thumb over my bottom lip, staring at me in awe, like I'm something he lost that he never expected to find again.

"And maybe," he says, leaning in closer, "maybe you will find my own love worthy too. Because the truth is, Laila, that I'm in bloody love with you."

His words light me up inside. It's instantaneous. I dreamed of what it could feel like if he ever told me he loved me, and I didn't think it would hit me like this. So sharp, so fast, and so deep. All at once the ice around my heart thaws, the icicles around my ribs shatter, and I feel, really feel, what being loved by this man feels like.

It feels like heaven.

"You are?" I whisper, afraid that maybe I heard him wrong.

He grins at me, that crooked, cocky smile that makes my knees weak. "Yeah. I am. I am fatally, fantastically, and stupidly in love with you, Laila. The 'stupidly' part has taken over a lot lately and for that I am sorry."

I laugh. It's my loud laugh, and it bounces off the ship and around the walls of the museum, and it just makes him laugh in return, the sweetest sound.

But then my laugh is swallowed up by his lips pressing against mine, pulling me into a kind of kiss that just cements his words, makes me feel them with the gentle slide of his tongue, the way he's cradling my face, possessive and sure.

He pulls away an inch, presses his forehead against mine.

"I understand if you need more time. If you stopped loving me and I have to earn it back. I have more groveling to do. I have a whole plan."

"Shhh," I say, pressing my finger against his lips. "I mean, I won't say no to more groveling if it leads to nights like this. But I still love you, you know. That didn't change. I couldn't stop loving if I tried."

He gives me a sheepish smile. "And did you try?"

"You bet I did," I say. Then I give him a quick kiss. "Turns out, you're impossible to unlove, James Hunter."

"Well, thank god for that," he says with a grin before burying his nose in my neck and placing his lips there.

"Now," he says, his mouth moving against my skin, "we have some time before the first course. I had arranged for there to be an appetizer but, well . . . perhaps I'd rather eat you instead."

My brows rise, heat flushing through my body. I'm giddy, joyful, and in seconds, impossibly turned on. I haven't been with James since the night everything went to shit, and even though I have done my best to keep him out of my heart, out of my head, my body has been calling to him.

"I don't mind being on the menu," I tell him, and he pulls back to flash me his wonderfully wicked grin, the one that gets me weak at the knees. He looks over at the table and the waiters, then grabs my hand and leads me into the depths of the museum.

Here, after hours, when the place is mostly dark, empty, and totally silent, save for some sounds coming from behind closed doors, where I assume the kitchen is, it feels like another world. It's hard to believe it's the same crowded and chaotic place I took the boys.

And it's even harder to believe that I'm here with James, that he's leading me into the polar area dressed in a tuxedo.

He brings me over to the ice caves and ushers me inside and out of view of the waiters, and then quickly presses me up against the wall.

"Ever had sex in an ice cave before?" he asks in a husky voice as he hikes my dress up to my waist, biting and licking my shoulders, my neck.

I giggle. "No. First time for me. You?"

"Also an ice cave virgin," he says, pulling down my underwear until it's gathered at my feet. "So hopefully you'll take it easy on me. Keep in mind, I won't be taking it easy on you."

And at that he drops down to his knees.

Oh my god.

He grabs my thighs with his big strong hands and parts them, burying his face to where I'm already wet with anticipation over actually having the real thing and not just a fantasy I've pulled out my vibrator for. He sucks and licks his way up the inside of my leg until he reaches my pussy, and then he plunges his tongue inside me, pushing it in as deep as he can, moving it around, tasting, eating me, and then I lean my head back against the wall and close my eyes, running my hands through his thick hair, and whimper.

I am completely helpless against him.

"James," I moan. "Oh my god."

"Mmm," he says, licking and swirling his tongue around my clit.

I tilt my head back a little more and close my eyes, enjoying the feel of his hot mouth on me, the way he so completely and thoroughly devours me. He's been just as starved for me as I have been for him. I move my hands to his shoulders and squeeze them tightly as the pressure builds inside my core, and a few moments later he reaches up with his hands and grabs my ass, squeezing it in kind.

"I love that you're in a tux," I tell him through a breathy moan. "Feels like I'm being eaten out by James Bond."

He chuckles against me, the vibrations starting to uncoil the hot cord inside me, and he pulls my hips against his mouth so that his face is even deeper in my pussy. His tongue lashes against my clit and then darts down to the very bottom of my slit, sucking the tender skin between his lips, and my whole body jerks and I can't stop myself as I come.

It feels like I come harder than I ever have before.

"James!" I gasp, trying not to scream and draw attention to ourselves, gripping his head firmly between my hands and tugging his hair like the mane of a wild horse.

While I'm still a quivering, boneless mess, he pulls me up off the wall and turns me around. Then he wraps his arms around me, kissing my neck from behind.

He holds me like that for a long, tender moment, and then he tugs my hair back gently with one hand and brings his mouth to the side of my throat. I hear the sound of his zipper as he pulls it down, and then he makes another sound, moving back, and I can feel his erection pressing against my backside.

"Tell me what you want," he growls in my ear.

"Fuck me," I say breathlessly. "I want you to fuck me like you're making up for all the time we've missed, all the time we've been idiots."

"I can do that," he says, and I can hear the smile on his lips.

He grabs my hips and pulls my ass back farther, and then he pushes his cock into where I'm so very wet and apparently still needy, even after I've just come.

"My god," I moan as his cock fills me, stretching me to my limits.

James takes my arms and brings them up above my head. Pinning my wrists there on the wall, he begins to move his hips, thrusting into me again and again, hard and fast, his cock pounding into me.

God it feels so good. I've missed this so much.

"I love you," James says, his hips rocking against me, his voice both breathless and pained. "I love you so much, my Laila love."

"I love you too," I say, shivering at his words, at the feel of him deep inside me, taking me for all it's worth.

I love him.

He loves me.

This is my dream coming true.

He takes my hair in his hand, gathering it up and bringing it over one shoulder, and then he pulls my head back and my chin up so that he can kiss me, his tongue probing deeply into my mouth, and I can taste whisky on his lips, like he had to calm his nerves before tonight.

"I can't get enough of you," he says, his cock pounding into me. "I can't waste any more time not being with you, not being inside you."

"You have me," I say breathlessly, feeling him hard and deep inside me.

"I'm going to take you so hard, my Laila love," he says, and I can feel the sweat beading on his forehead as it presses against my neck, the desperation of wanting me, on fire for me.

"Do it," I tell him. "I want it. I want to feel you."

"Fuck!" he groans, and pulls my body back hard against him, his hips slamming against me, and I can feel his balls bouncing off my ass.

He buries his face in my neck again, and he starts to pump into me wildly, his body jerking and thrusting against mine, and in the heat of everything I forget myself and start grinding back against him, meeting his every brutal thrust, moaning as he buries himself inside me over and over again.

His hands leave my wrists and grab on to my hair, twisting the strands around his fingers.

"I love you," he pants, his thrusts becoming quicker and more urgent. "I love you and I never want to stop."

I can't think straight. I can only feel.

He's moving faster and faster and my entire body is flushed with the heat of our passion.

I'm going to come.

I can feel it coming like a thunderstorm.

"Oh my god," I gasp as my whole body begins to shake.

"Come," James says, thrusting between my legs, his cock buried in deep, a hand reaching around and pressing in messy, slippery strokes against my clit.

"Fuck!" I cry out as every muscle in my body tenses and I start to come around him, gasping his name and gripping the wall like I'm going to crumble to pieces.

"Oh, I'm coming, I'm coming," James grunts, slamming into me, and I feel his cock twitch and pulse as he comes, spilling into me over and over again.

We're loud. There's no way the staff didn't hear us. But I'm assuming Magnus arranged this dinner for James, so perhaps he warned them in advance of what might happen.

James pulls out of me, leaving me feeling both sated and hollow, and I turn around to face him, wobbling slightly, leaning my body into his, wrapping my arms around his waist.

"Laila love," he says to me, breathing heavily, putting his hand at the back of my head and pressing a wet kiss into my forehead. "I can't bloody see straight and yet I'm far from being done with you."

"We have dinner plans," I remind him, but I make no effort to pull down my dress, even as I feel him start to spill out of me. I have to admit, nothing turns me on more.

"Plans changed," he says, pulling back to grin at me, his eyes heavy lidded but brimming with lust. "You're not just the appetizer. You're also the main course and the dessert. You're a whole fucking feast."

He kisses me at that, and I kiss him back, soft and slow to start, then harder, deeper, messier, and I know it's only a matter of minutes before we're right back at it.

This man has an appetite.

He also has my whole heart.

And now, finally, I have his.

Epilogue

. . . .

JAMES

One year later

"ARE YOU READY?!" MAGNUS YELLS AT ME AT THE TOP OF his lungs, trying to be heard above the roar of the wind and the engines.

I manage to tear my eyes away from the open door and look at him. He's giving me the thumbs-up, his expression manic as he nods. He wants me to be ready. I don't think I'll ever be ready to jump out of an airplane.

I manage to give him a thumbs-up, though I can't force the smile.

Ottar pats me on the back, making me jump. He leans in, even though he's already close because I'm going tandem with him. "I told you you'd end up doing something like this one day," he yells.

"Never a dull moment," I mutter.

Obviously none of this was my idea, and I tried to back out

as gracefully as I could, but once Magnus had it in his head to go skydiving, I was forced to go along. He says it was for his protection, but I mean, come on. He's the one throwing himself out of a plane. I can't do much to protect him from that.

Anyway, it was either this or BASE jumping, and I figured I'd have better luck with a commercially operated skydiving company than with Magnus, who just runs off cliffs with a backpack attached, hoping to pull that cord right away.

I have to say, in the time that I've been working as Magnus's protection officer, it's been a wild ride, but all this time I feel like he's been building me up to this, to see what I'm really made of. I mean, sure, I nearly died saving his own son from drowning, but let's see what jumping out of an airplane will do for my character.

The skydiving instructor pats Magnus on the back, and then Magnus lets out a rip-roaring cry and leaps from the airplane, disappearing from sight.

Oh shit, oh shit, oh shit.

The instructor yells at us to come closer to the door, and we do. I don't know what kind of a wild world we live in where Ottar is the one pulling the cord because he's got more experience doing this, but here we are.

"You ready?" the instructor says.

"Yes!" Ottar yells in my ear.

"Not really," I manage to say.

But it doesn't matter because we're literally standing on the edge of the open side of the airplane and someone is counting down, and I think I'm just going to have a heart attack right here and now. Sorry, Magnus, I failed the ultimate bodyguard test and *died* before I even hit the ground.

Then we're jumping.

Falling.

And the sun is in my eyes and the wind is in my ears, buffeting my face, and the sky is so blue and the fields outside Oslo are coming up faster and faster, spreading as far as the eye can see, turning into mountains and fjords.

Bloody hell.

I'm beside myself with feeling, my heart in my throat, the adrenaline running in me like it never has before. I can hear Ottar yelling in my ear. When I look down I see Magnus, freewheeling like Tom Cruise before he pulls his chute. Then Ottar pulls ours.

We're yanked back as the chute opens and the rush stops and everything goes . . . calm.

We just float.

And I'm beside myself with happiness in ways I can't even describe. It's not just that the endorphins are running amok inside me, it's everything that's led up to this moment and everything that will happen afterward.

Because this isn't the scariest thing I'm about to do today.

No, I have a diamond ring in my suit pocket, waiting for me below.

Magnus, Ottar—they both know I'm going to propose to Laila tonight. They're pretty good at keeping secrets in the long run, because for the last six weeks straight I've literally been telling them I'm going to propose to her and I haven't yet.

But now? After jumping from an airplane, I realize I'm brave enough to do all the things that scare me. And asking Laila to marry me doesn't scare me anymore. Wanting to spend the rest of my life with her. None of that scares me anymore.

I'm ready.

We touch down on the soft earth, and I try to keep my legs moving, but Ottar's extra weight pushes me forward until we're both rolling on the ground. Okay, not the most graceful landing.

"You did it!" Magnus yells at us, coming over and helping us to our feet. I unclip from Ottar, and then Magnus pulls me into a hug. "I'm so proud of you," he says, getting all emotional.

"Okay, okay, ease up there," I tell him. "I survived."

"No thanks to me," Ottar says.

"All thanks to you, Ottar," I tell him, giving him a grateful nod. "Thank you for pulling the chute on time."

He chuckles then shrugs. "Well, I figured if I didn't, you wouldn't be able to propose." He squints at me. "You are proposing tonight, aren't you?"

"Yes," I tell him. "For real this time."

"Ha," Magnus says, patting me on the back. "I'll believe it when I see it. Come on, that took a little longer than I thought. We better get back home so you can catch your other flight. Hopefully you don't jump out of that one."

Other than deciding that I want Laila to marry me, a lot of other things have changed over the year.

We still work together at Skaugum Estate. We're obviously a couple, though our work doesn't always have us interacting all day long, especially as Magnus gets more and more involved with the king and queen, a transition that will happen sooner rather than later with the king's health in decline. I spend a lot of time in Oslo, but when I come home each night, we're at least sharing the same bedroom now. No more whispering—and, erm, other stuff—through the walls.

Laila has really found her groove as the nanny. Bjorn is on medication for ADHD, which helps with his impulsivity, and Laila does a lot of focus work with him. It takes patience, but she's more than up for it, and as a result she and Bjorn have grown a lot closer. Tor too has become a great kid, more sensitive than we thought he'd be, but he's a good foil to Bjorn.

Then there's everyone else at the estate: Ottar, Lady Jane, Einar, Olaf, Sigrid. After Laila lost her grandmother they really stepped up in giving her a sense of community, and in the end, they did the same for me. Though both Laila and I may not have any close relatives left, we've learned not only to become each other's family but also that found family is as valid and as important. It just happens to be that our family is now a royal one (and a bunch of zany motherfuckers at that).

That said, we don't spend all our time there anymore. No, we spend our weekends at the house in Todalen.

Every Friday night, unless there is an event, we fly in the royal private jet up to Todalen and stay the weekend. We have a car we leave at the airstrip, and then we just drive down and have a real, proper weekend together. Just the two of us. Most of the time we don't even leave the bedroom, let alone the house (Skaugum Estate still lacks a certain amount of privacy). But some days we have coffee with the neighbors, or we go kayaking on the fjord, or we go hiking. Just spending the time with each other doing the simple things.

It's my favorite part of my life at the moment. And I can only hope and pray that it's a part of our life that will grow. I want these quiet days with her forever.

It's May, so the sun is out late these days, but even so, we want to get up to Todalen before dinner. The drive back to

Skaugum from the skydiving place is about an hour, and I'm a nervous wreck. I was nervous before, but now that the adrenaline from jumping out of the plane is running through my veins, I'm nearly bouncing in my seat. I can kind of understand why Magnus is addicted to doing this kind of wild shit.

Then again, I've been nervous every Friday for the last six weeks, since I first bought the ring, wondering when I'd find the right moment on the weekend to pop the question. I've been trying to think of something romantic, and elaborate, and memorable, but I'm not that good at that sort of thing, and I'm definitely not the type of guy who would do the kind of proposal that people film or tell stories about.

But while I've been waiting for the right moment, the right moment hasn't really come. I'm starting to think I need to borrow a page from Magnus's rule book and just do it on pure impulse. The proposal itself isn't going to get Laila to say yes. She already knows her answer.

We get back to the estate in just enough time, and Laila is already waiting on the steps with our bags. Magnus and Ottar get out of the car, both of them giving me knowing looks that I hope Laila doesn't pick up on, and then we're being taken to the airfield.

"I'd ask you to tell me all about your adventure," Laila says to me as we wave goodbye to Einar and board the narrow steps onto the plane, "but I think I'd rather wait until the plane has landed."

"Fair enough," I tell her.

She looks me up and down. "But I can definitely tell you that you're buzzing pretty good. You better keep that energy up for later," she adds with a wink.

Oh, she has no idea.

The plane ride is quick as always, which helps with the guilt. Magnus and his family have been more than generous in providing transportation for us like this when it's available. We have no illusions of who we are on the social ladder. They're the royals upstairs; we're the staff downstairs. But because we've been folded in like family, and because the royals go out of their way to help us, we really do live this strange life of being normal commoners with a lot of special perks. I don't think Laila and I will ever get used to having a private jet at our disposal, and the moment we do, then we need to reevaluate who we are. We're both very adamant about not losing touch with where we came from, even all the ugly bits.

For Laila, though, as the plane touches down, as we drive through the winding roads toward the long, dark slice of water that is Todalsfjorden, every weekend reminds her where she comes from and why it's so important to her. Now she has a sense of home in two places—one being here, the physical house where her soul feels most at peace, and the other at Skaugum, not quite within the physical walls, but with the actual people.

I'm starting to feel the same way.

And that's when it hits me.

I yank the car over onto the tiny pullout on the side of the road, right along the fjord.

"What happened?" Laila asks, looking up from her phone in surprise. "Did we run out of gas?"

I shake my head, my hands trembling as I turn off the ignition. "No," I say. "There's something . . . I need to show you."

I mean, I can't propose to her in the car—not when there's

this lovely, deep fjord beside us, the water calm, reflecting the towering, craggy mountains on the other side. Suddenly it all seems so perfect.

I unbuckle my seat belt and get out of the car, walking to the water's edge. There are two large rocks there, artfully balancing against each other.

"What are you doing?" Laila asks, walking over to me.

I'm not sure. Suddenly I have the notion that maybe *I am* one of those people who would film a proposal.

"Uh, go stand on that rock over there," I say to her. "I want to pose for a picture."

"Okay," she says warily, but she still walks over. "Which rock?"

"The taller one," I tell her. I set up my iPhone on the hood of the car, balancing it in the windshield wipers as I hit record.

Then I walk over to her.

"You're doing a self-timer?" she asks, incredulous. She's always the one taking a million photos of us. I think I have one photo of us together on my phone, and it was one that she took.

"Why not," I tell her.

I step up onto the shorter rock. It's not very steady, and it wobbles back and forth under my boots, but at least I'm a little bit shorter than her this way. Beats having to get down on one knee.

"Are we posing?" she asks me, eyes bright and curious as I take both her hands in mine. "How long did you set that self-timer for?"

But I ignore her. I barely hear her. All I can think about is that ring burning a hole in my pocket and the words I want her to hear but I'm not sure how to say.

Just say it, I tell myself. *Be the blunt bastard that you are.*

"Laila," I tell her, trying to smooth out my voice.

I squeeze her hands, staring into her eyes. And all it takes is that because suddenly her whole demeanor changes. She's not scared, but she's . . . waiting, eyes already going wet.

"Laila love," I tell her, taking in a deep breath. "We've known each other quite a while now. We've loved each other for quite a while. And I think we've found a home in each other too. I've always said that the reason we connect so well is because we both know what it's like to lose family, lose our loved ones, feel alone in the world. Our upbringings were very different from each other's, but we're both bound by that searching for family."

I let go of her one hand and stick mine in my jacket pocket, closing it around the velvet box.

She brings her free hand up to her mouth, already gasping.

"Laila, I've found my family in you. Everything I've spent my life looking for, I've found in you. In your big heart, in your beautiful soul, you've made room for me, and I've made room for you. And I think we're at the point now where there's nothing holding us back. No fear, no regret, nothing but the future. And I need you to be a part of mine forever."

She's crying now, tears streaming down her face, so fucking beautiful, but at least they seem to be tears of joy.

I let go of her other hand and pull out the box, opening it for her to see. It's actually a vintage ring that was combined with an opal gemstone for her birthday, and it practically shines in her face.

"James," she says through a choked whisper, staring down at the ring, hands shaking.

"Laila Bruset," I say to her, having to blink back the heat behind my eyes. "Will you marry me?"

She nods, crying. "Yes, yes, yes," she says, gasping.

The adrenaline from earlier is nothing compared to what I'm feeling right now. Because I also have joy. Joy that I never knew I was capable of feeling.

Before I drown in it, I take the ring and slip it on her finger.

It sits there like it's meant to be there, like it will stay there forever. One can only hope it will.

She holds her hand out, admiring the ring, crying some more, and then she throws her arms around me, kissing me. "James, James, I love you."

But while I'm about to answer her back, that I love her more than anything in the world, my future wife, her movement knocks me off-balance.

I teeter on the rock, and I don't know if it's because of the emotions of the proposal itself, because she said fucking YES, or because I jumped out of an airplane earlier today, but my balance is shot.

I go falling off the rock, trying to break my fall, but instead I go tumbling down into the water.

SPLASH.

I land in the fjord face-first, the water shockingly cold. I immediately find my footing, trying to stand on slippery rocks.

Meanwhile Laila is yelling, trying to run down the slope after me, except she loses her footing and can't slow down. She ends up falling into the water right beside me.

Thank god it's shallow, and she's already on her feet, laughing her head off, trying to help me up to mine. Eventually we both stagger out of the water, freezing cold, soaking wet, collapsing on the ground in each other's arms.

"You didn't change your mind, did you?" I ask, wiping the wet hair off my forehead. "Because that was probably the most ungraceful move I've ever made."

She laughs, kissing me happily, her lips tasting like salt. "I've told you before, I like it when you seem like a mere mortal."

"So I guess that means you'll take me for better or for worse."

"I'll take you for everything, James," she says to me, cupping my face. "I love you."

"I love you too," I tell her, pressing my lips to hers, feeling the happiness bubble up between us.

That and the shivers.

"Come on," I tell her, getting to my feet and helping her up to hers. "Let's go home and celebrate. I may have stashed a bottle of champagne somewhere for whenever I got the courage to pop the question."

"You've been planning this awhile?" she asks as we head toward the car.

And that's when I remember I filmed the whole damn proposal.

"Oh shit," I swear, running over to the phone. I quickly turn to stop the video and slip the phone into my coat. "You have to promise me that no one ever sees this footage."

She claps happily. "Oh that is going up on YouTube right away. We'll get a million hits!"

"No, Laila," I tell her as we get in the car.

"You at least have to show me."

"We can watch it at home with the champagne."

"Then *we'll* put it on YouTube," she says with a devious smile. "Can you imagine it? Bodyguard to the Norwegian prince falls in a fjord during proposal to royal nanny."

"I can imagine it, actually." Magnus would never let me hear the end of it. I narrow my eyes at her playfully, even though I'm still grinning like a fool. "You wouldn't dare."

"I'm starting to think you don't know me at all," she says, waving her hand at me. "We're getting married now. For better or for worse, remember?"

I shake my head, but I'm laughing.

For better and for worse and for everything else in between. That's us.

Acknowledgments

It's amazing how your life can change over the course of writing a book. When I first started writing James and Laila's story, I wanted to write a book that would make my Norwegian father proud. While I had written a book set in Norway before (*The Wild Heir*, which is about how Prince Magnus and Princess Ella met), I wanted a book that was set in his quaint and quirky hometown of Todalen in Norway, a love letter to the place my father grew up and where most of my dear relatives on the Halle side still live to this day. In fact, the house that Laila's grandmother owned is 100 percent based on the house that my father grew up in and is still in the family. (Fun fact: When Norwegians inherit houses from their family, they rarely ever sell it. Instead they keep it in the family, often for everyone to share. So lovely!)

But just as I started writing this book, my brother died. And then two months later my father died. And completing this book was the last thing on my mind as I navigated wave after wave of monstrous grief. I won't bore you with how awful things were and how writing seemed impossible (imagine the worst brain fog times one thousand and that's what grief does to you from the inside out). Eventually, though, time passed and I came up for air and found my footing again. I fell back in love with James and Laila's story, and as difficult as it was to write at times (especially when it came to scenes about Laila's grandmother), I was happy I was able to set a book in the home of my family, as well as tie it to characters of mine (Magnus and Ella) who I had missed so much.

Yet I couldn't have done any of this without the support of my editors, Sarah Blumenstock and Cindy Hwang, who were beyond gracious and encouraging with me as I navigated my new reality. They truly cheered me on with every word, and I am so grateful for their belief in me, as well as their patience. Likewise, my agent, Taylor Haggerty, was also amazing (as usual!) with her steadfast support and understanding. I'm quite blessed to work with such wonderful women.

Of course, I have to thank my mother for her unwavering strength and Finnish sisu for going through all that she has, and my husband, Scott, who has truly been my rock (and my mother's) through the lowest of the lows. Your love is transcendent and I am honored to be your wife.

Finally, to my charming aunt Else, to all my lovely cousins (I won't dare name you all because I'll leave someone out by accident, but you know who you are), and everyone else who's a part of the Halle family in Norway, thanks for always being so welcoming and loving even though you're half a world away. I know my father is what connected us but even with him gone, I see and feel him in all of you. He had an insatiable zest for life, despite all the challenges, and I hope none of us ever lose that same spirit that he had.

KEEP READING FOR AN EXCERPT FROM

The Royals Next Door

AVAILABLE NOW FROM BERKLEY ROMANCE.

NICKY GRAVES JUST THREW UP IN MY HANDBAG.

It's my fault, really. I knew he was sick, even though he tried to muster up some eight-year-old bravado and pretend he wasn't. I know that when I was his age, if my forehead felt remotely hot, I'd be in the nurse's office all day, waiting for my mom to come and get me. Any excuse to miss school.

But Nicky loves school (and since I'm his second-grade teacher, I *should* be honored by this), so he pretended he was fine until he wasn't.

I saw it happen in slow motion too. I was reading to the class from one of their favorite series, Mercy Watson, talking about the pig's love for butter, when Nicky's face went a wicked shade of green. His hand shot up to his mouth, and before I could do anything, he was running to the trash can beside my desk. Which would have been great had I not left my purse beside the trash and had Nicky possessed a LeBron James style of pinpoint accuracy.

"I'm sorry, Miss Evans!" Nicky wails, standing beside what used to be a nice leather bag I picked up in Mexico years ago when I was on vacation with my ex, Joey. I suppose it's fitting that in the end it's just a pile of vomit, which is exactly what our relationship turned out to be. Metaphors 101.

"It's okay, Nicky," I tell him, trying to sound calm even though I can feel the class descending into panic as cries of "Ewwww!" and "Nicky puked! Sicky Nicky!" and "I'm gonna barf!" fill the room.

I practically throw the book down and run over to him, trying to hold it together myself. This is not my favorite part of the job, and I'm probably the only elementary school teacher who still gets easily grossed out. I grab an entire box of tissues and somehow manage to get Nicky cleaned up, call the nurse's office and his mother to come get him, and calm down the class.

It isn't until the bell rings that I have time to deal with the purse of puke.

I'm staring at it, wondering if I should call it a wash and just throw it all away, when there's a knock at the door. It's the first-grade teacher, Cynthia Bautista, poking her head in, sympathy all over her face. Maybe a tinge of disgust.

"You okay? I heard you had a sickie today."

I gesture to the bag, which I still haven't touched. "Well, I'm in the market for a new purse."

She walks in and eyes it, flinching. "Oh. Fuck me." Then she covers her mouth and bursts out laughing. "I'm sorry. It's not funny."

"Don't worry, if it had happened to you, I'd be laughing too."

Cynthia is one of the few teachers here who I'd consider a friend. Not that I'm a hard person to get along with—people-pleasing is something that's been ingrained in me since I was a child—but there aren't that many people who "get" me, especially where I live, especially in the school system. There's a very rigid set of rules and hierarchy at SSI Elementary, and I'm still treated like a newcomer, even though I've worked here and lived here long enough. They say that most people who move to Salt Spring Island only last a few years, and if you make it to five, then you're considered a "real islander." I've made it to five, and I haven't managed to get close to anyone. People seem to think I'll eventually go back out with the tide.

"I think you're going to have to throw it away," Cynthia says, her nose scrunched up. "Anything valuable in there?"

I sigh, nodding. "My wallet. Some makeup. A book. Tic Tacs."

My antianxiety medication, I finish in my head. But she doesn't need to know *that.*

Then I remember. "Oh, wait. Maybe . . ." I crouch down and gingerly poke at the outside pocket where I remember sliding my bank cards this morning after getting my morning coffee at Salty Seas Coffee & Goods. My bank card and credit card seem untouched by the contents of Nicky's stomach. Unfortunately, those are the only things saved.

"Shit." I slap the cards on my desk and give Cynthia a tired look. "Feel like doing me a favor?"

"Hell no," she says, shaking her head adamantly. Cynthia is a pretty tough cookie, emigrated here from the Philippines by herself when she was twenty, went through an awful divorce, and is now raising her ten-year-old daughter by herself. "That bag and everything in it is a lost cause. You can always get another driver's license. And makeup. And books. And Tic Tacs."

She's right. I glance at the clock. It's just past three, which means there's plenty of time to get to the insurance place and get a new driver's license. Luckily our school is right in the middle of our tiny town and close to everything. "I guess I'll go do that now before I forget. Do we have a toxic waste receptacle here?" I eye the purse.

Cynthia gives me a look like I'm ridiculous. "You want to try to get your license now? Have you even stepped outside today?"

I shake my head. During recess and lunch hour I stayed at my desk and read my book, preparing for the podcast I'm doing tonight. I'd already read it, but I wanted to skim through it to beef up my talking points in the review.

"Why, what's happening?"

This island is small, and nothing much ever happens here. Perhaps there's some hippie protest about a cell phone tower or something.

Cynthia's eyes go wide, and she gets this excited, knowing look upon her face. "You haven't heard?"

I stare at her blankly and cross my arms. Obviously not. "*What?*"

"You know Prince Edward and MRed?"

Do I know Prince Edward and MRed, aka Monica Red, aka Monica, Duchess of Fairfax? "Cynthia, I live *on* a rock, not under a rock."

"Well, apparently you live under one too. They're here! Like, today. Now. And looking for real estate. The whole island has been losing their mind over it. Paparazzi have been arriving in float planes all morning, the ferries are full of lookie-loos or however you call it. The town is at a standstill."

My tired brain can hardly comprehend any of this.

You see, Prince Edward, the younger, stoic son of Queen

Beatrix and her husband, Prince Albert, recently married a Grammy-winning singer named MRed, and the press has been up in arms about it. Not only is Monica Black, but she's American and she had a successful career, which may have included a lot of risqué songs, scantily clad videos, performances gone viral, etc. In other words, the UK media has been absolutely brutal to the both of them, with racism and slut-shaming at every turn. I mean, I'm by no means a royal fanatic, but I've been keeping up with it (they dominate the news everywhere), and I don't see the media ever attacking Eddie's older brother, Prince Daniel, who remains a womanizing bachelor.

At any rate, it was reported everywhere that Monica and Eddie were leaving the UK for a yearlong break for undisclosed reasons. A sabbatical of sorts. Some people thought they'd go to Seattle, to be near her parents. Others thought the ski resort town of Whistler, where the royal family spent winter vacations when Eddie and Daniel were young. Others yet thought India, where the couple often did charity work.

Never in a million years did I think they would pick this island in British Columbia, Canada, a small yet eccentric haven between Vancouver Island and the mainland.

Honestly, I still can't believe it. None of this seems right.

"Are you sure?" I ask Cynthia. "Maybe it's just an actor or something." Our island is known for being the perfect hermit's hideaway (and I can attest to that—if I didn't have to work, I think I'd rarely leave the house). There are lots of known authors who toil away in their writing studios, and ex-musicians who sometimes play the local pub, and everyone from Barbra Streisand to Raffi has had a summer home here at some point.

"No, it's Eddie and Monica," Cynthia says adamantly. "Don't

believe me? Just walk to town and you'll be swallowed up by the frenzy."

She sounds breathless when she says "frenzy," and there's a feverish sheen to her eyes. Something tells me that Cynthia is absolutely loving this. Our quiet little town turned into a paparazzi-driven chaos? That sounds awful to me. I can't even handle the crowds when summer holidays hit, and that's two weeks from now.

"Okay. I guess I'll just go home and hope I don't run into any cops."

"Nah, they're all out trying to contain the madness." She says this gleefully, tapping her fingertips together like Mr. Burns from *The Simpsons*.

We say goodbye, and I pick up the puke purse and take it down to the nurse's office, where Judy is still tidying up (school nurse by day, restaurant server who never gets my order right at the Sitka Spruce Restaurant by night). She doesn't even bat an eyeball at it and says she'll dispose of it for me, like she's getting rid of a dead body. At this point, that's what it kind of feels like, and I get out of there before she changes her mind.

The school after three p.m. is probably my favorite place to be. There are usually a few students straggling about, killing time and waiting to be picked up, but today is warm, sunny, and dry (opposed to the usual cold, gloomy, and wet), so any kids who are left are outside. It's just me in the halls, enjoying being out of the house and away from any stress and responsibilities, and getting to be alone at the same time.

I take a moment to slowly walk down the hall, smiling at all the art the kids have showcased on the walls, and then I'm out the door and heading to my car in the parking lot. It's a 2000

Honda Civic hatchback that I've always called the Garbage Pail (since it's silver and dented), and I added fuzzy green seat covers for that Oscar the Grouch feel. Almost everyone on the island has an electric car, and it's definitely on my list of things to get (along with the goal of saving money), but since I essentially take care of both myself and my mother under one income, a new car seems like just another one of my dreams, along with traveling the world and falling in love with someone who deserves it.

Still, I have great affection for the Garbage Pail. I could get the dents fixed, but on this island, no one bats an eye, and it does really well on gas. Hanging from the mirror is a pair of fuzzy dice that my father won for me at an arcade when I was a teen, before he ditched out on us, and my glove compartment is stuffed with Tic Tacs, which I have a borderline addiction to, ferry receipts, and who knows what else.

I get in, and even though I'm not driving through town to get home, I already know what Cynthia means. On the sides of the main road leading into the center, cars are lined up and parked in haphazard lines. This isn't normal for a Thursday afternoon in June. It looks more like the crowds we get during our Saturday market during the peak of summer, but on steroids, and I guess instead of people perusing the organic vegetables or hemp-based clothing or homemade vegan vagina purses (yes, those are a thing and they're exactly what they sound like), these visitors have their cameras and phones all ready, hoping to catch a glimpse of the renegade royals.

I shake my head and turn off the road, glad that I don't have to deal with any of that today. I still think that maybe Cynthia's mistaken about all of this. I mean, I like living here because it's gorgeous and affordable and I can be a recluse and no one thinks anything of it, but I'm not sure why Prince Eddie and MRed would be attracted to this place. I mean, yeah, it's beautiful and secluded. But you're also kind of *stuck* here too.

My house is located at the end of a peninsula called Scott Point, one of the most affluent and tightly knit communities on the island.

Naturally, I'm like a sliver you can't get rid of along the narrow finger of the peninsula. Yes, we own the house, an adorable cedar-shingle three-bedroom that used to be the servants' quarters to the mansion next to it, but I still drive the Garbage Pail among all the shiny Range Rovers and Teslas (full disclosure: the GP used to be my mother's car until she wrecked my Kia Soul, but anyway . . . long story), and my mother and I aren't exactly overly friendly with our neighbors. We don't belong here, but we make it work.

It sure is stunning, though. The only way through is via a narrow road that cuts through the middle of the peninsula like an artery lined with evergreen arbutus trees, their peeling red bark as thin and delicate as Japanese rice paper. On either side are houses hidden by tall cedar fences, each with a witty name like Henry's Haven and Oceanside Retreat carved up on custom-made signs. Between the houses you can catch glimpses of the ocean, the sun glinting off it in such a way that shivers run down your spine. That glint at this time of day tells me that summer is in full swing, and summer is my dreaming period.

I'm already dreaming about getting a mug of tea and heading down to the dock to enjoy the sun when I suddenly have to slam on my brakes.

Instead of the usual deer or quail family crossing the road, there's a very tall, broad-shouldered tree of a man standing in the middle of the road at the top of the small hill, holding his hand out to me like he's trying out for the Supremes.

Shit. Pins and needles start to form in my lungs, my heart pounding. My anxiety has no problems jumping to the worst-case scenario, and it's always that something has happened to my mother while I was at work. There's not a moment when that exact fear isn't lurking at the back of my mind, so the fact that there's a very grim-faced stranger in a dark suit striding downhill toward me makes me think my worst nightmare is going to come true.

My window is already rolled down, so I hear him say, "Excuse me, miss?" in a very strong, raspy British accent. He's more curt than sympathetic, which makes me calm just a little.

"Yes? What's wrong?" I ask him, trying not to panic.

Now that he's up close, I can get a better look at him. His suit is navy blue with a touch of teal, looking sharp and well-tailored, with a pressed white shirt underneath and a dark gray tie. It's the kind of suit that screams money, and not the kind of money that the people on this street have, more of a worldly, next-level kind of money. The kind that class brings.

He's also way more imposing up close, built like a Douglas fir, barrel-chested and sturdy in a graceful way. My eyes trail up to his face and see that it matches the brusqueness of his voice. He's got aviator sunglasses on that reflect my own bewildered expression (and make me realize my hair is a blond rat's nest from driving with the window down), but even so, I can *feel* his eyes on me. If they're anything like the wrinkles in his forehead and the seemingly permanent line etched between his dark arched brows, then I'm definitely intimidated.

There's also something about him that's vaguely familiar, but for the life of me I can't recall why. It's like he reminds me of a famous actor or something.

"I need you to turn around," he says stiffly, making a motion for me to pivot and go.

"But I live here," I protest.

The line between his brows deepens, and his full mouth sets into a hard line. This man is no joke. He jerks his very strong, manly, bearded chin down the road. "I'm going to need you to turn around," he repeats.

I blink at him. "I'm sorry, but who even are you? I'm not turning around. I live here. And if you don't let me go home to my mother, who, by the way, suffers from DPD and BPD, she's going to end up calling the police when I don't show up. Hell, I'll call the police right now and report you."

The man stares at me, and I stare right back at my frazzled reflection, my eyes drifting briefly to notice that his ears stick out, just a little. That bit of information is enough to take the intimidation factor down a notch.

When he finally speaks, I expect him to ask me to leave again, but instead he asks, "What's DPD?"

I sigh. I didn't mean to drag my mother's mental illness into this. In fact, there are very few people around me who know exactly what she has, so the fact that I told *him*—this very commanding, rude British stranger in a suit—the truth feels wrong.

"It stands for dependent personality disorder. And before you ask about BPD, that stands for borderline personality disorder."

He raises his chin, and I'm not sure if this is an act of defiance or if he's going to ask me further questions that he can obviously go and Google later. Then he says in his low, raspy voice, "What's your address?"

I'm about to tell him, but I stop myself. "Wait a minute, you never told me who you are. Why should I tell a stranger my address? You think I want to see your face peeping through my window while I'm sleeping?"

His frown amplifies. "You think I'm a Peeping Tom?"

"I don't know. Is your name Tom?"

"It's Harrison," he says reluctantly. "Harrison Cole, PPO. And I'm afraid that unless you prove you live where you say you do, you'll have to turn around. I've been turning away cars all day, and I have no problems doing it to you."

Wow. What an asshole. I clear my throat. "Sorry, Harrison Cole? Is that a made-up name or your real name?"

He grunts in response, and if his brows furrow any deeper, I'm afraid his face might split in two.

I continue, no longer intimidated by him and his overtly manly, gruff ways. "And since you asked me what DPD stood for when you should have minded your own business, I'm going to have to ask you what a PPO is. Petty paralegal oaf? Perfectly pissy oligarch?"

"Personal protection officer," he booms. "By order of Her Majesty, the Queen of the United Kingdom."

I blink at him as things slowly come together in my brain. "Like a bodyguard? Are you . . . oh my god, are you Eddie and MRed's bodyguard?"

He doesn't say anything, and he doesn't have to. It dawns on me, one big bright lightbulb going on in my head, that the reason I thought he looked familiar isn't because he's an actor but because I have seen him in the tabloids and on the news.

Usually out of sight but sometimes in the background behind Eddie and Monica. He's the one the public (or at least the voracious users of the #FairfaxFans hashtag on Twitter) has dubbed the Broody Bodyguard and Sexy Secret Agent, and I've stumbled across more than a few fanfics about him. (And by *stumbled*, I mean purposefully devoured. For my podcast . . .)

And he's standing here, in front of me, telling me to go. Which means that the royal couple have to be farther up the road!

"I'll let you go to your house if you can prove you live there," the infamous Broody Bodyguard eventually says. "Let me see your driver's license."

Oh . . . that.

Shit.

Karina Halle is a screenwriter, a former music and travel jour-
nalist, and the *New York Times*, *Wall Street Journal*, and *USA
Today* bestselling author of *River of Shadows*, *The Royals Next
Door*, and *Black Sunshine*, as well as eighty other wild and romantic reads, ranging from light and sexy rom-coms to horror/
paranormal romance and dark fantasy. Needless to say, whatever genre you're into, she's probably written a romance for it.
When she's not traveling, she and her husband split their time
between a possibly haunted 120-year-old house in Victoria,
British Columbia, and their condo in sunny Los Angeles.

VISIT KARINA HALLE ONLINE

AuthorKarinaHalle.com
AuthorHalle
MetalBlonde

Ready to find
your next great read?

Let us help.

Visit prh.com/nextread